A CARTOON NETWORK ORIGINAL

VOLUME FOUR

OVER THE GARDEN WALL Volume Four, June 2018. Published by KaBOOM!, a division of Boom Entertainment, Inc. OVER THE GARDEN WALL, CARTOON NETWORK, the logos, and all related characters and elements are trademarks of and © Cartoon Network. (S18) All rights reserved. Originally published in single magazine form as Over the Garden Wall Ongoing No. 13-16. © Cartoon Network. (S17) All rights reserved. KaBOOM!™ and the KaBOOM! logo are trademarks of Boom Entertainment, Inc., registered in various countries and categories. All characters, events, and institutions depicted herein are fictional. Any similarity between any of the names, characters, persons, events, and/or institutions in this publication to actual names, characters, and persons, whether living or dead, events, and/or institutions is unintended and purely coincidental. KaBOOM! does not read or accept unsolicited submissions of ideas, stories, or artwork.

BOOM! Studios, 5670 Wilshire Boulevard, Suite 400, Los Angeles, CA 90036-5679. Printed in China. First Printing.

ISBN: 978-1-68415-185-1, eISBN: 978-1-64144-000-4

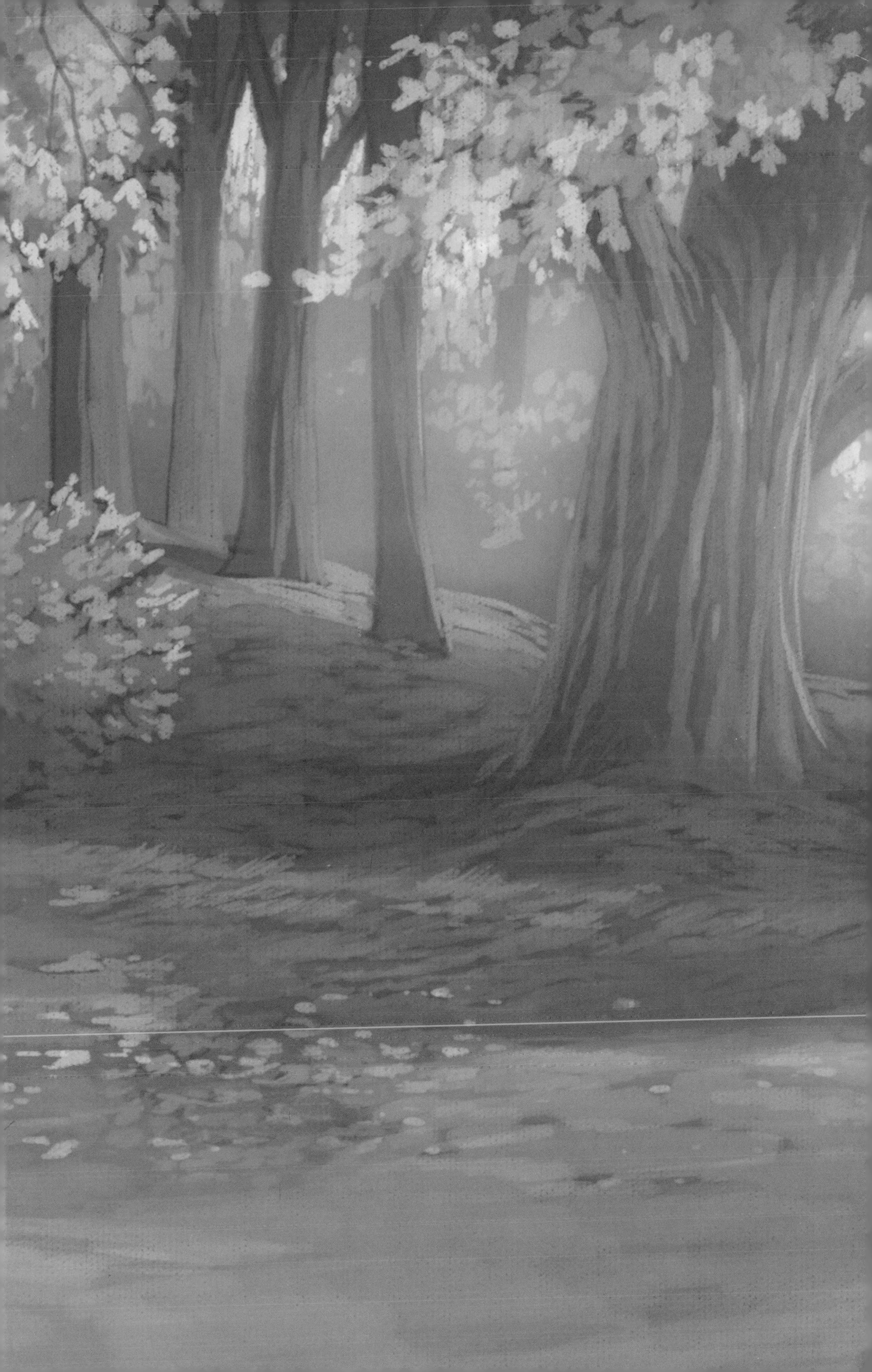

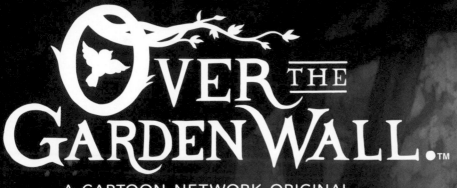

OVER THE GARDEN WALL™

A CARTOON NETWORK ORIGINAL

CREATED BY PAT MCHALE

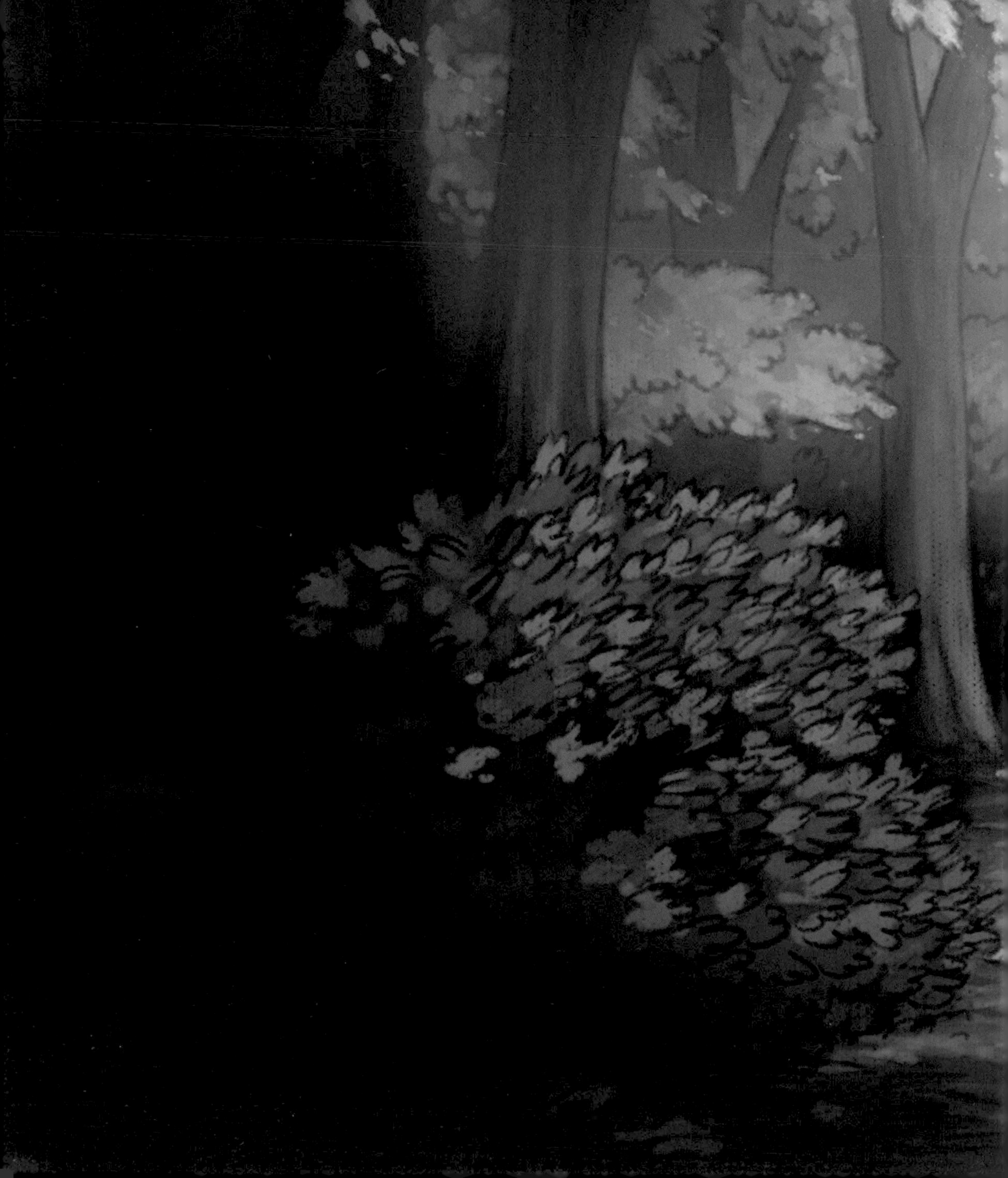

"Hunt for Hero Frog: Greg"
written by Danielle Burgos
illustrated by Jim Campbell

"Hunt for Hero Frog: Wirt"
written by Kiernan Sjursen-Lien
illustrated by Cara McGee
colors by Whitney Cogar,
Eleonora Bruni, Laura Langston
& Joana Lafuente
letters by Warren Montgomery

"Three Wise Men"
written by George Mager
illustrated by Kiernan Sjursen-Lien
colors by Laura Langston
letters by Warren Montgomery

cover by Meg Omac

designer Jillian Crab
associate editor Matthew Levine
editor Whitney Leopard

With special thanks to Marisa Marionakis,
Janet No, Curtis Lelash, Katie Krentz,
Pernelle Hayes, Adrienne Lee, Stacy Renfroe,
and the wonderful folks at Cartoon Network.

HUNT FOR HERO FROG

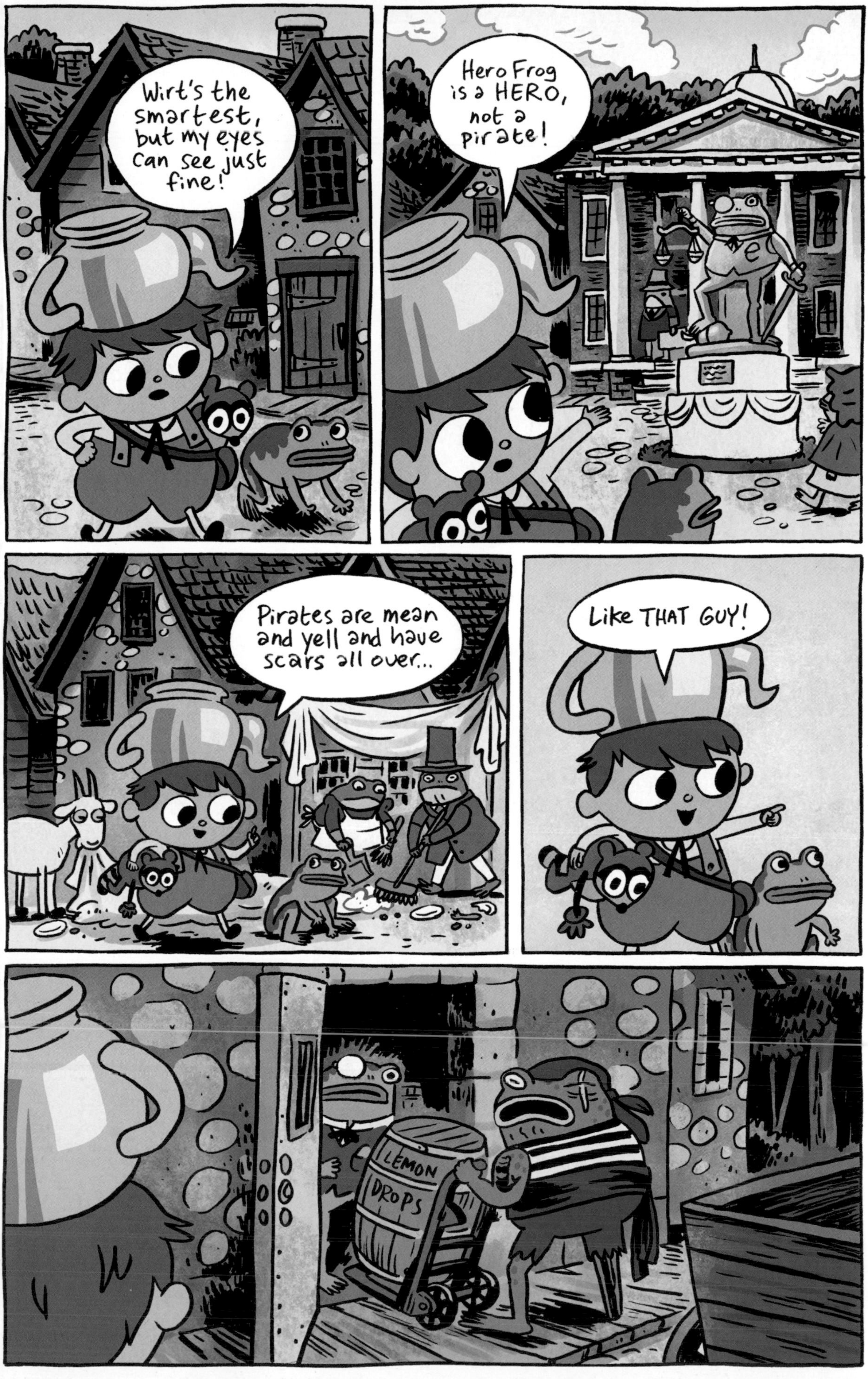
Wirt's the smartest, but my eyes can see just fine!
Hero Frog is a HERO, not a pirate!
Pirates are mean and yell and have scars all over...
Like THAT GUY!
LEMON DROPS

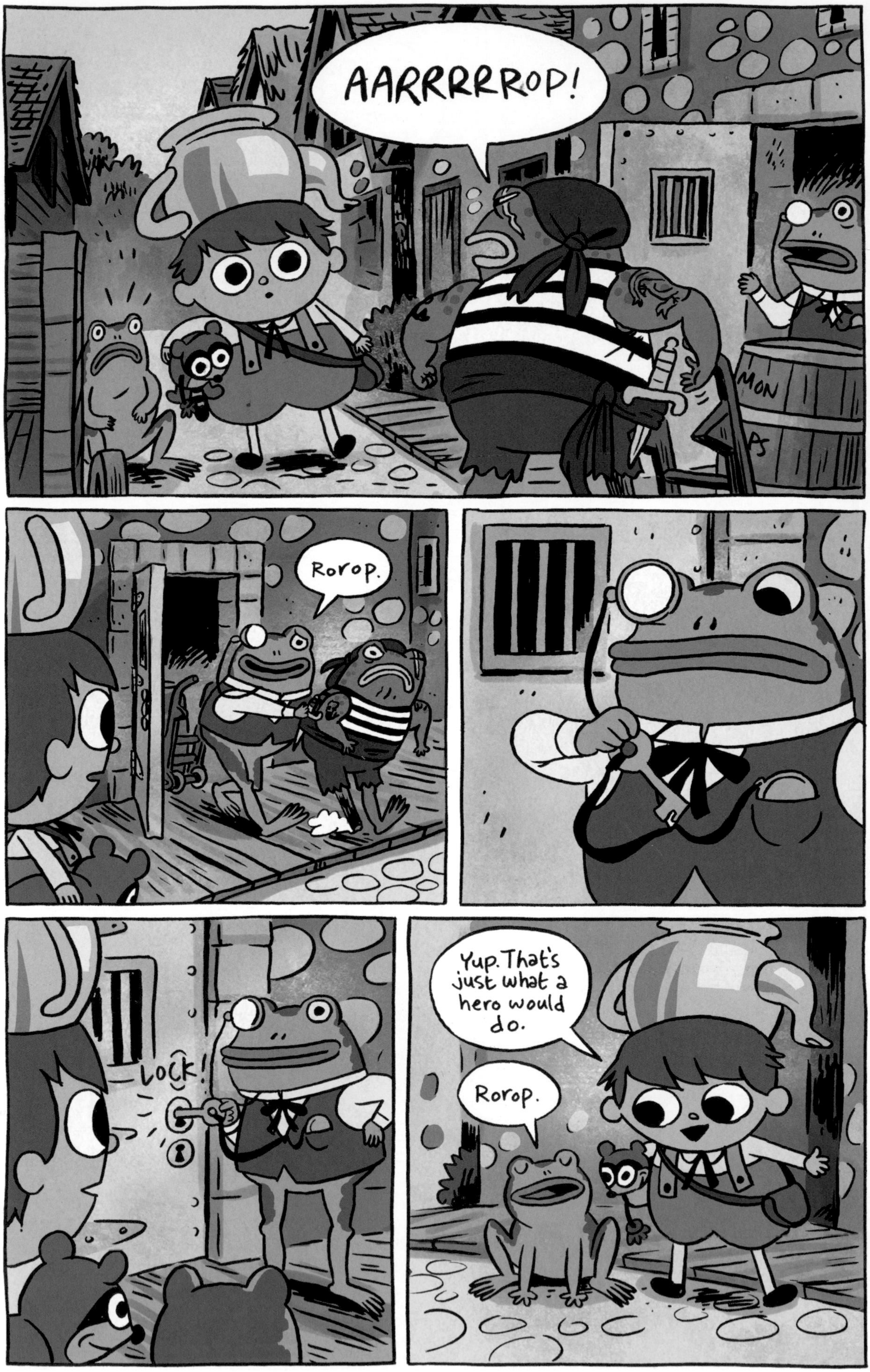
AARRRRROP!
MON
Rorop.
LOCK!
Yup. That's just what a hero would do.
Rorop.

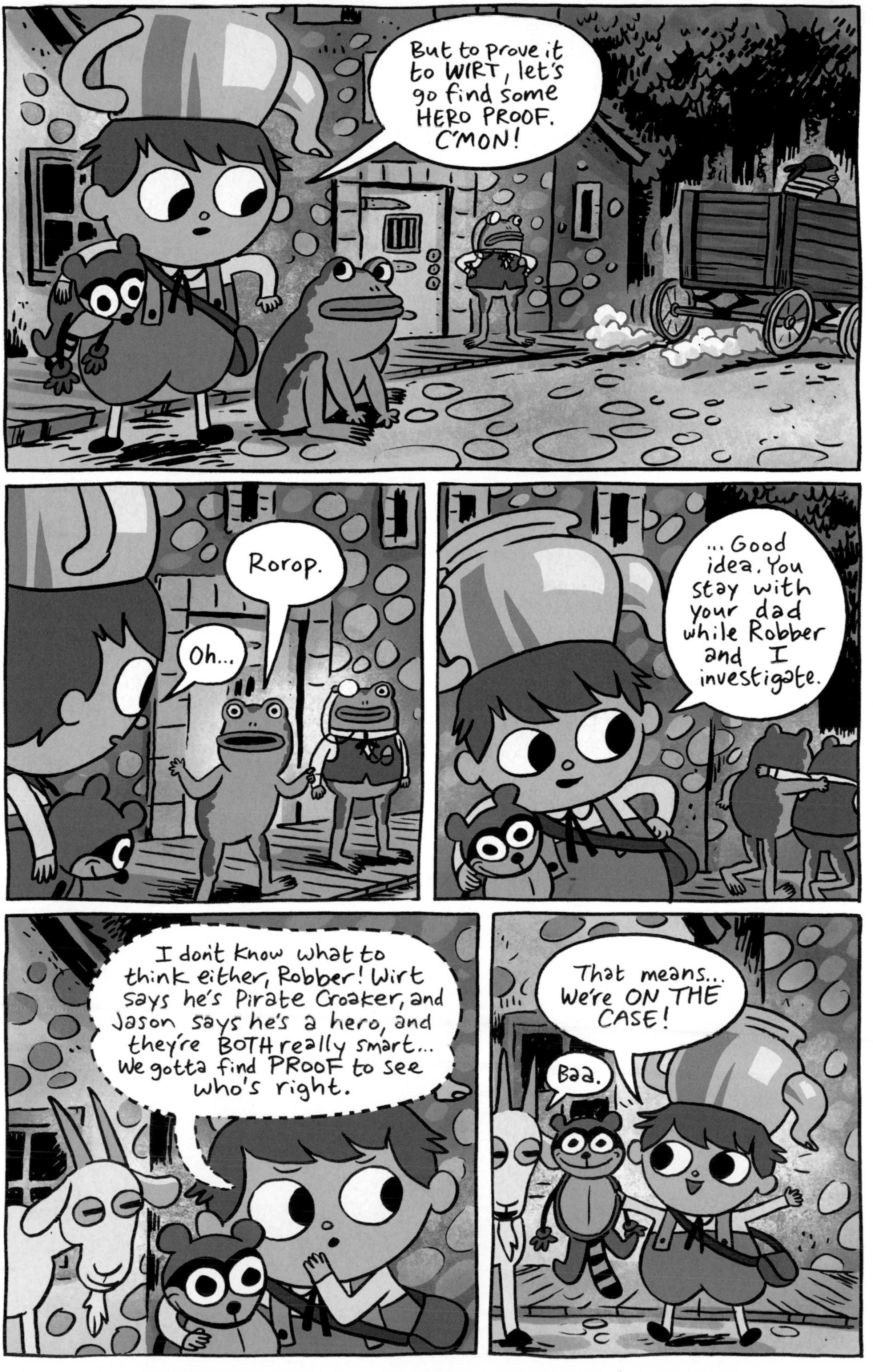
But to prove it to WIRT, let's go find some HERO PROOF. C'MON!
Oh...
Rorop.
...Good idea. You stay with your dad while Robber and I investigate.
I don't know what to think either, Robber! Wirt says he's Pirate Croaker, and Jason says he's a hero, and they're BOTH really smart... We gotta find PROOF to see who's right.
Baa.
That means... We're ON THE CASE!

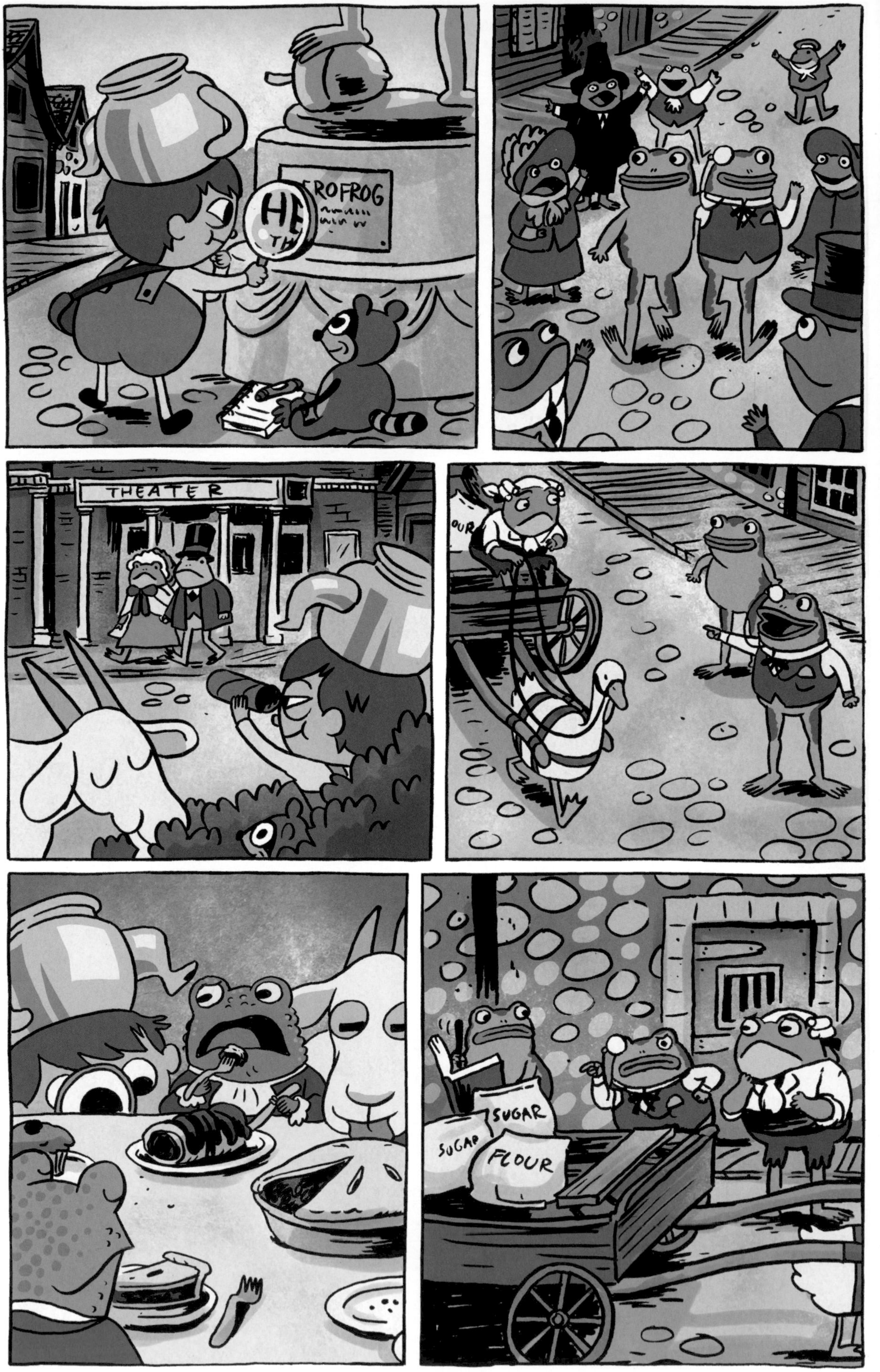

EROFROG
HE
TH
THEATER
OUR
SUGAR
SUGAR
FLOUR

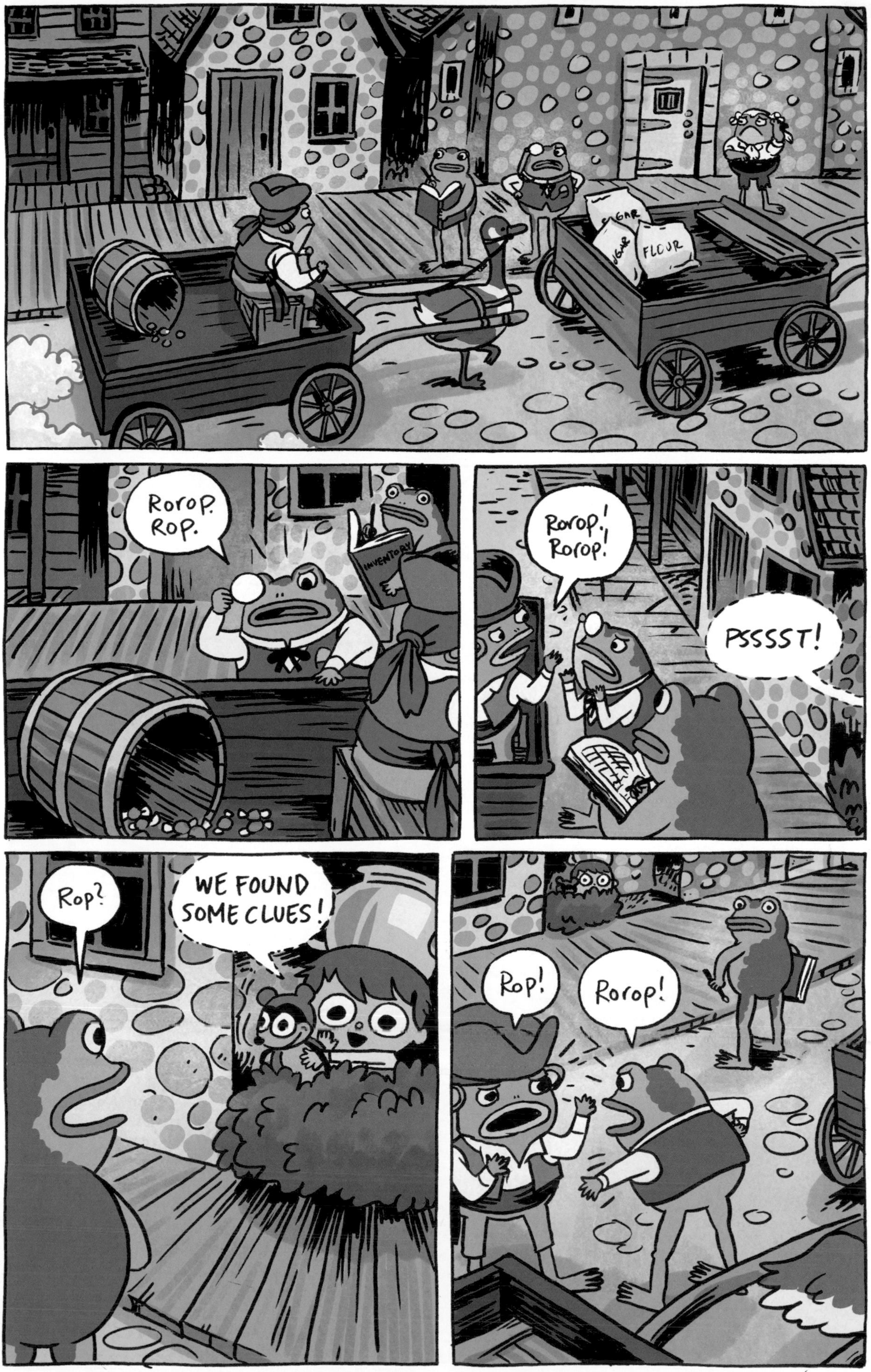
SUGAR
SUGAR
FLOUR
Rorop. Rop.
INVENTORY
Rorop! Rorop!
PSSSST!
Rop?
WE FOUND SOME CLUES!
Rop!
Rorop!

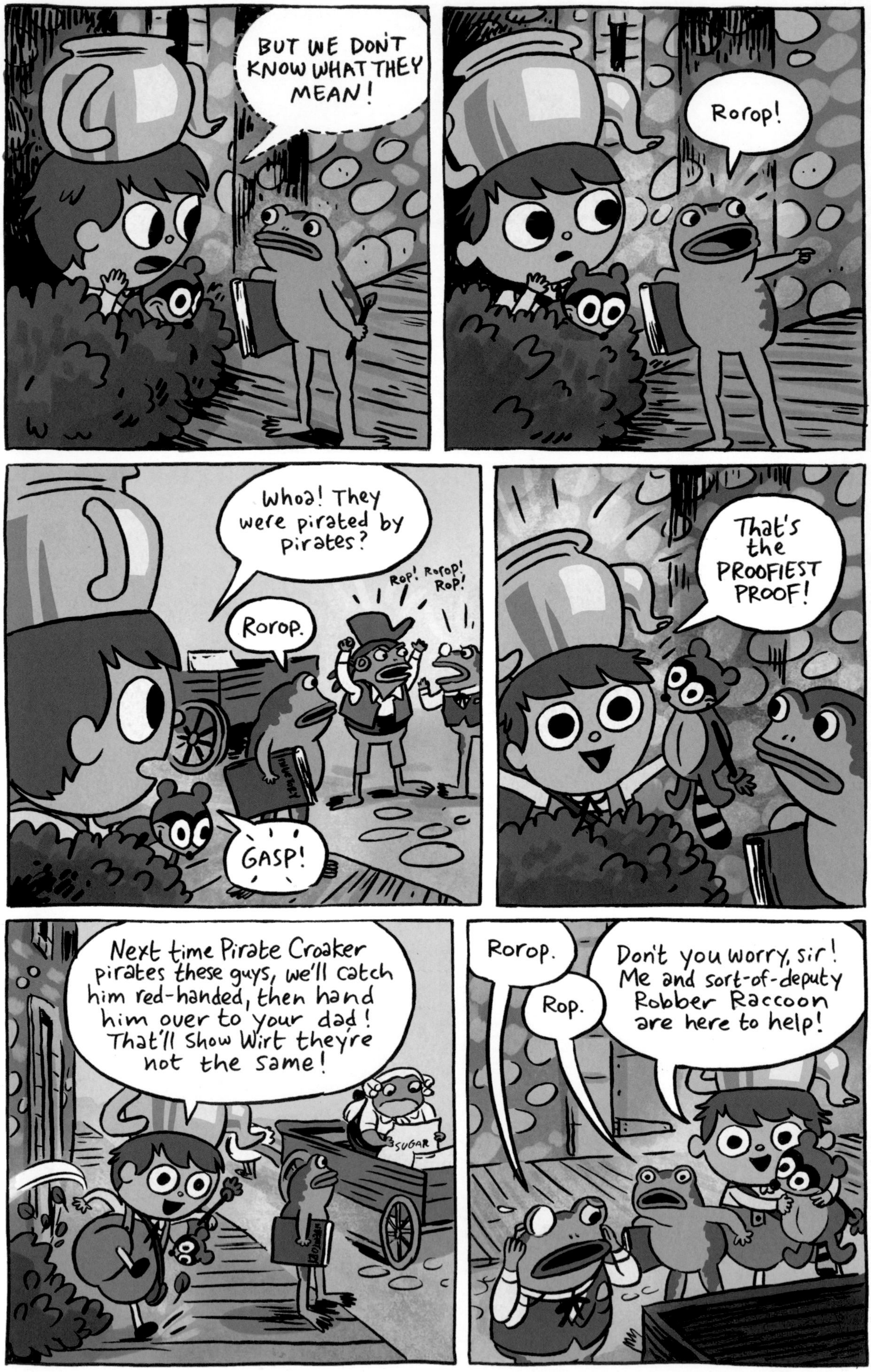

BUT WE DON'T KNOW WHAT THEY MEAN!
Rorop!
Whoa! They were pirated by pirates?
Rorop.
Rop! Rorop! Rop!
GASP!
That's the PROOFIEST PROOF!
Next time Pirate Croaker pirates these guys, we'll catch him red-handed, then hand him over to your dad! That'll show Wirt they're not the same!
SUGAR
Rorop.
Rop.
Don't you worry, sir! Me and sort-of-deputy Robber Raccoon are here to help!

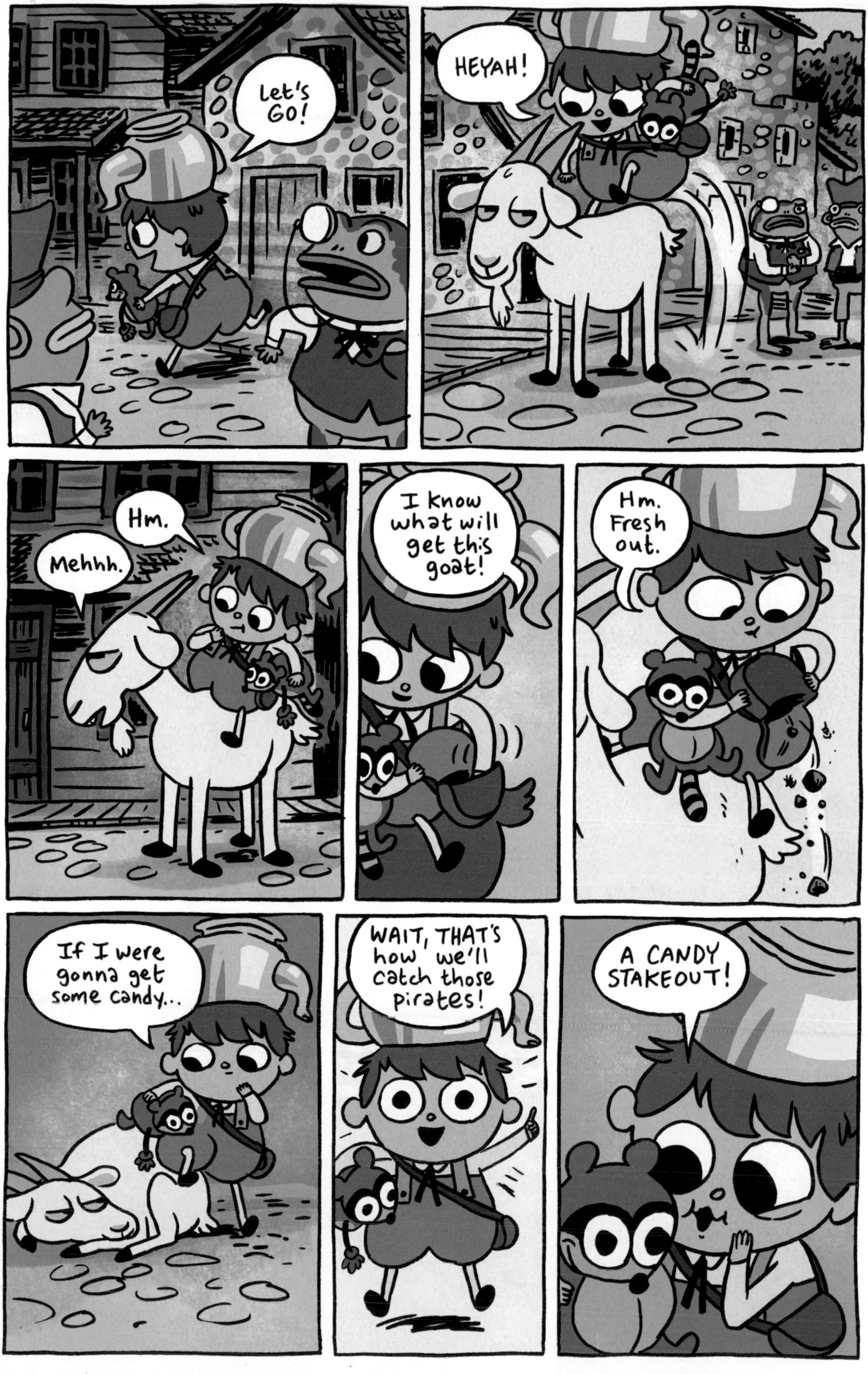
Let's GO!
HEYAH!
Hm.
Mehhh.
I know what will get this goat!
Hm. Fresh out.
If I were gonna get some candy...
WAIT, THAT'S how we'll catch those pirates!
A CANDY STAKEOUT!

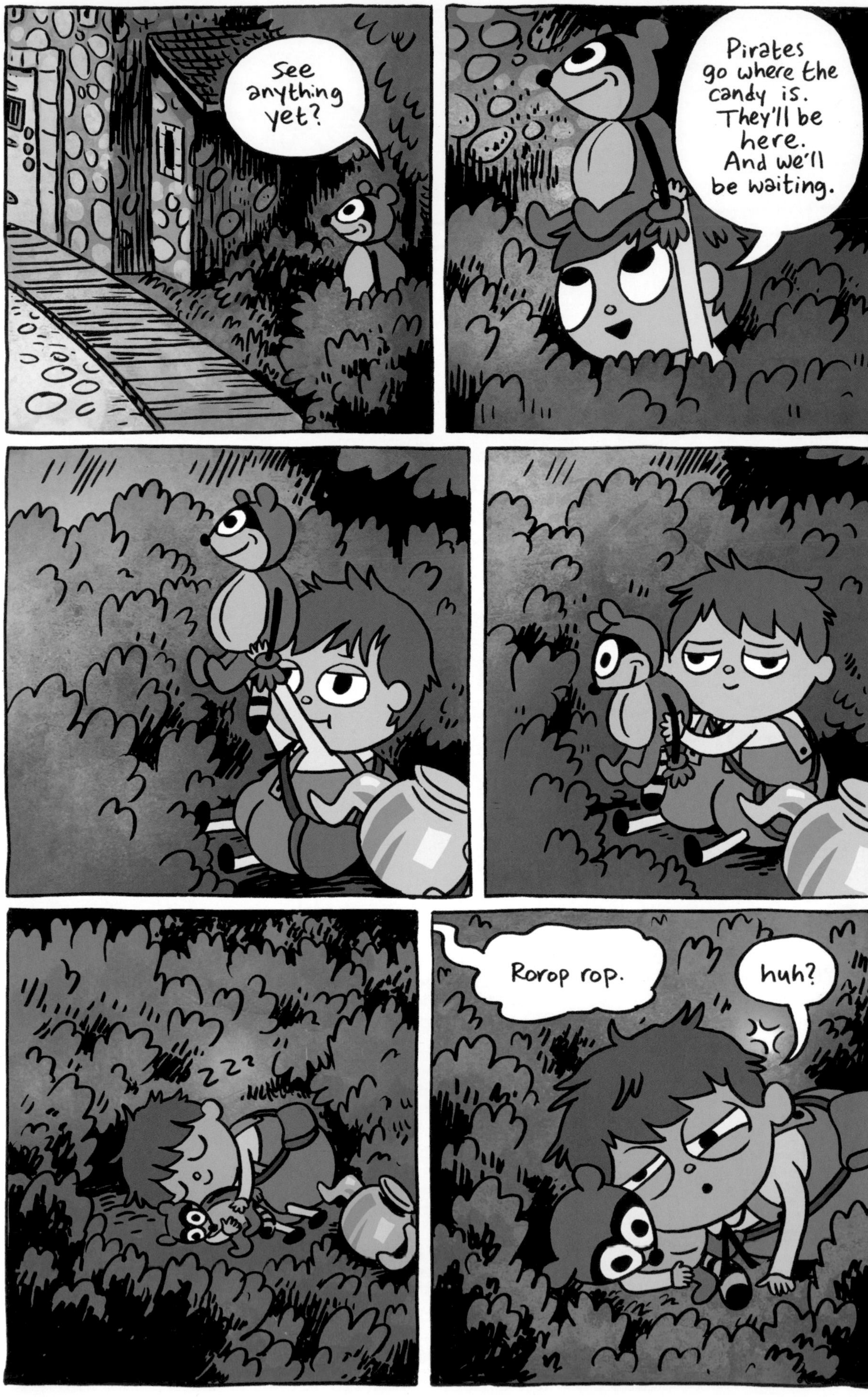
See anything yet?
Pirates go where the candy is. They'll be here. And we'll be waiting.
zzz
Rorop rop.
huh?

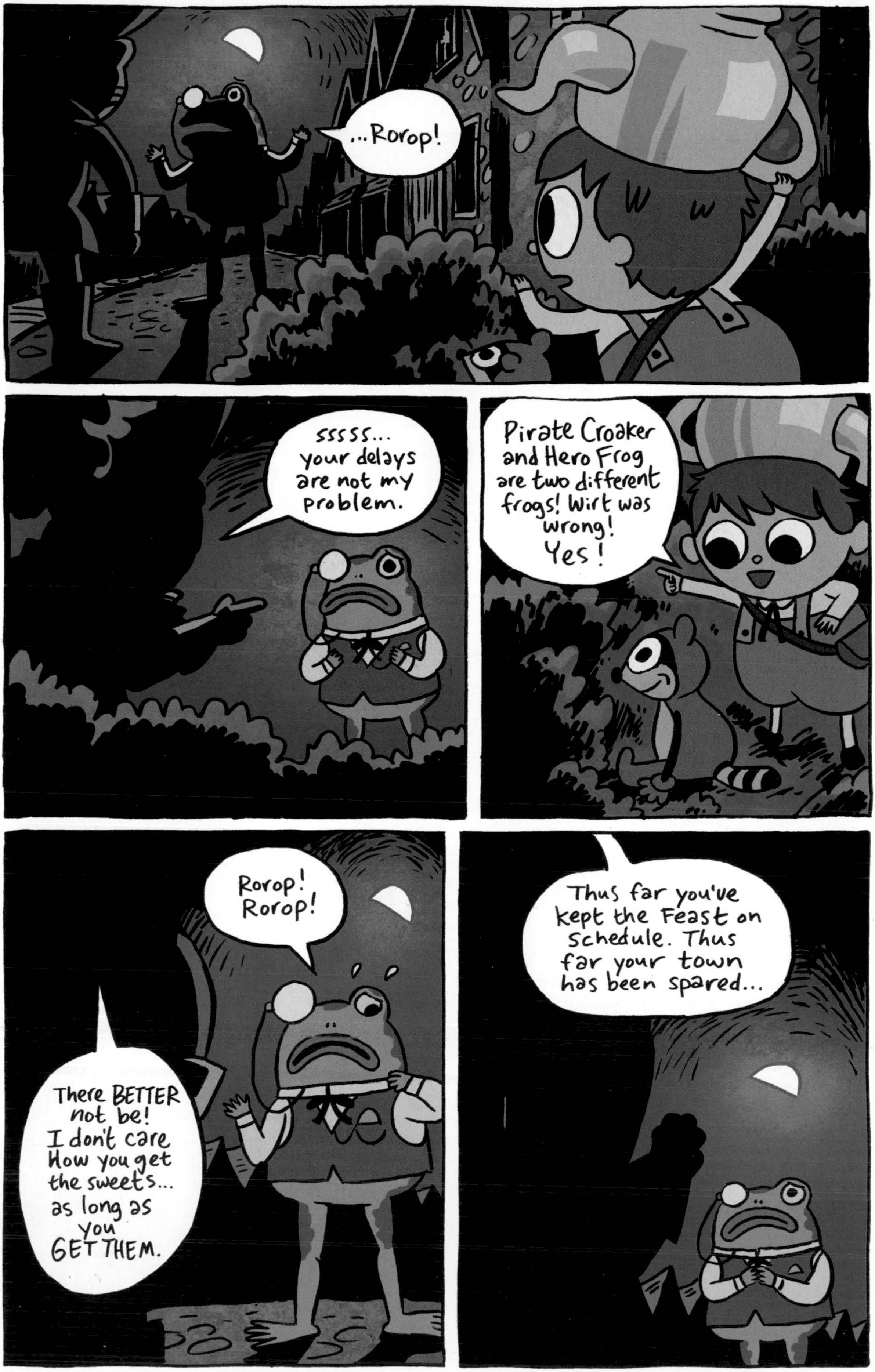
...Rorop!
sssss... your delays are not my problem.
Pirate Croaker and Hero Frog are two different frogs! Wirt was wrong! Yes!
Rorop! Rorop!
There BETTER not be! I don't care How you get the sweets... as long as you GET THEM.
Thus far you've kept the Feast on schedule. Thus far your town has been spared...

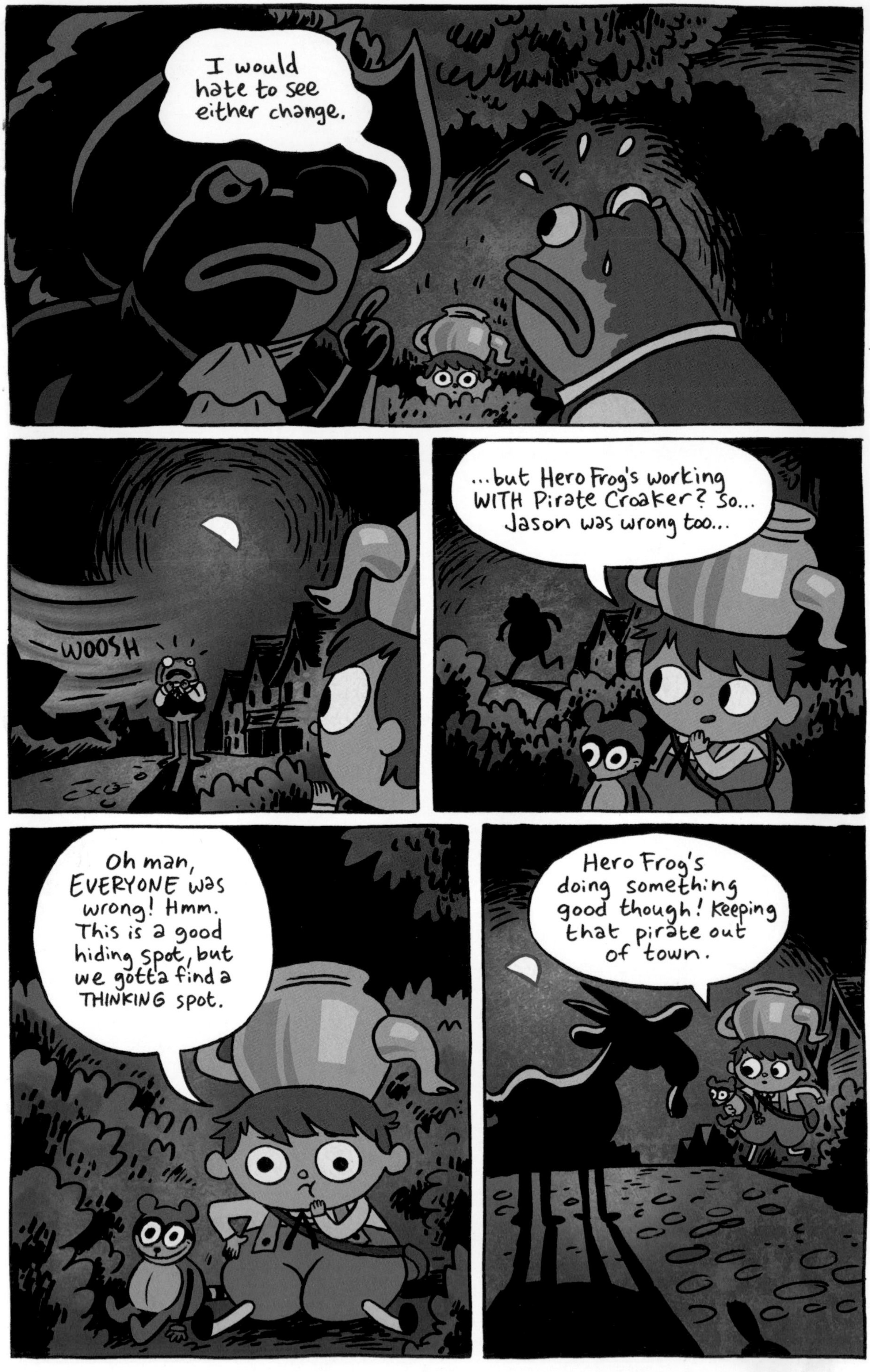
I would hate to see either change.
WOOSH
...but Hero Frog's working WITH Pirate Croaker? So... Jason was wrong too...
Oh man, EVERYONE was wrong! Hmm. This is a good hiding spot, but we gotta find a THINKING spot.
Hero Frog's doing something good though! Keeping that pirate out of town.

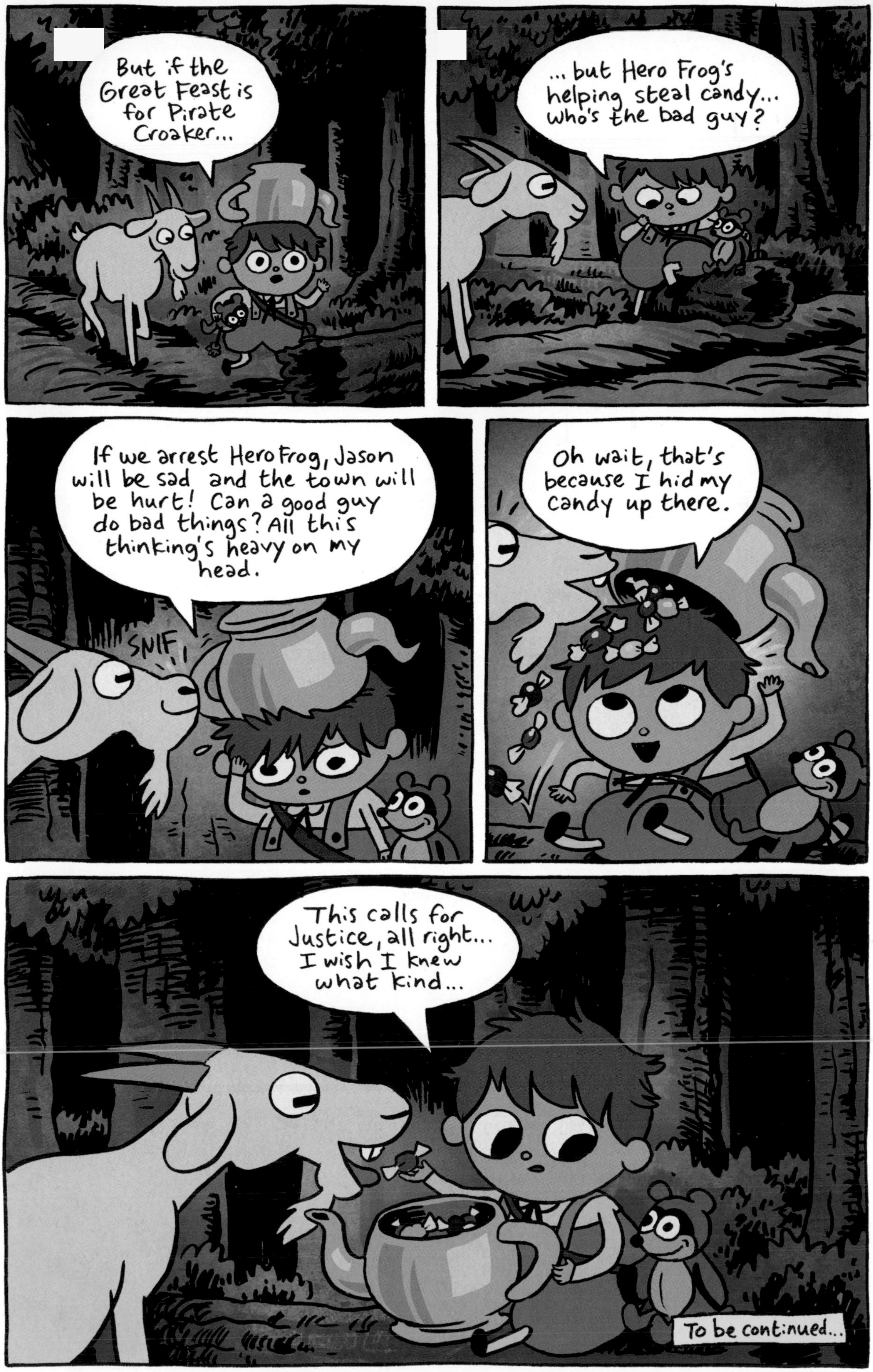
But if the Great Feast is for Pirate Croaker...
... but Hero Frog's helping steal candy... who's the bad guy?
If we arrest Hero Frog, Jason will be sad and the town will be hurt! Can a good guy do bad things? All this thinking's heavy on my head.
SNIF
Oh wait, that's because I hid my candy up there.
This calls for Justice, all right... I wish I knew what kind...
To be continued...

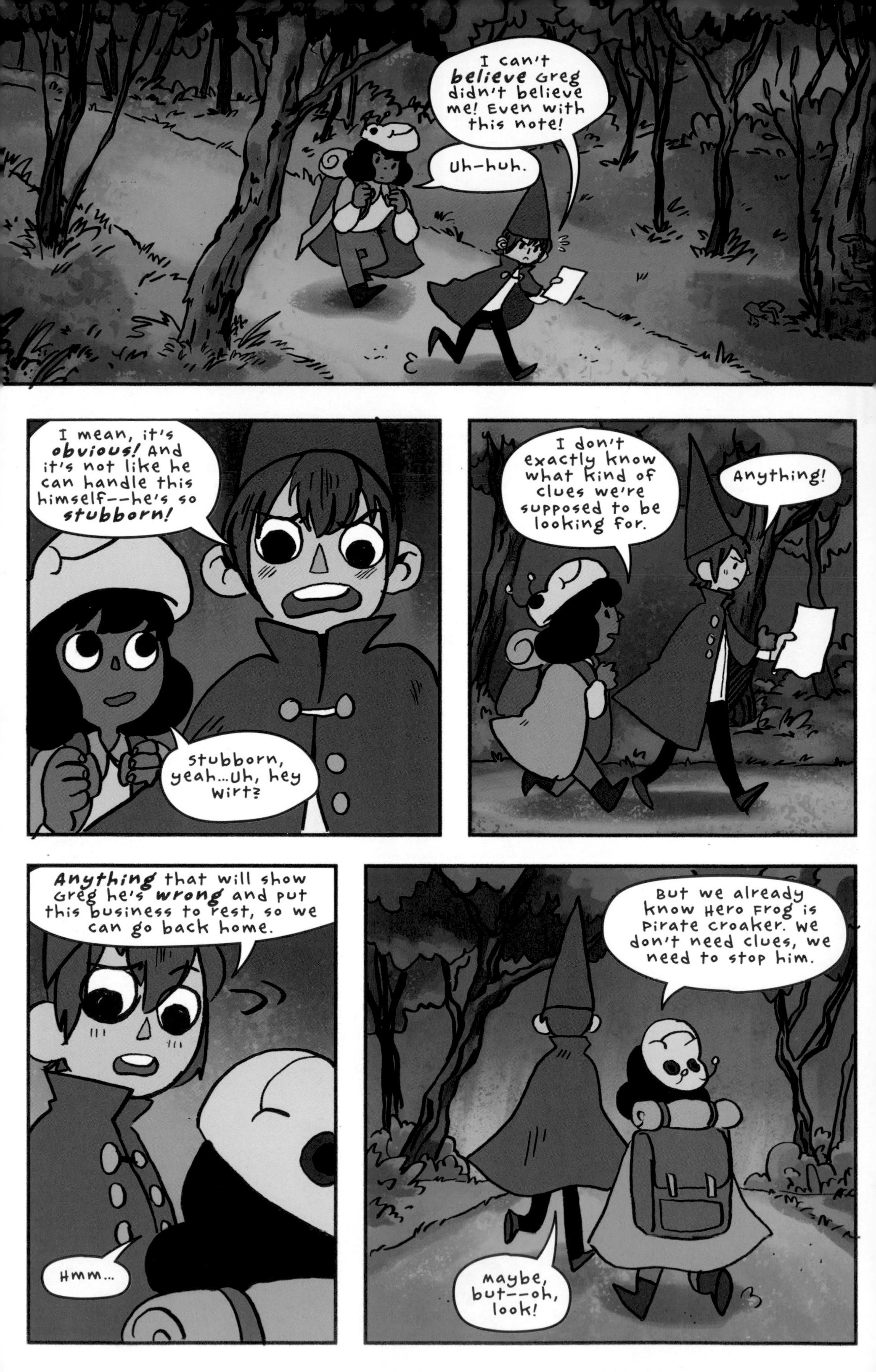

I can't **believe** Greg didn't believe me! Even with this note!
Uh-huh.
I mean, it's **obvious!** And it's not like he can handle this himself--he's so **stubborn!**
Stubborn, yeah...Uh, hey Wirt?
I don't exactly know what kind of clues we're supposed to be looking for.
Anything!
Anything that will show Greg he's **wrong** and put this business to rest, so we can go back home.
Hmm...
But we already know Hero Frog is Pirate Croaker. We don't need clues, we need to stop him.
Maybe, but--oh, look!

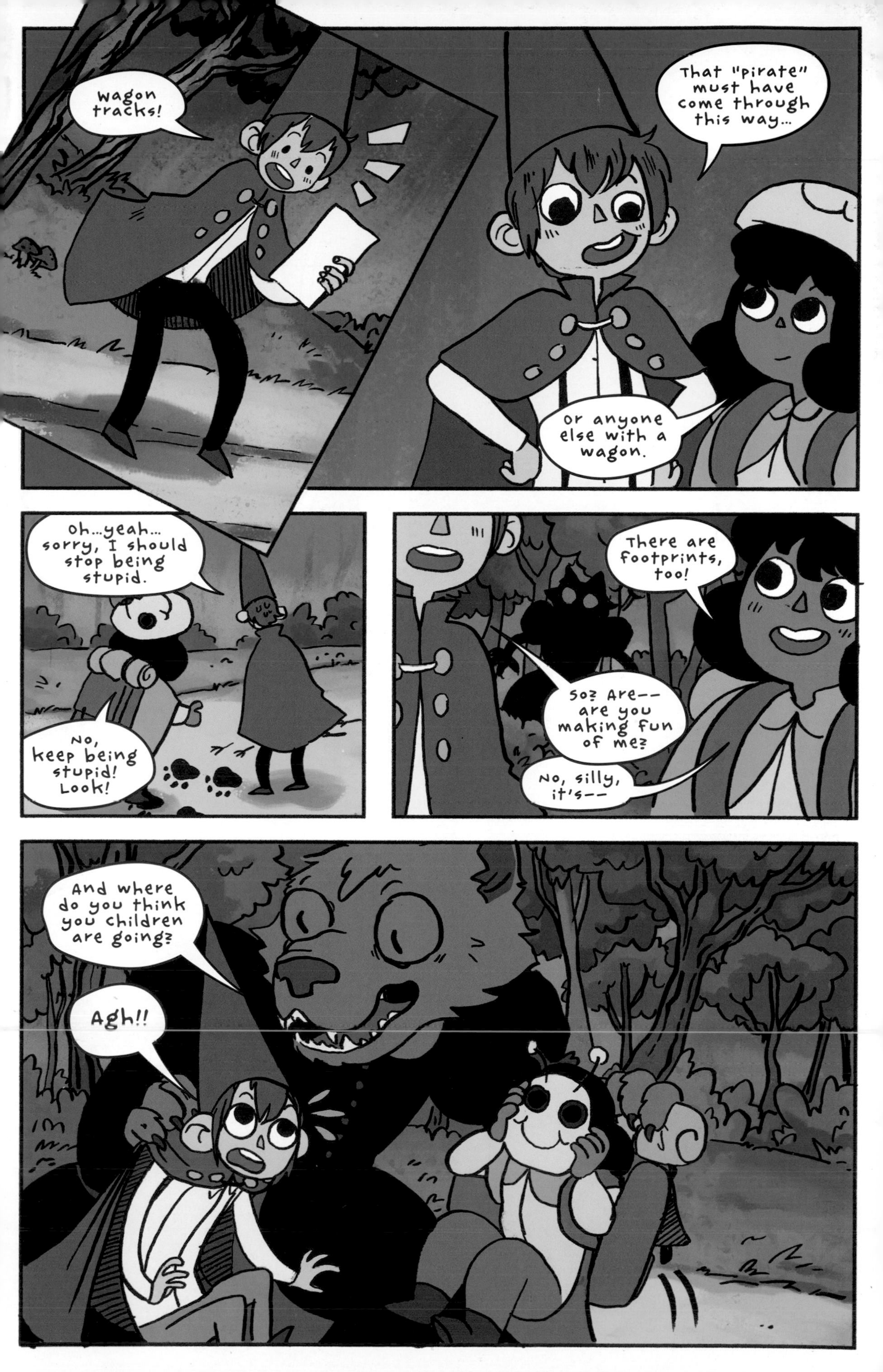
Wagon tracks!
That "pirate" must have come through this way...
Or anyone else with a wagon.
Oh...yeah... sorry, I should stop being stupid.
No, keep being stupid! Look!
There are footprints, too!
So? Are-- are you making fun of me?
No, silly, it's--
And where do you think you children are going?
Agh!!

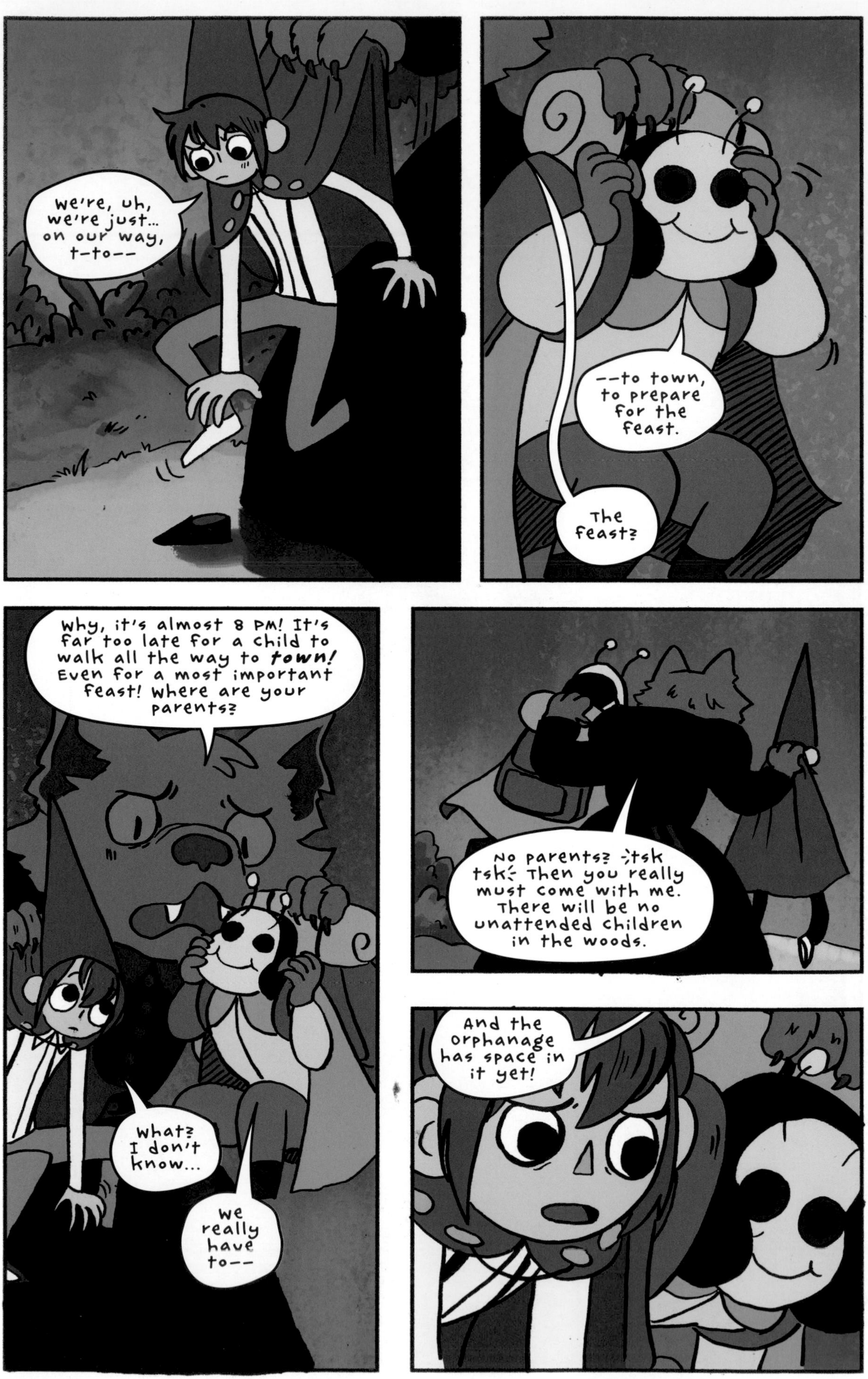
We're, uh, we're just... on our way, t-to--
--to town, to prepare for the feast.
The feast?
Why, it's almost 8 PM! It's far too late for a child to walk all the way to *town!* Even for a most important feast! Where are your parents?
What? I don't know...
We really have to--
No parents? -tsk tsk- Then you really must come with me. There will be no unattended children in the woods.
And the orphanage has space in it yet!

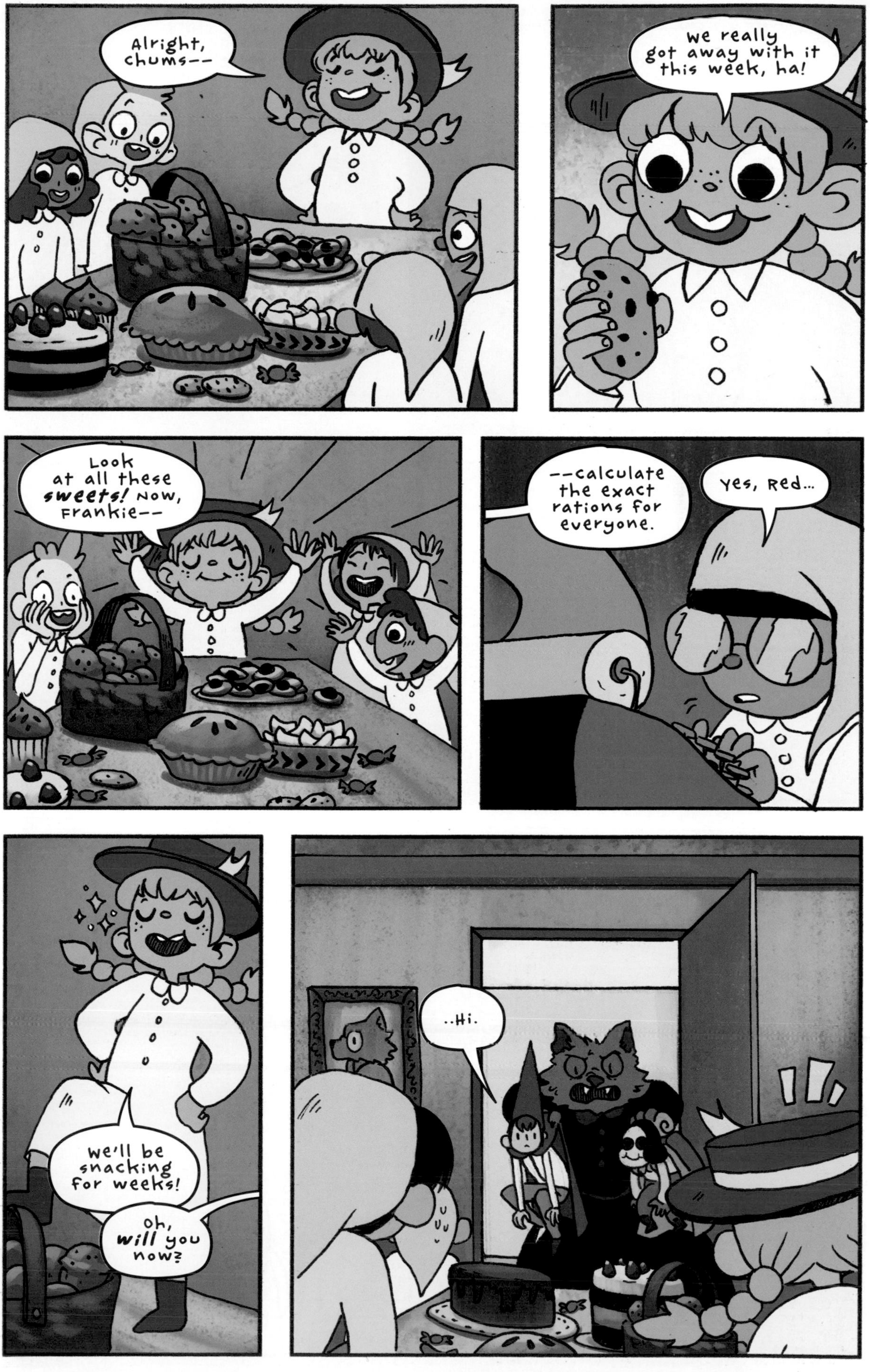
Alright, chums--
We really got away with it this week, ha!
Look at all these sweets! Now, Frankie--
--calculate the exact rations for everyone.
Yes, Red...
We'll be snacking for weeks!
Oh, will you now?
..Hi.

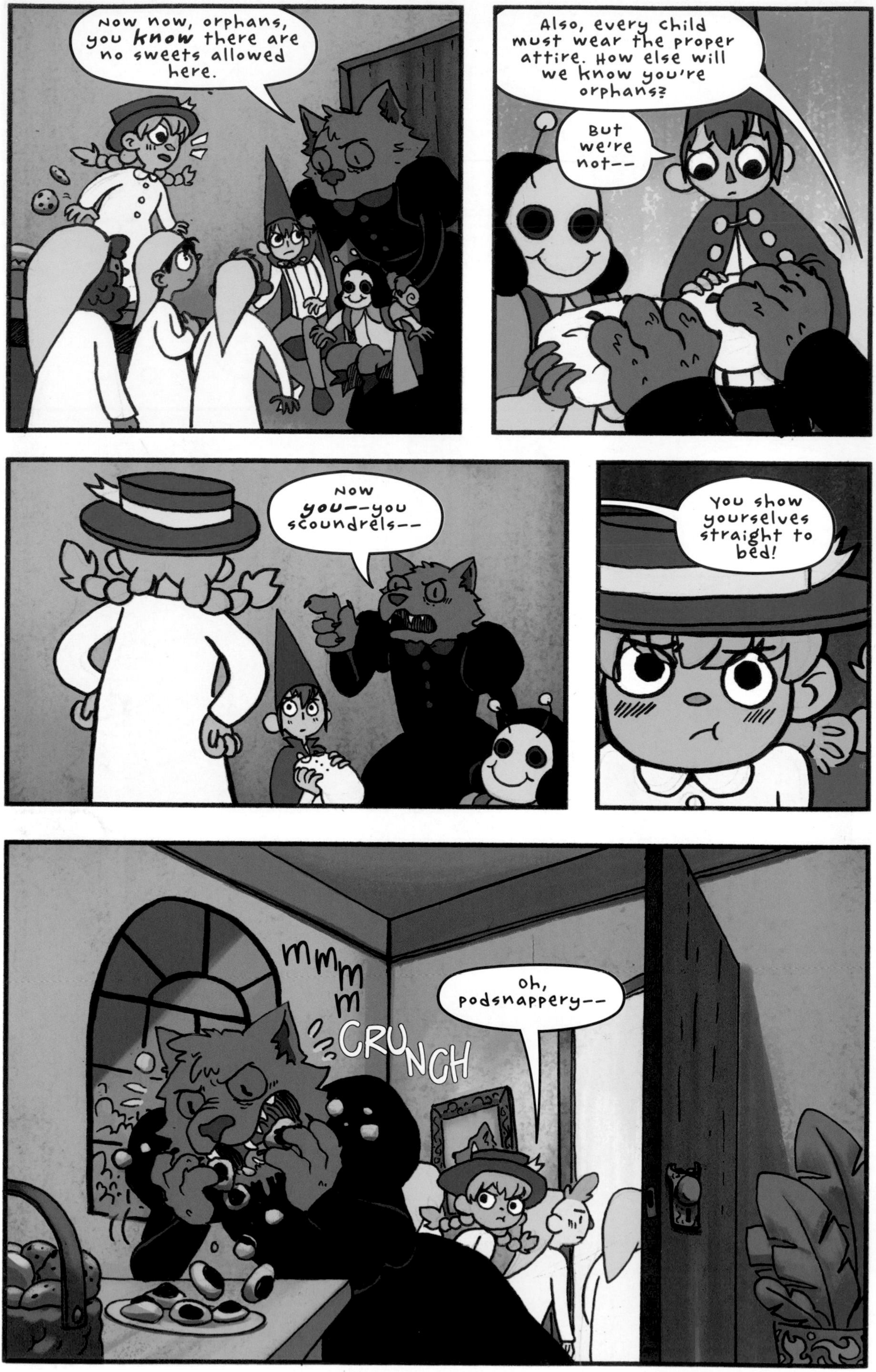
Now now, orphans, you *know* there are no sweets allowed here.
Also, every child must wear the proper attire. How else will we know you're orphans?
But we're not--
Now *you*--you scoundrels--
You show yourselves straight to bed!
MMMMM
CRUNCH
Oh, podsnappery--

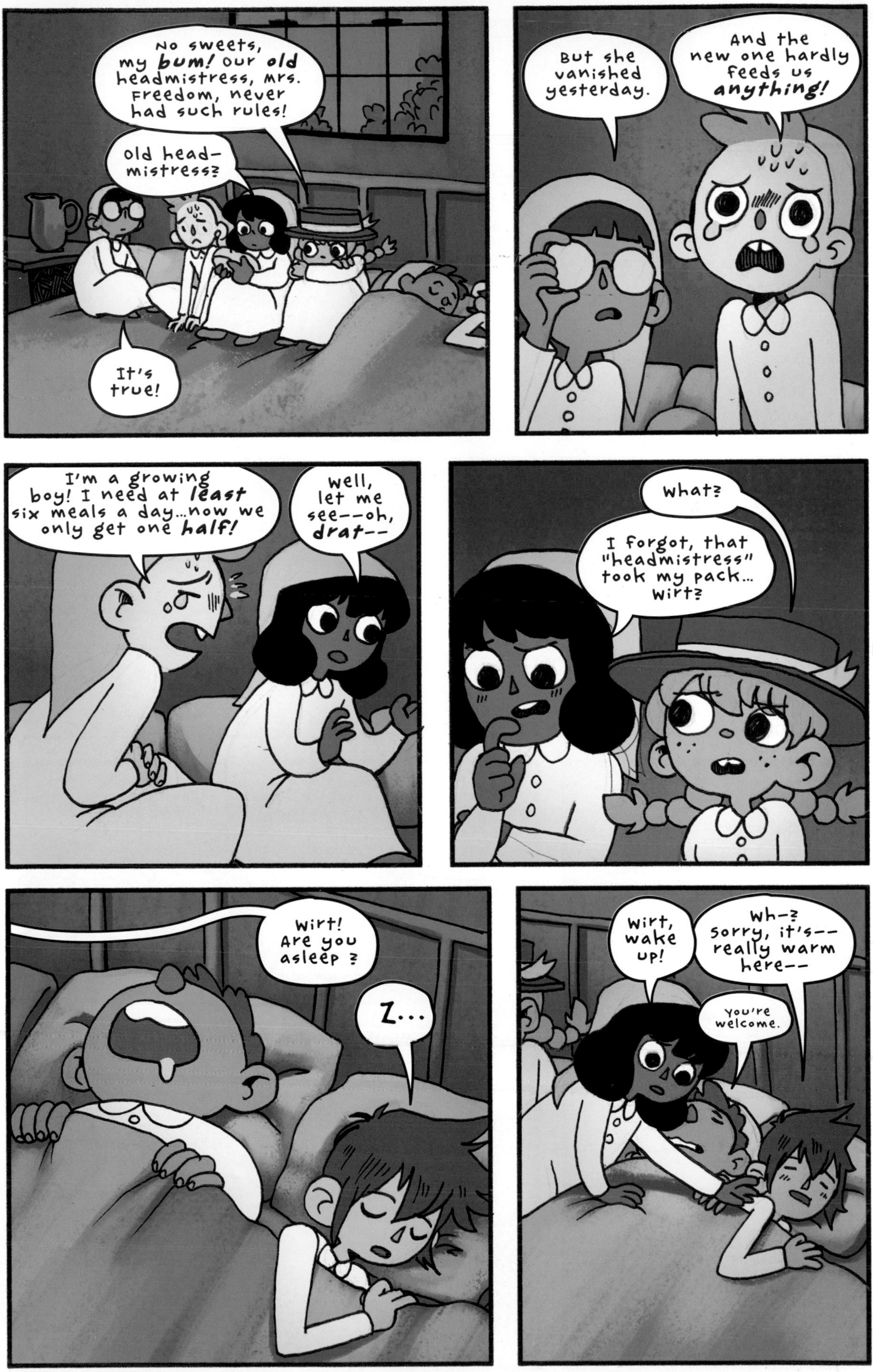
No sweets, my **bum!** Our **old** headmistress, Mrs. Freedom, never had such rules!
Old head-mistress?
It's true!
But she vanished yesterday.
And the new one hardly feeds us **anything!**
I'm a growing boy! I need at **least** six meals a day...now we only get one **half!**
Well, let me see--oh, **drat**--
What?
I forgot, that "headmistress" took my pack... Wirt?
Wirt! Are you asleep?
Z...
Wirt, wake up!
Wh-? Sorry, it's--really warm here--
You're welcome.

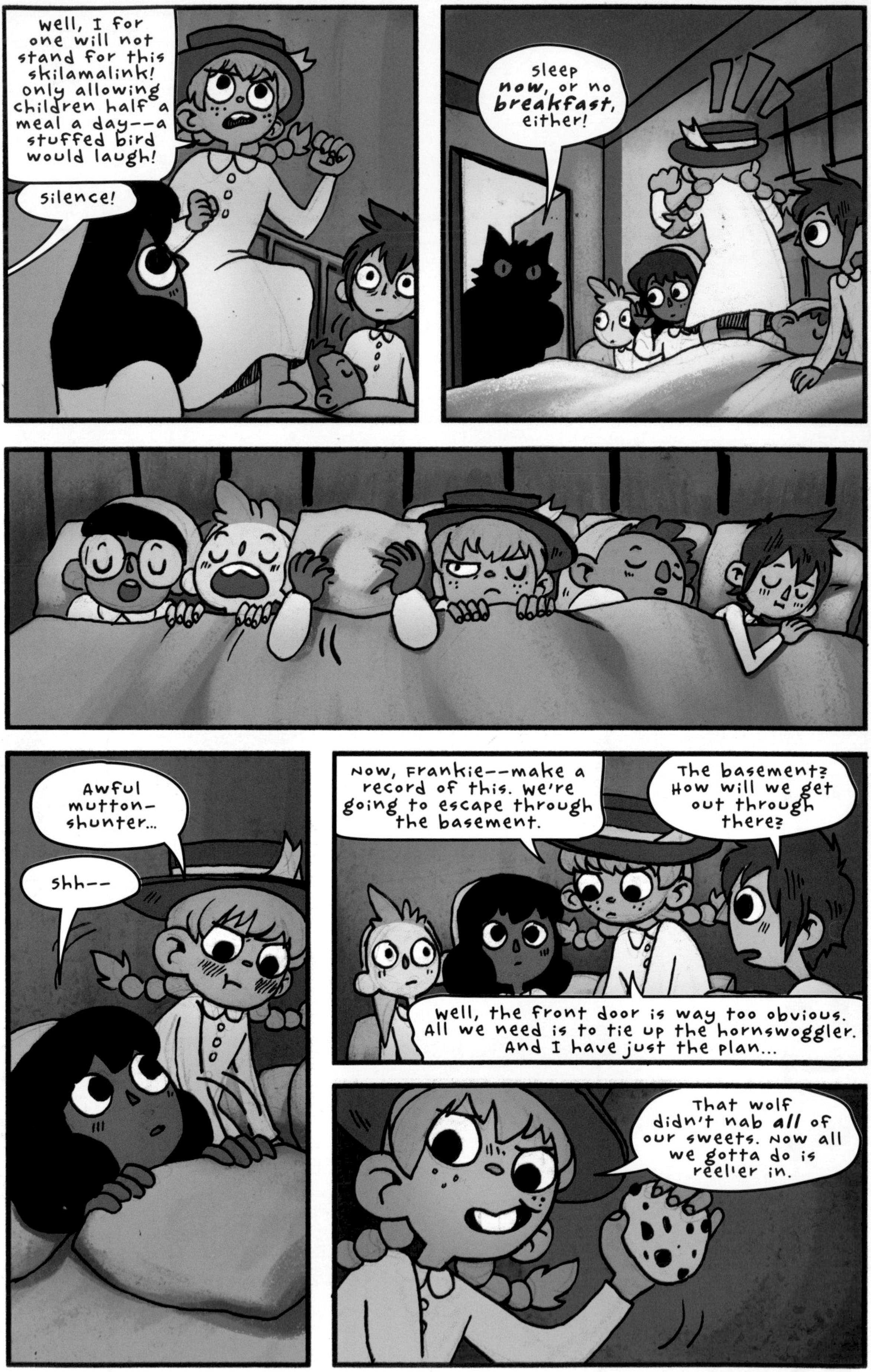
Well, I for one will not stand for this skilamalink! Only allowing children half a meal a day--a stuffed bird would laugh!
Silence!
Sleep now, or no breakfast, either!
Awful mutton-shunter...
Shh--
Now, Frankie--make a record of this. We're going to escape through the basement.
The basement? How will we get out through there?
Well, the front door is way too obvious. All we need is to tie up the hornswoggler. And I have just the plan...
That wolf didn't nab all of our sweets. Now all we gotta do is reel'er in.

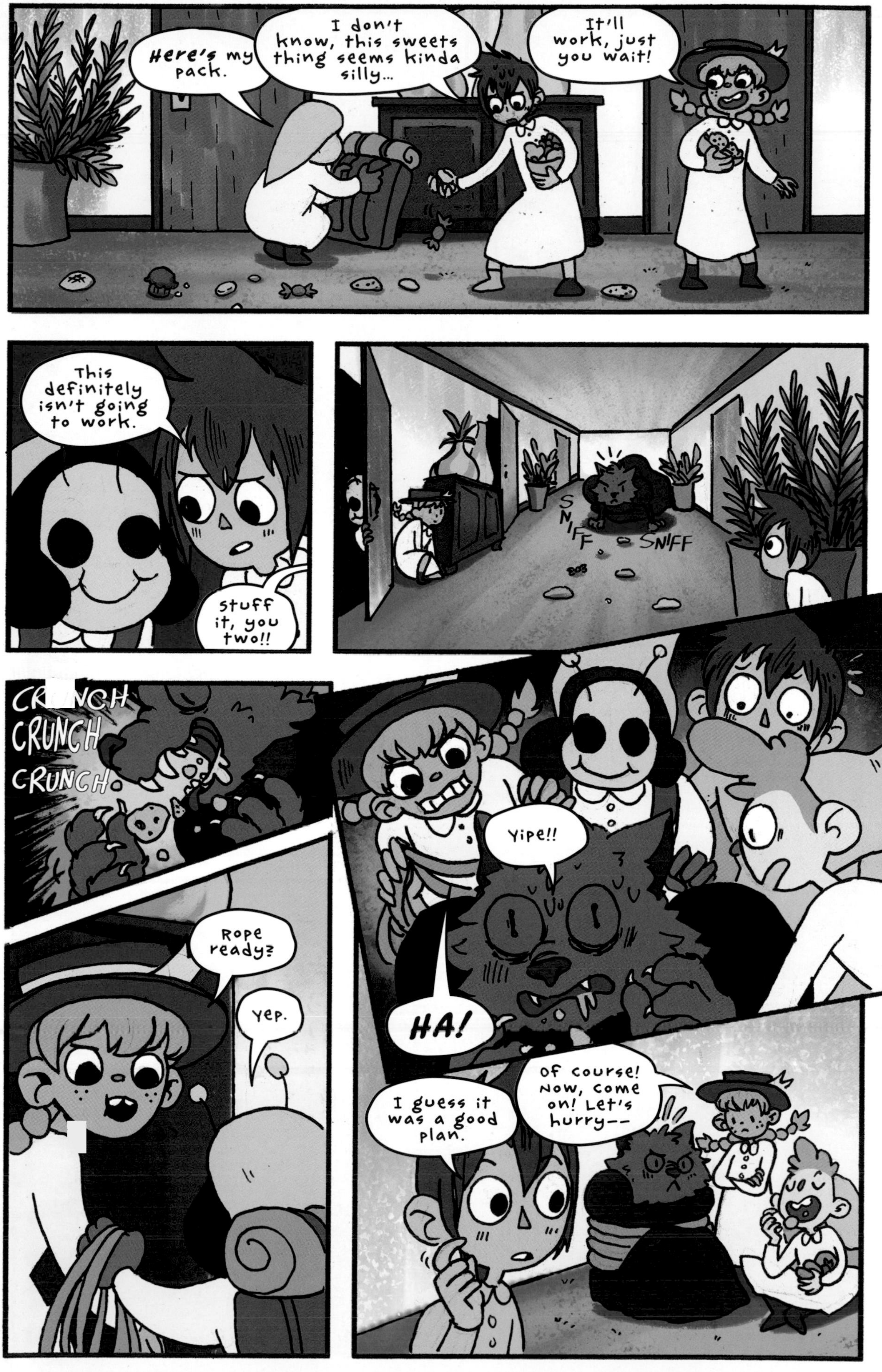
Here's my pack.
I don't know, this sweets thing seems kinda silly...
It'll work, just you wait!
This definitely isn't going to work.
Stuff it, you two!!
SNIFF
SNIFF
CRUNCH
CRUNCH
CRUNCH
Rope ready?
Yep.
Yipe!!
HA!
I guess it was a good plan.
Of course! Now, come on! Let's hurry--

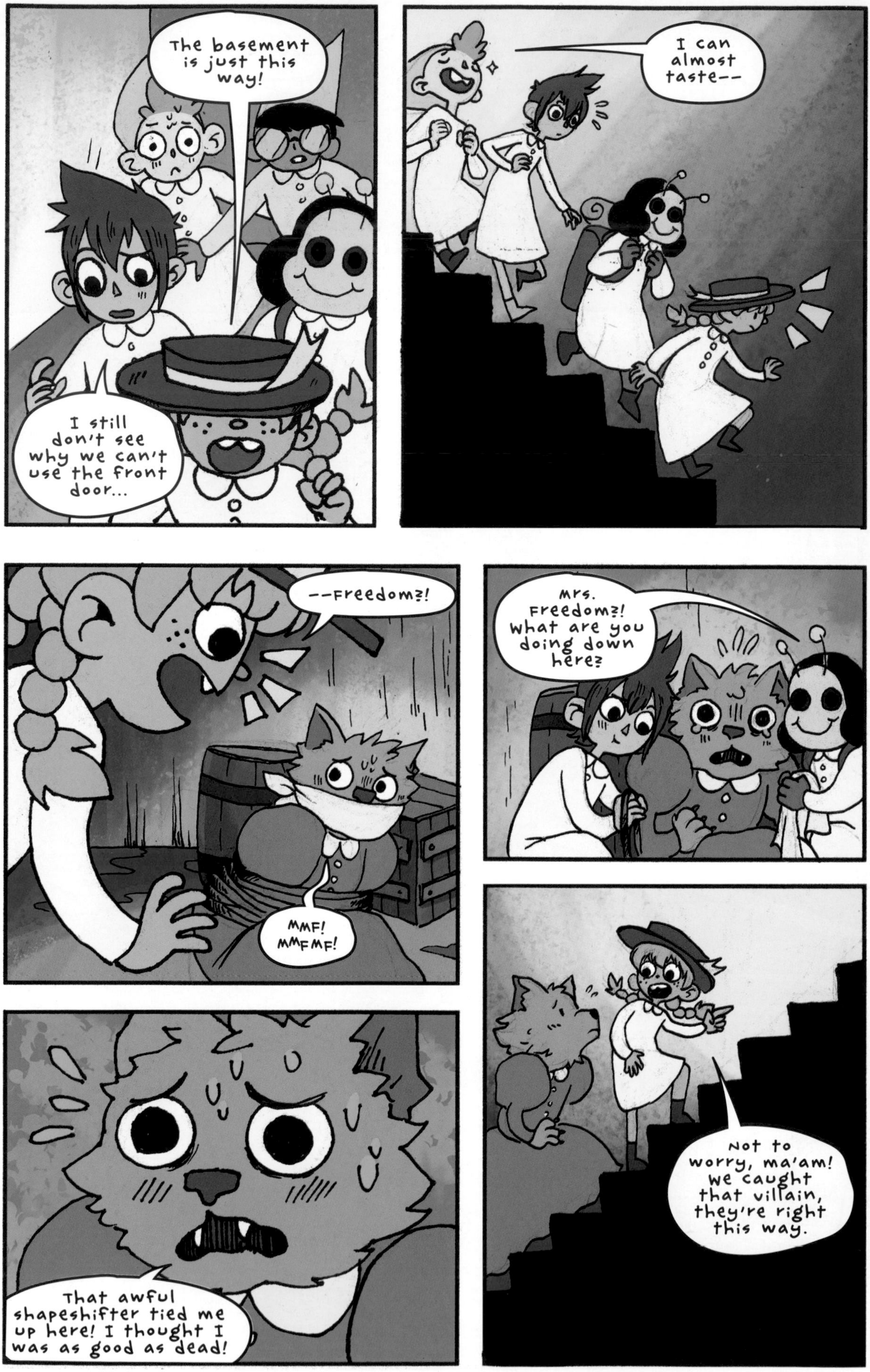
The basement is just this way!
I still don't see why we can't use the front door...
I can almost taste--
--Freedomz!
MMF! MMFMF!
Mrs. Freedomz! What are you doing down here?
That awful shapeshifter tied me up here! I thought I was as good as dead!
Not to worry, ma'am! We caught that villain, they're right this way.

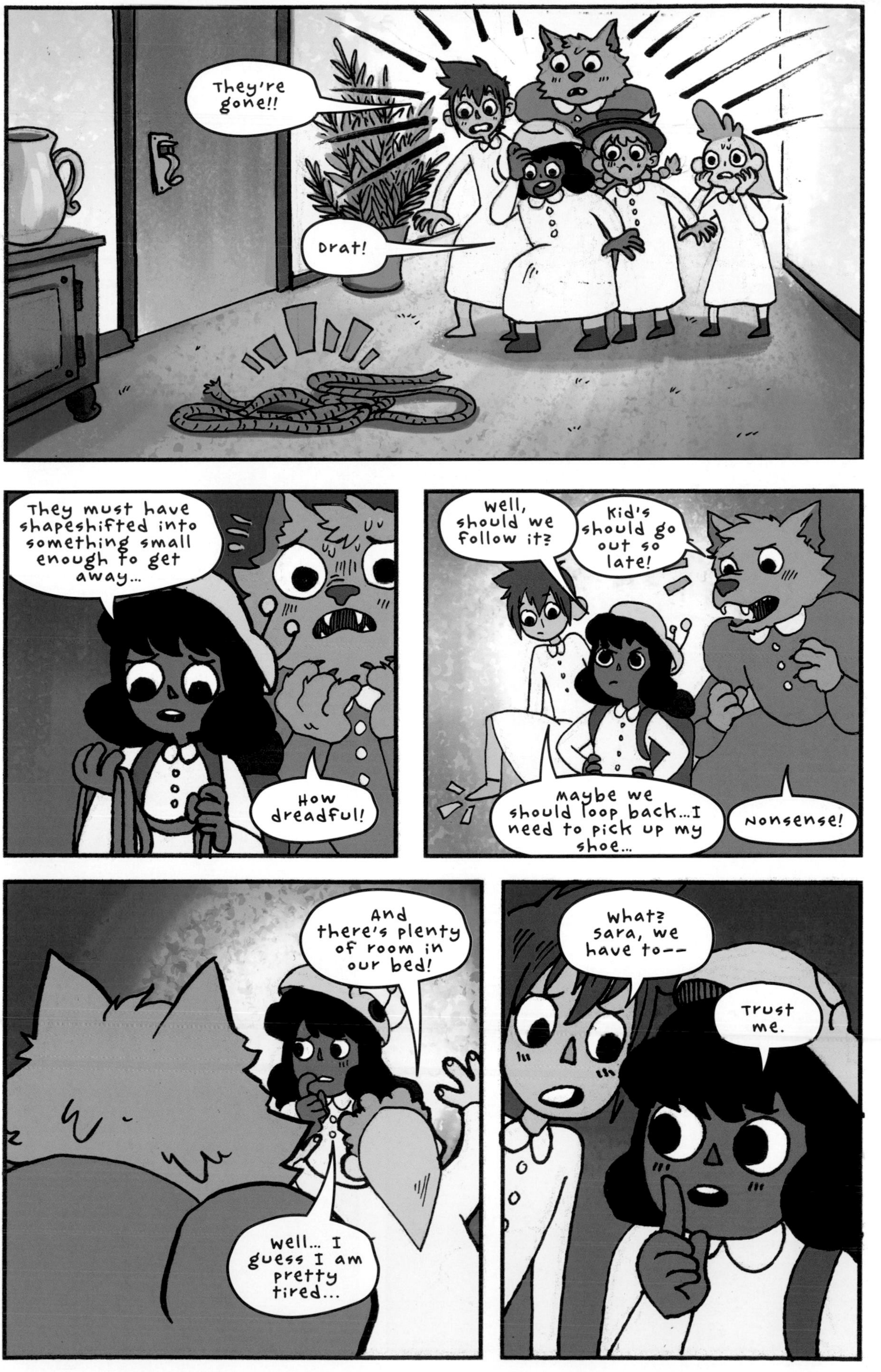
They're gone!!
Drat!
They must have shapeshifted into something small enough to get away...
How dreadful!
Well, should we follow it?
Kid's should go out so late!
Maybe we should loop back...I need to pick up my shoe...
Nonsense!
And there's plenty of room in our bed!
Well... I guess I am pretty tired...
What? Sara, we have to--
Trust me.

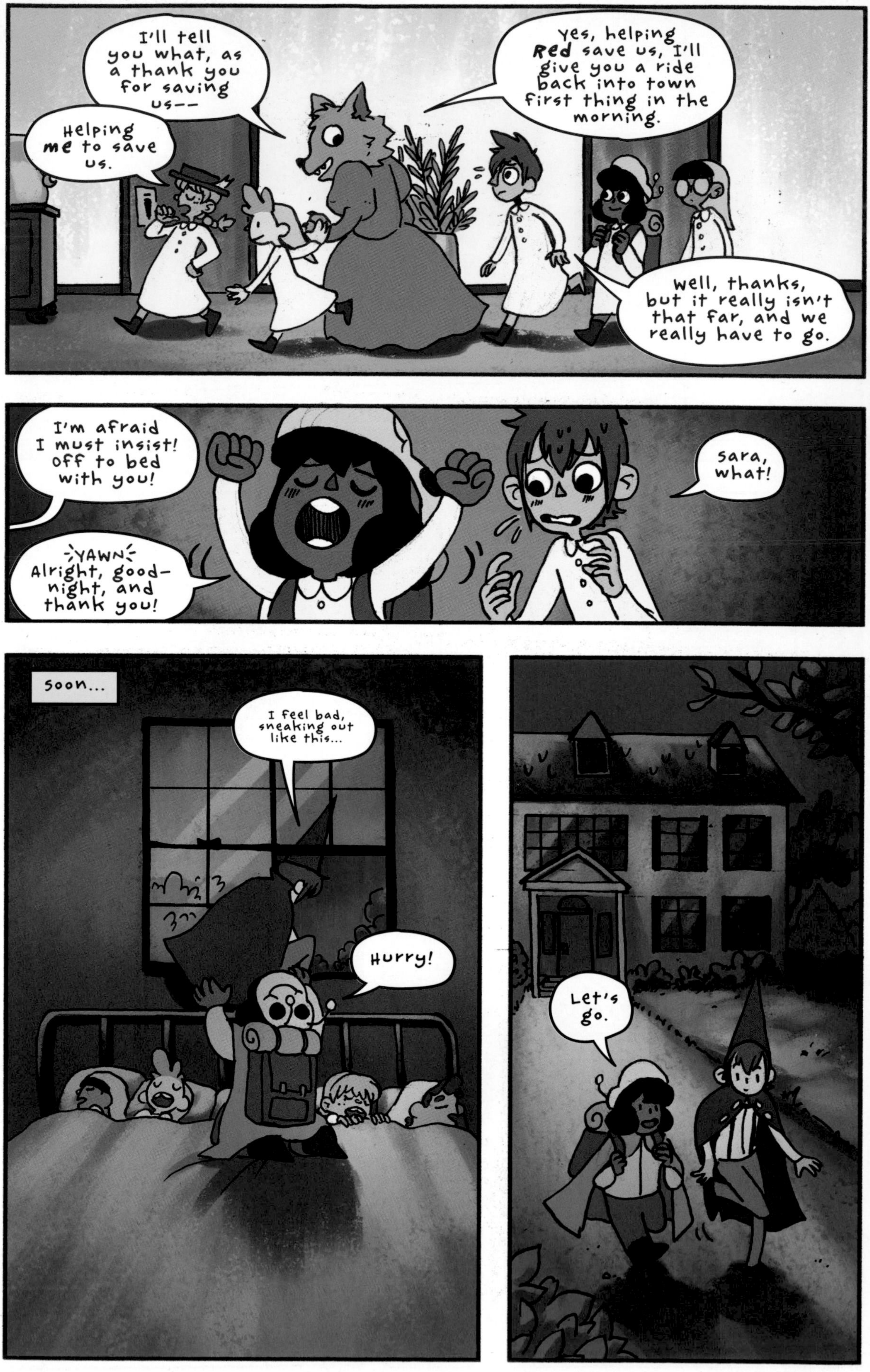
I'll tell you what, as a thank you for saving us--
Helping me to save us.
Yes, helping Red save us, I'll give you a ride back into town first thing in the morning.
Well, thanks, but it really isn't that far, and we really have to go.
I'm afraid I must insist! Off to bed with you!
YAWN
Alright, good-night, and thank you!
Sara, what!
Soon...
I feel bad, sneaking out like this...
Hurry!
Let's go.

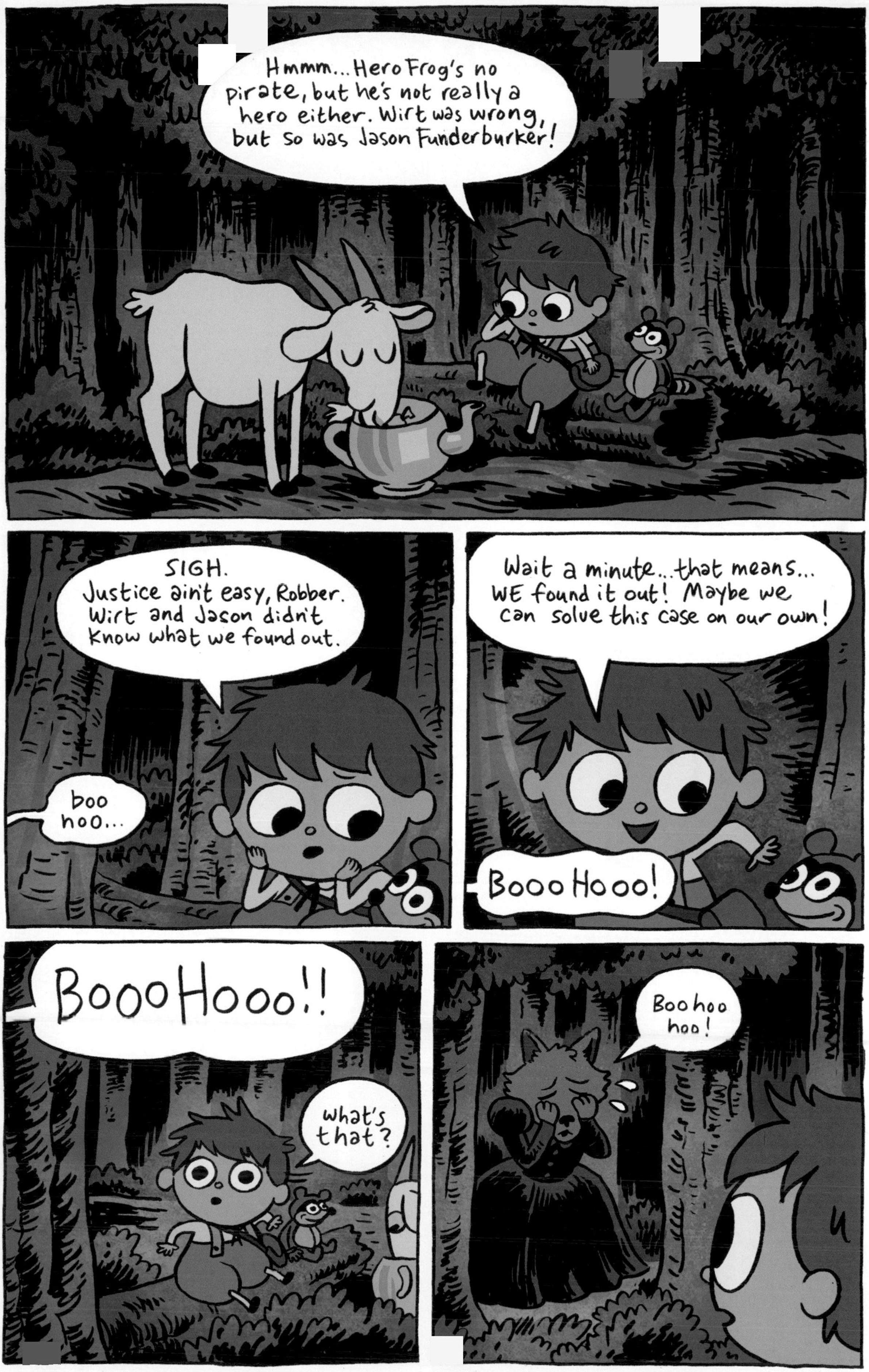
Hmmm... Hero Frog's no pirate, but he's not really a hero either. Wirt was wrong, but so was Jason Funderburker!
SIGH. Justice ain't easy, Robber. Wirt and Jason didn't know what we found out.
boo hoo...
Wait a minute... that means... WE found it out! Maybe we can solve this case on our own!
Booo Hooo!
BoooHooo!!
what's that?
Boo hoo hoo!

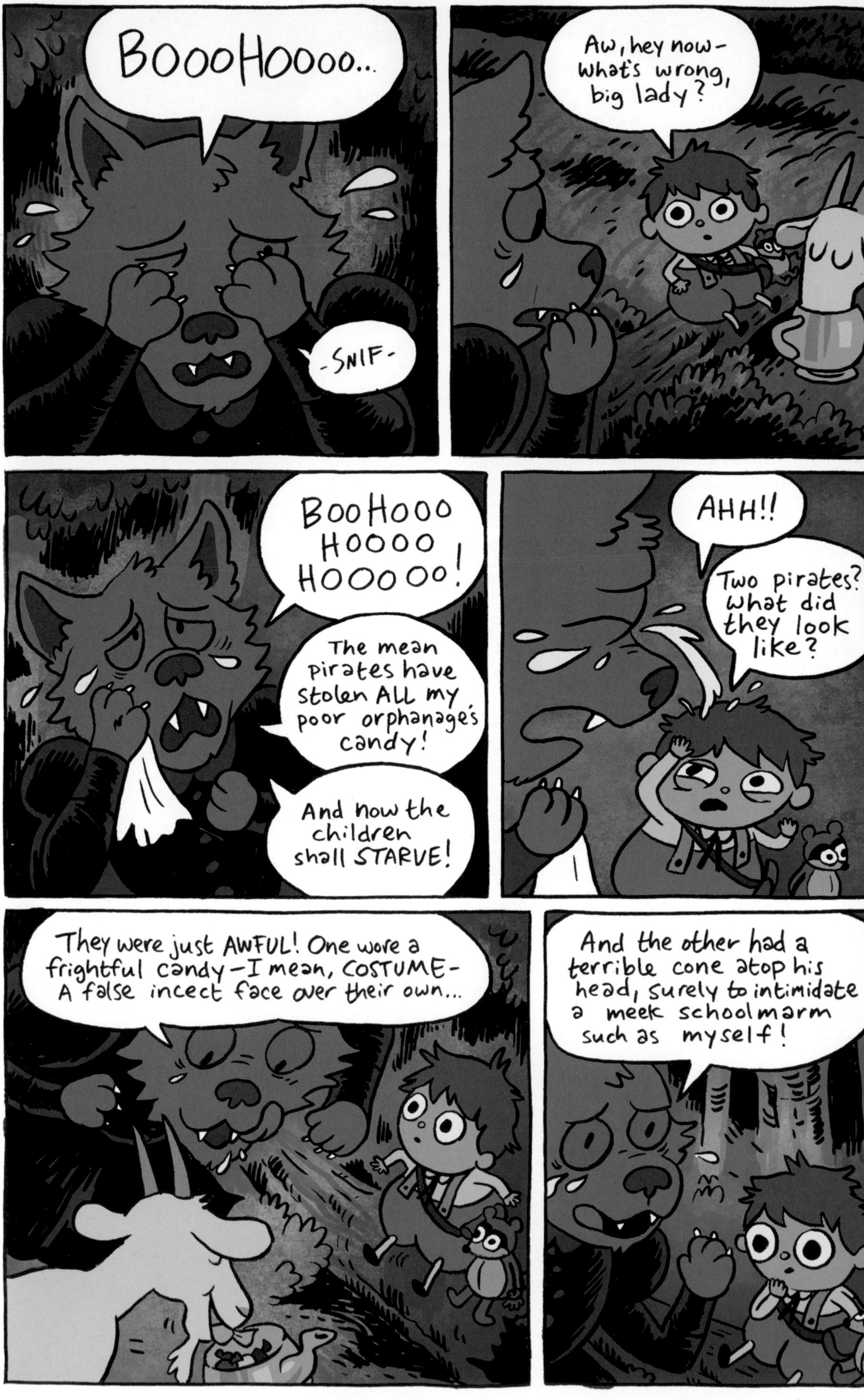
BOOOHOOOO...
-SNIF-
Aw, hey now- what's wrong, big lady?
BOOHOOO HOOOO HOOOOOO!
The mean pirates have stolen ALL my poor orphanage's candy!
And now the children shall STARVE!
AHH!!
Two pirates? what did they look like?
They were just AWFUL! One wore a frightful candy—I mean, COSTUME- A false incect face over their own...
And the other had a terrible cone atop his head, surely to intimidate a meek schoolmarm such as myself!

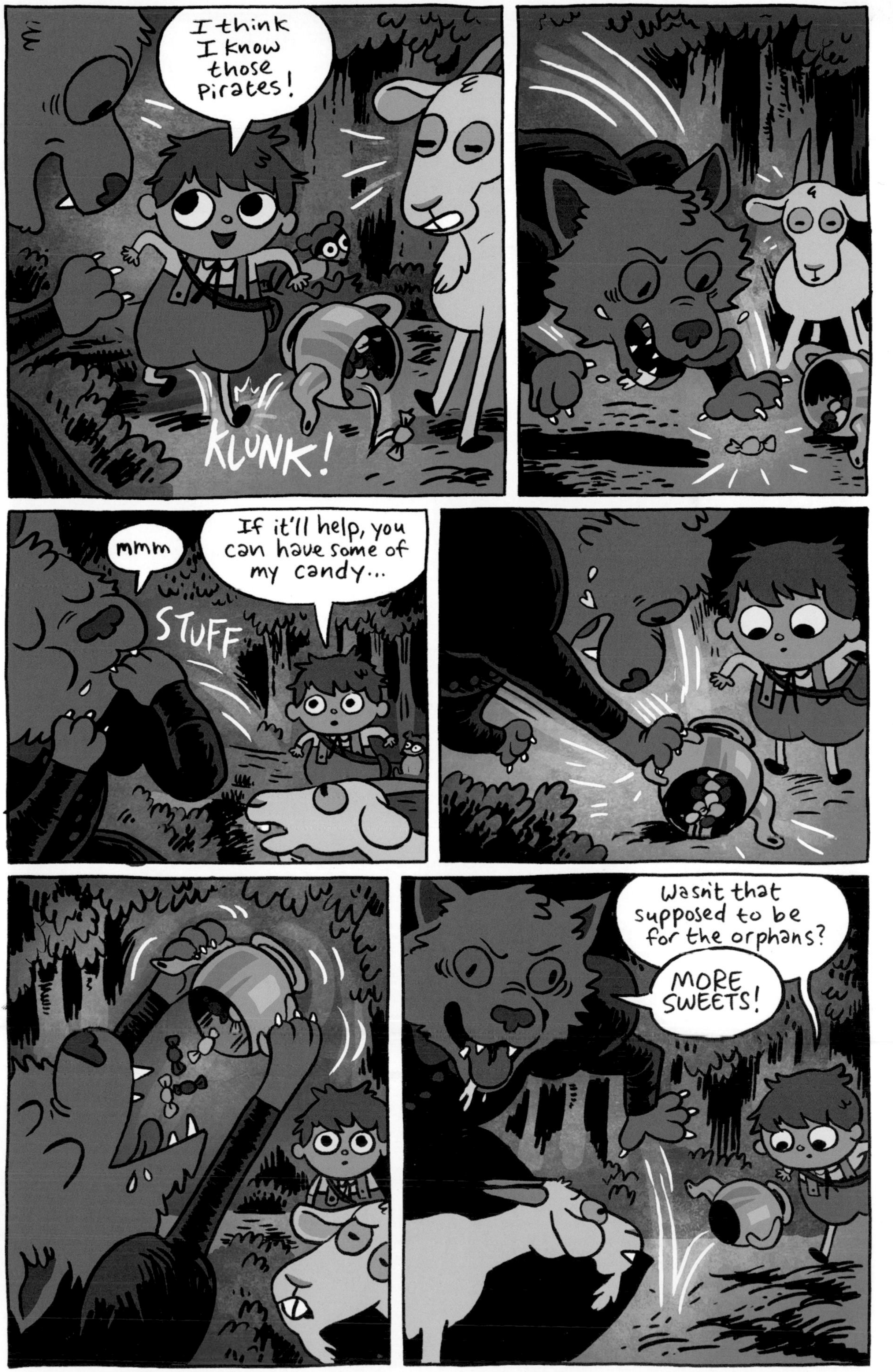
I think I know those Pirates!
KLUNK!
mmm
If it'll help, you can have some of my candy...
STUFF
Wasn't that supposed to be for the orphans?
MORE SWEETS!

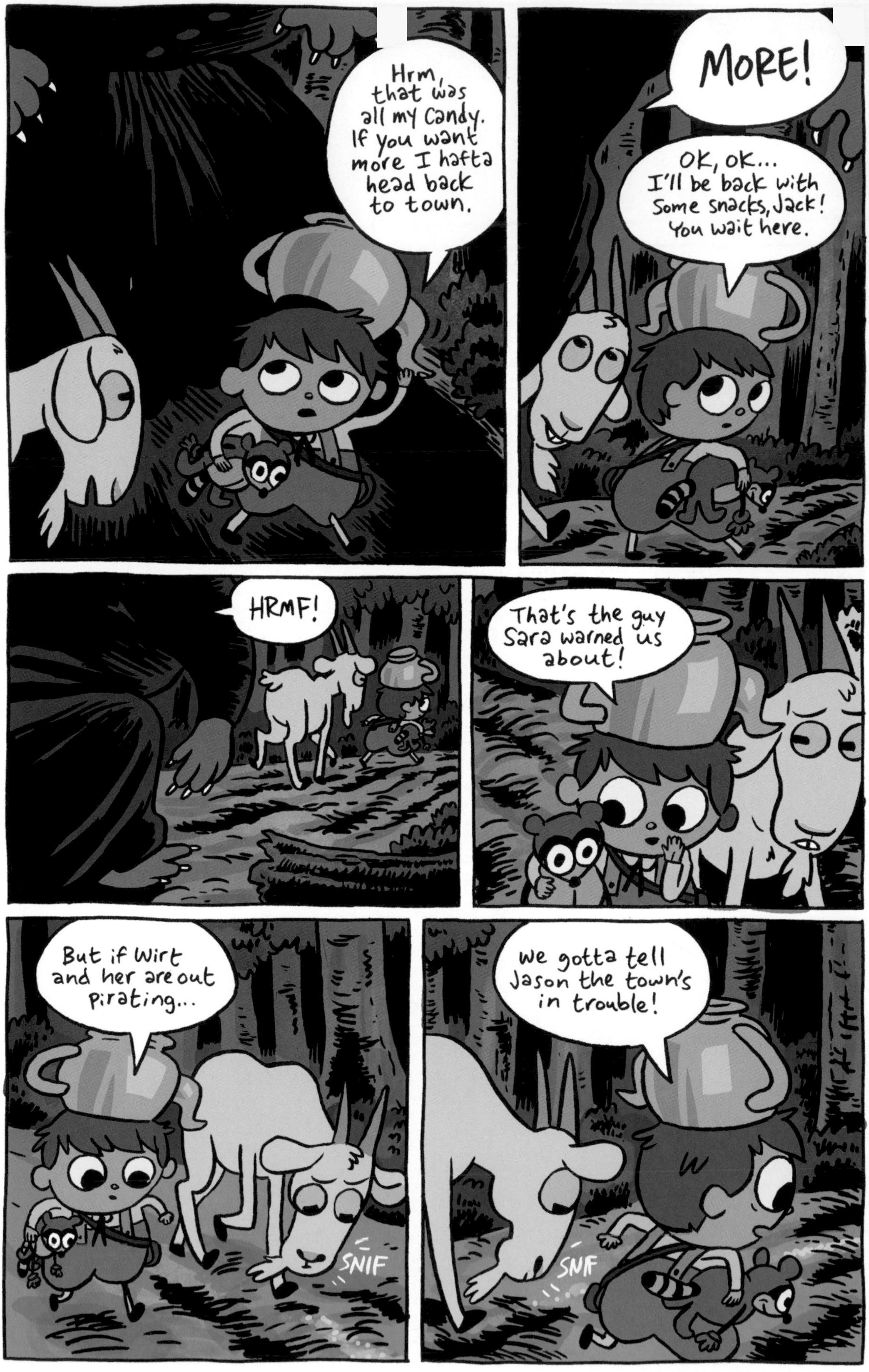
Hrm, that was all my Candy. If you want more I hafta head back to town.
MORE!
OK, OK... I'll be back with Some snacks, Jack! You wait here.
HRMF!
That's the guy Sara warned us about!
But if Wirt and her are out pirating...
SNIF
we gotta tell Jason the town's in trouble!
SNIF

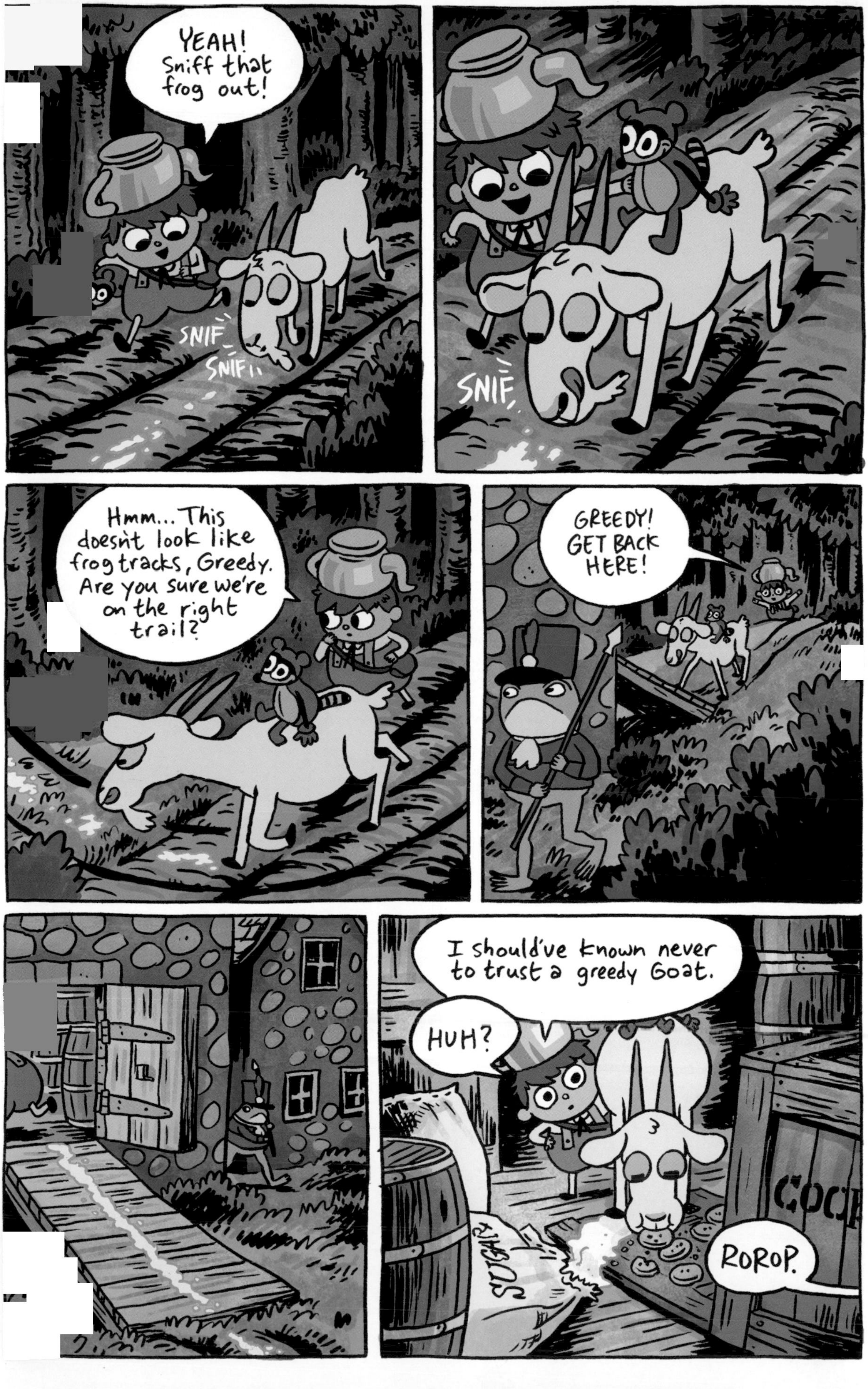
YEAH! Sniff that frog out!
SNIF SNIF
SNIF
Hmm... This doesn't look like frog tracks, Greedy. Are you sure we're on the right trail?
GREEDY! GET BACK HERE!
I should've known never to trust a greedy Goat.
HUH?
ROROP.

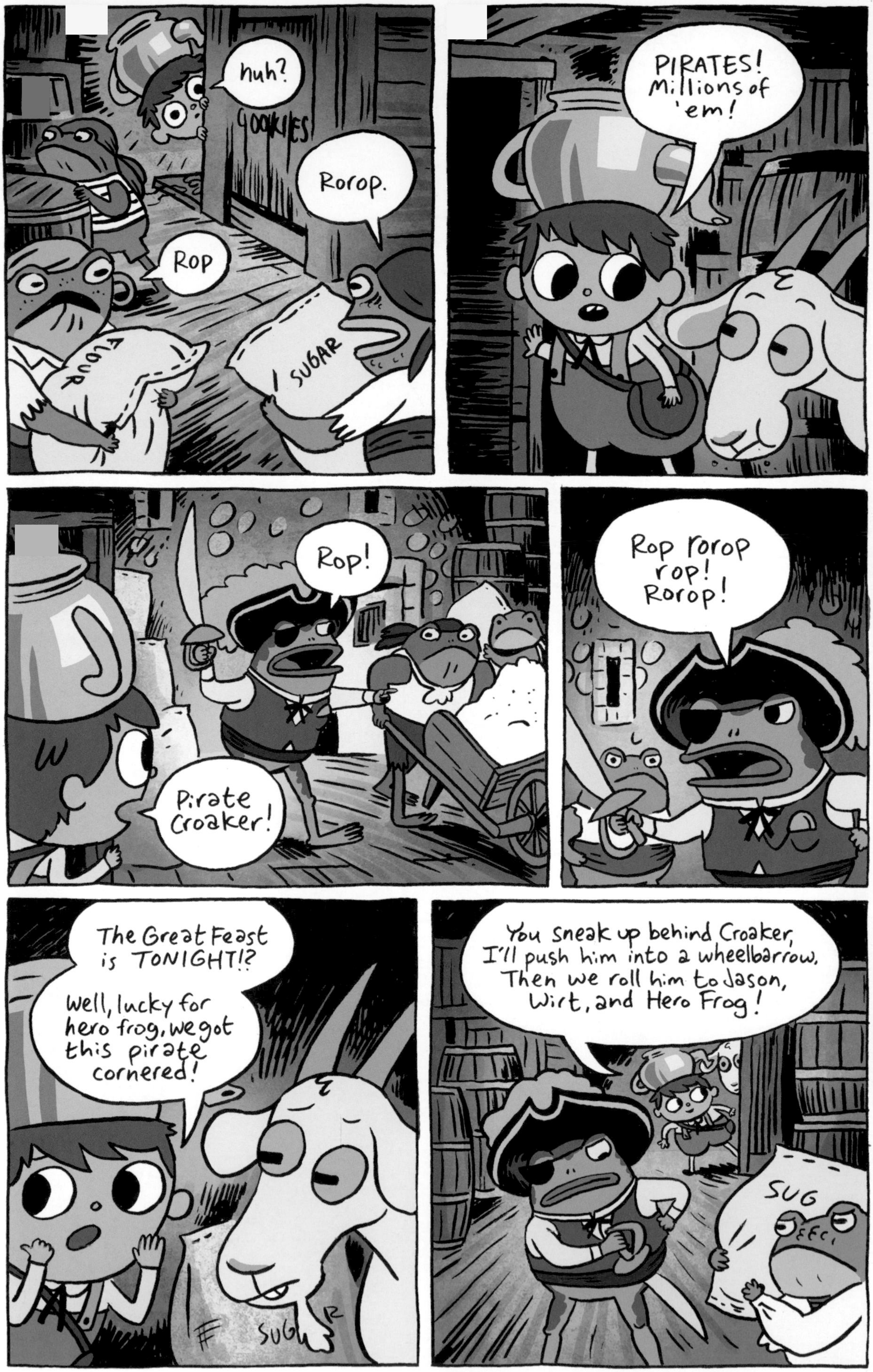
huh?
COOKIES
Rorop.
Rop
FLOUR
SUGAR
PIRATES! Millions of 'em!
Rop!
Pirate Croaker!
Rop rorop rop! Rorop!
The Great Feast is TONIGHT!?
Well, lucky for hero frog, we got this pirate cornered!
SUGAR
You sneak up behind Croaker, I'll push him into a wheelbarrow. Then we roll him to Jason, Wirt, and Hero Frog!
SUG

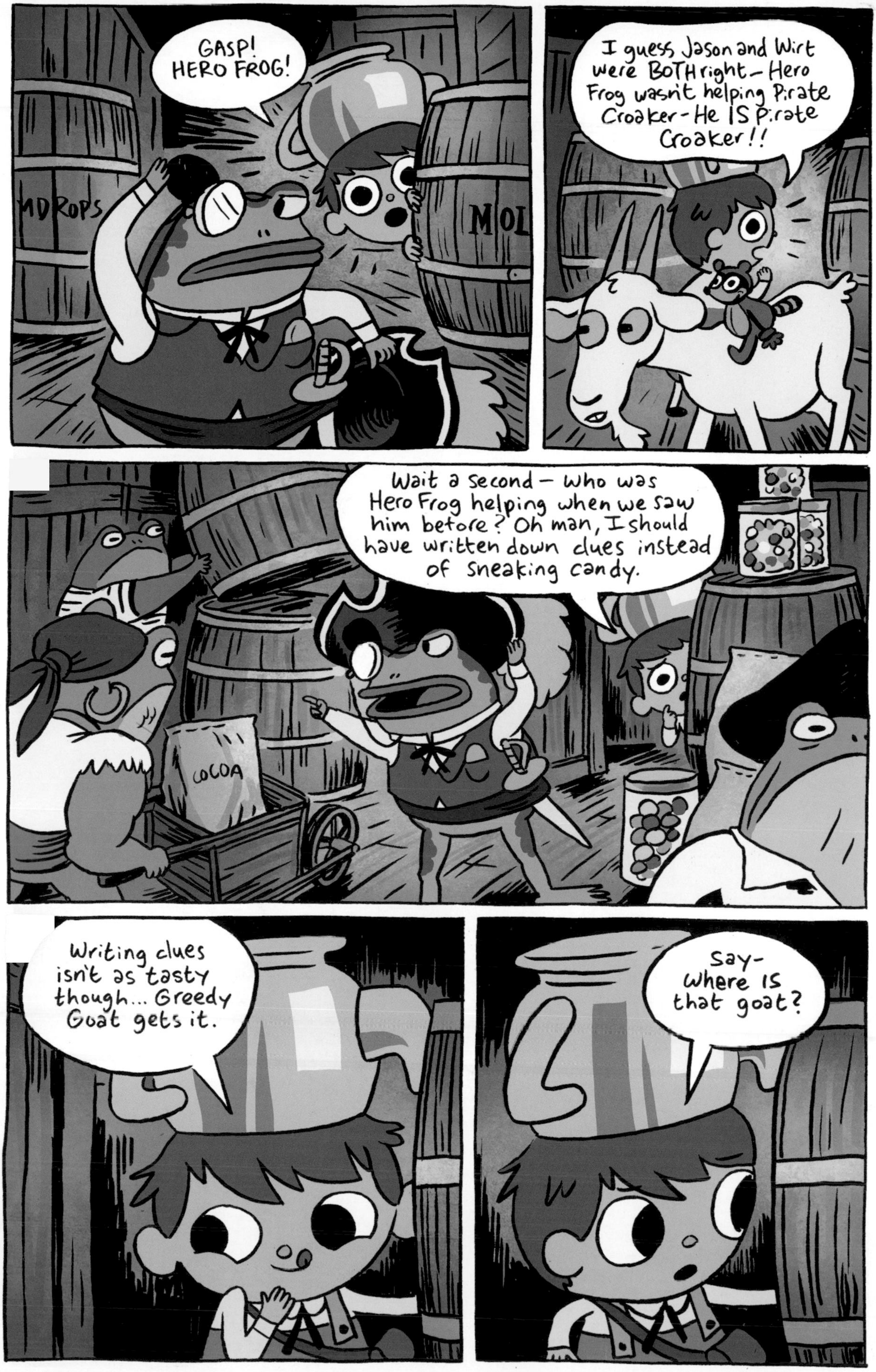
GASP! HERO FROG!
I guess Jason and Wirt were BOTH right— Hero Frog wasn't helping Pirate Croaker— He IS Pirate Croaker!!
MDROPS
MOL
Wait a second— who was Hero Frog helping when we saw him before? Oh man, I should have written down clues instead of sneaking candy.
COCOA
Writing clues isn't as tasty though... Greedy Goat gets it.
Say— Where IS that goat?

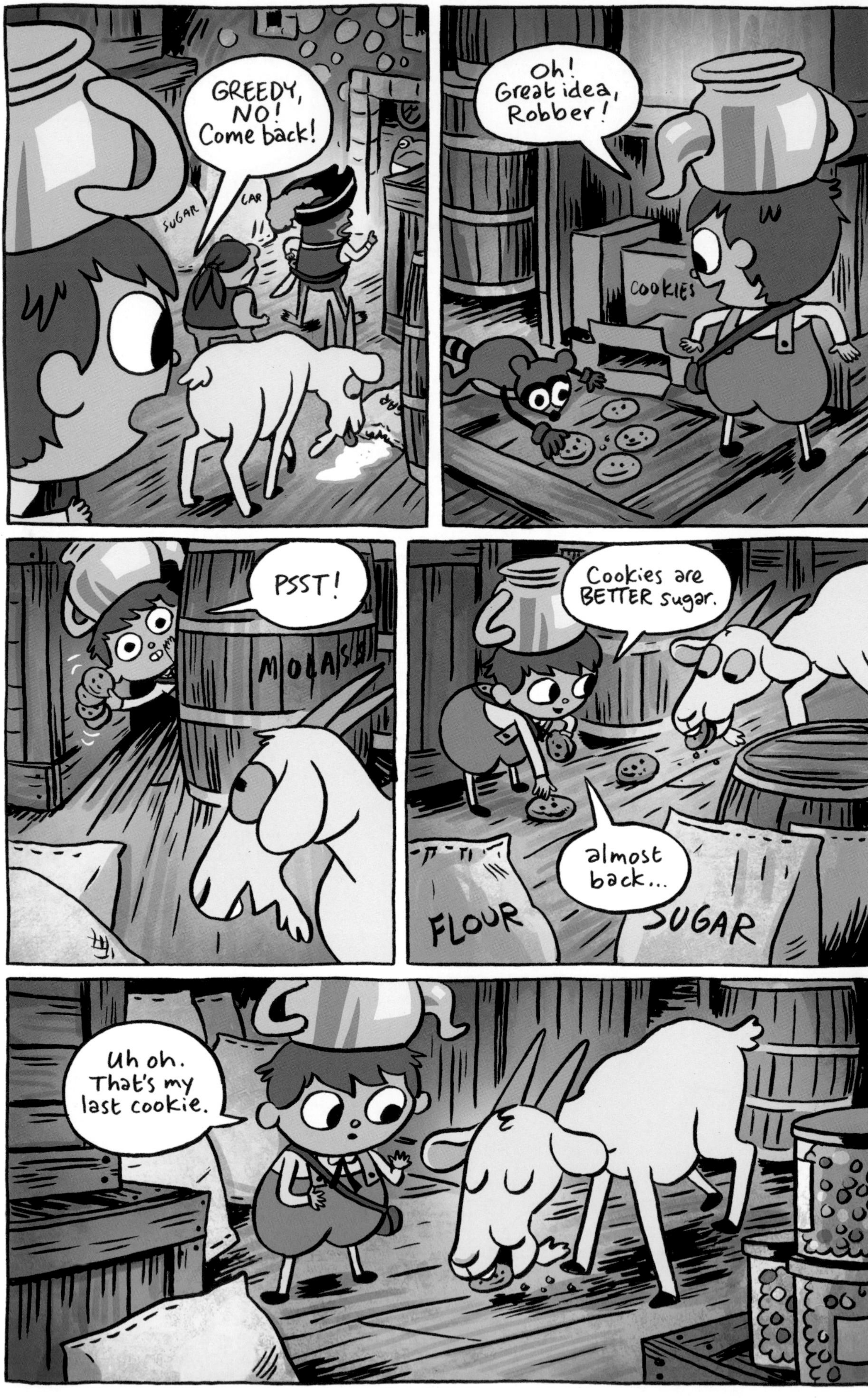
GREEDY, NO! Come back!
SUGAR
CAR
Oh! Great idea, Robber!
COOKIES
PSST!
MOLASS
Cookies are BETTER sugar.
almost back...
FLOUR
SUGAR
Uh oh. That's my last cookie.

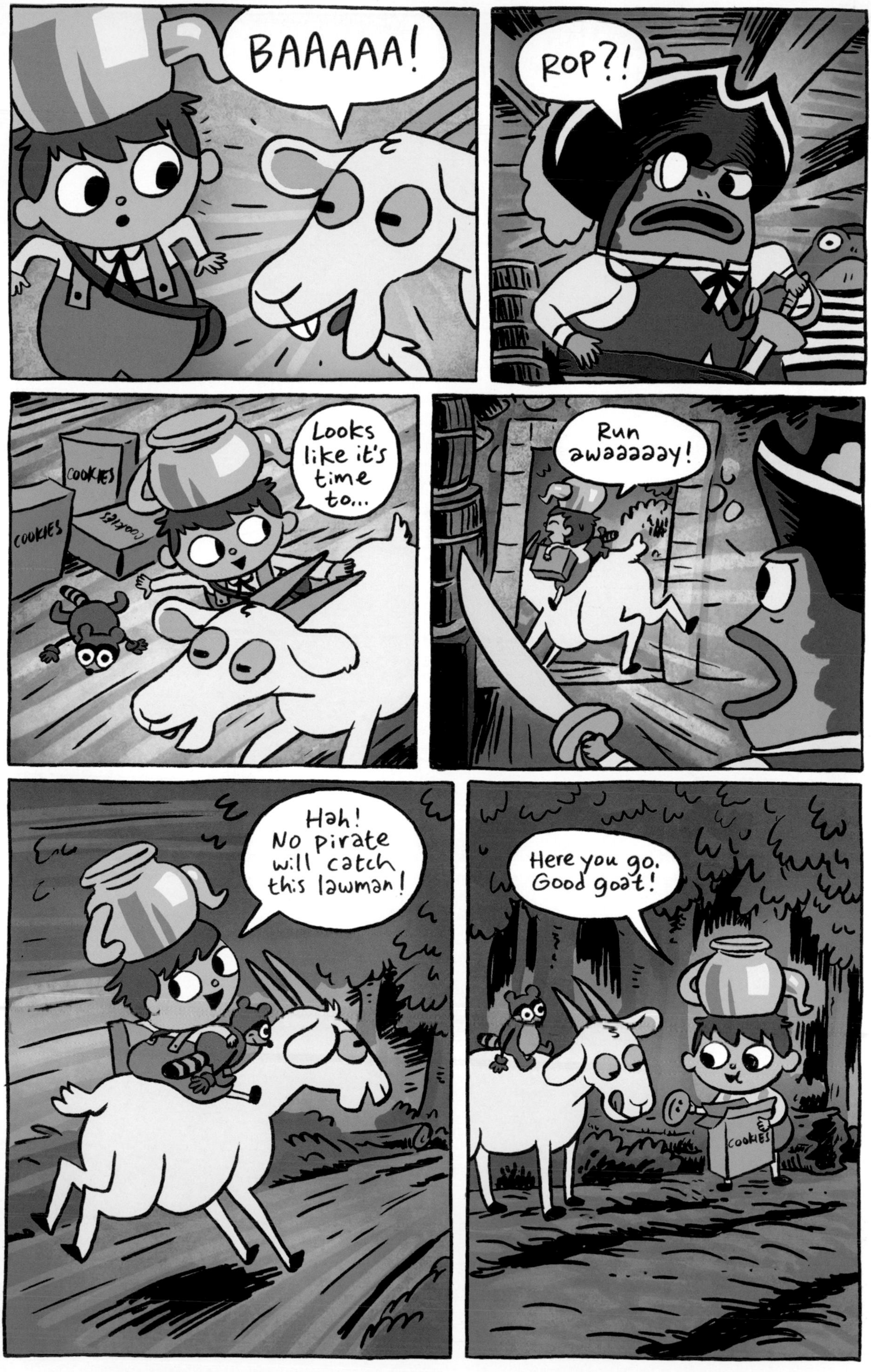
BAAAAA!
ROP?!
Looks like it's time to...
COOKIES
COOKIES
COOKIES
Run awaaaaay!
Hah! No pirate will catch this lawman!
Here you go. Good goat!
COOKIES

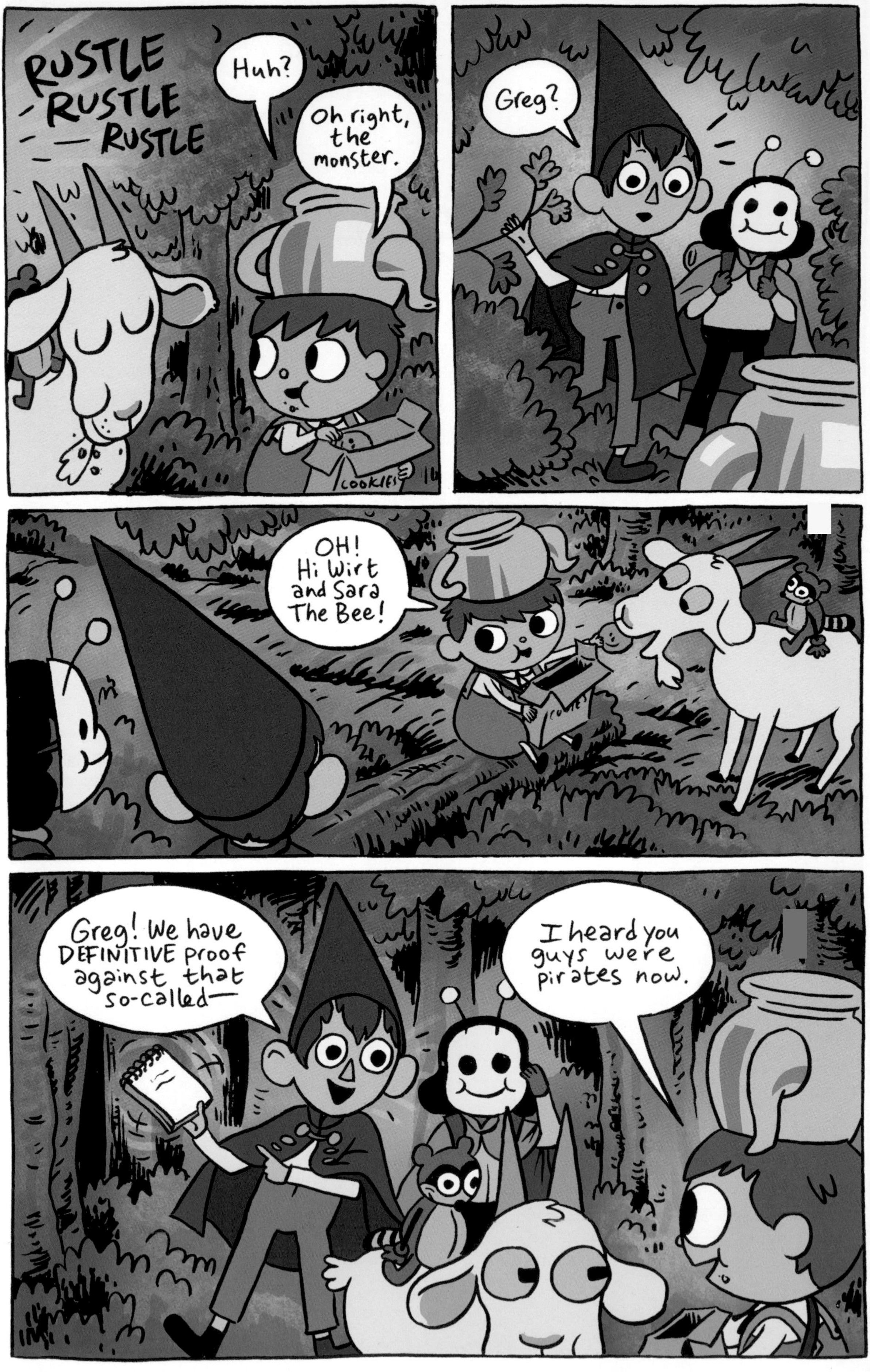
RUSTLE
RUSTLE
RUSTLE
Huh?
Oh right, the monster.
COOKIES
Greg?
OH! Hi Wirt and Sara The Bee!
COOKIES
Greg! We have DEFINITIVE proof against that so-called—
I heard you guys were pirates now.

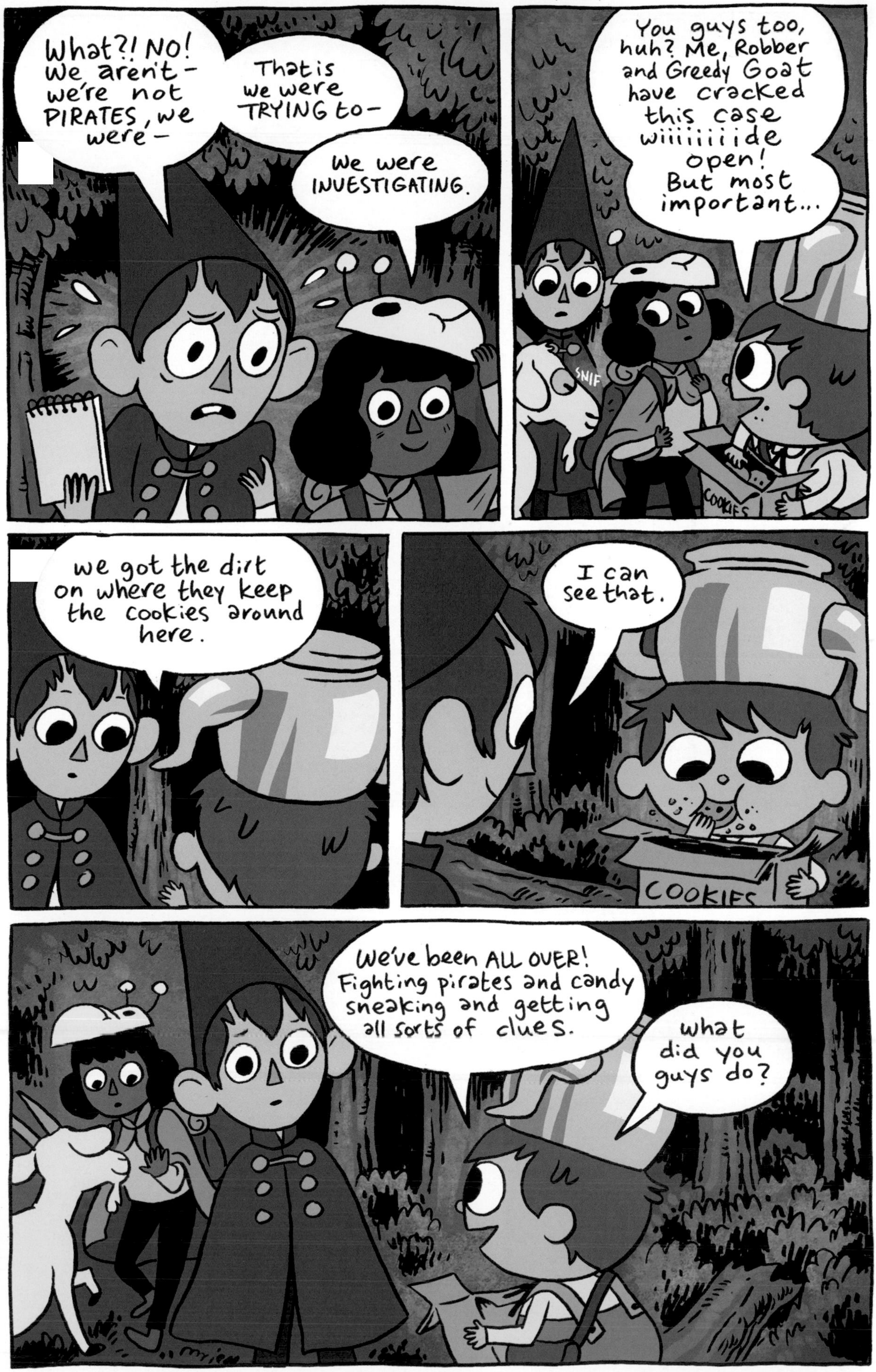
What?! NO! We aren't- we're not PIRATES, we were-
That is we were TRYING to-
We were INVESTIGATING.
You guys too, huh? Me, Robber and Greedy Goat have cracked this case wiiiiiiiide open! But most important...
SNIF
COOKIES
we got the dirt on where they keep the cookies around here.
I can see that.
COOKIES
We've been ALL OVER! Fighting pirates and candy sneaking and getting all sorts of clues.
what did you guys do?

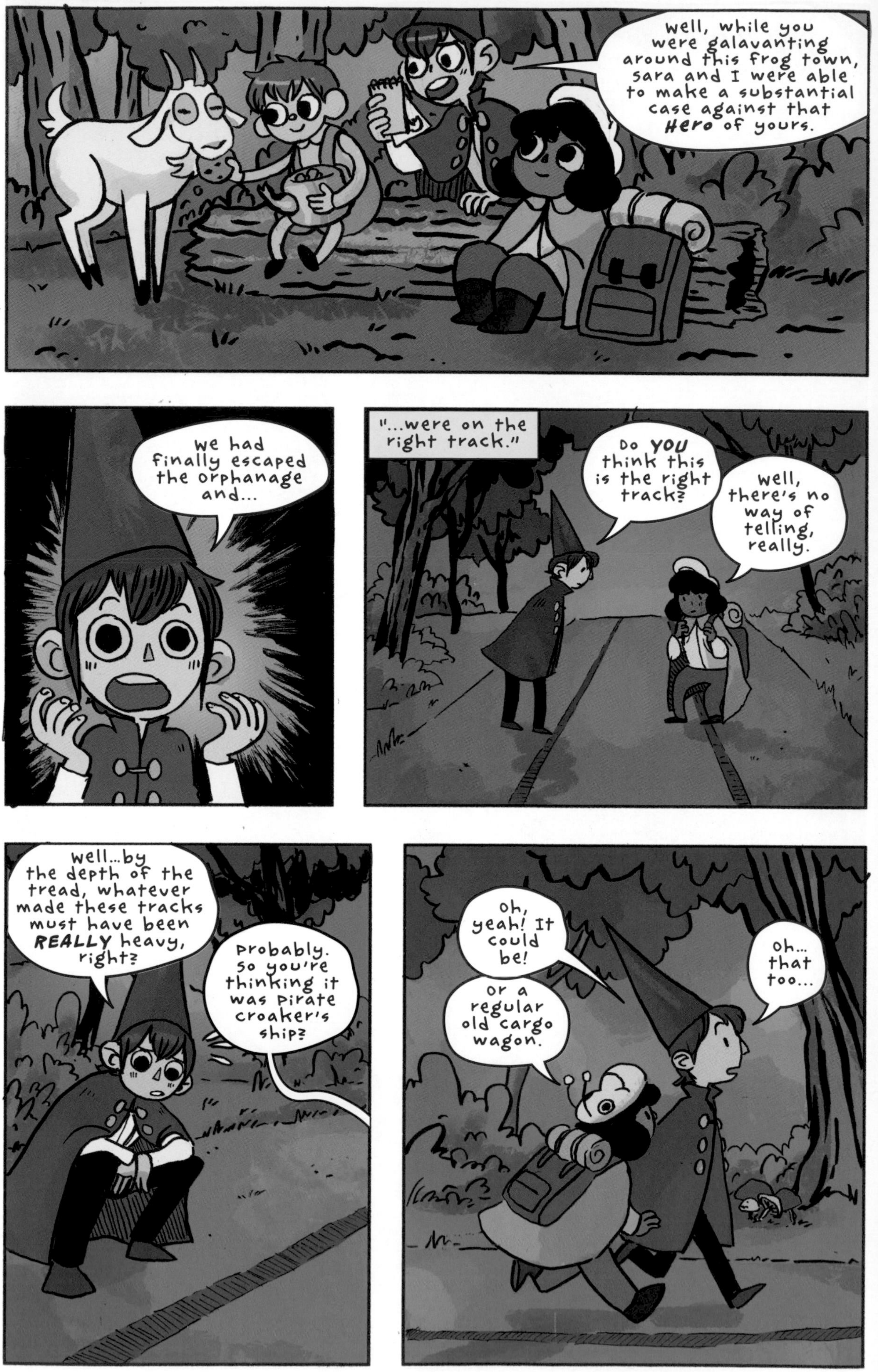
Well, while you were galavanting around this frog town, Sara and I were able to make a substantial case against that HERO of yours.
We had finally escaped the orphanage and...
"...were on the right track."
Do YOU think this is the right track?
Well, there's no way of telling, really.
Well...by the depth of the tread, whatever made these tracks must have been REALLY heavy, right?
Probably. So you're thinking it was Pirate Croaker's ship?
Oh, yeah! It could be!
Or a regular old cargo wagon.
Oh... that too...

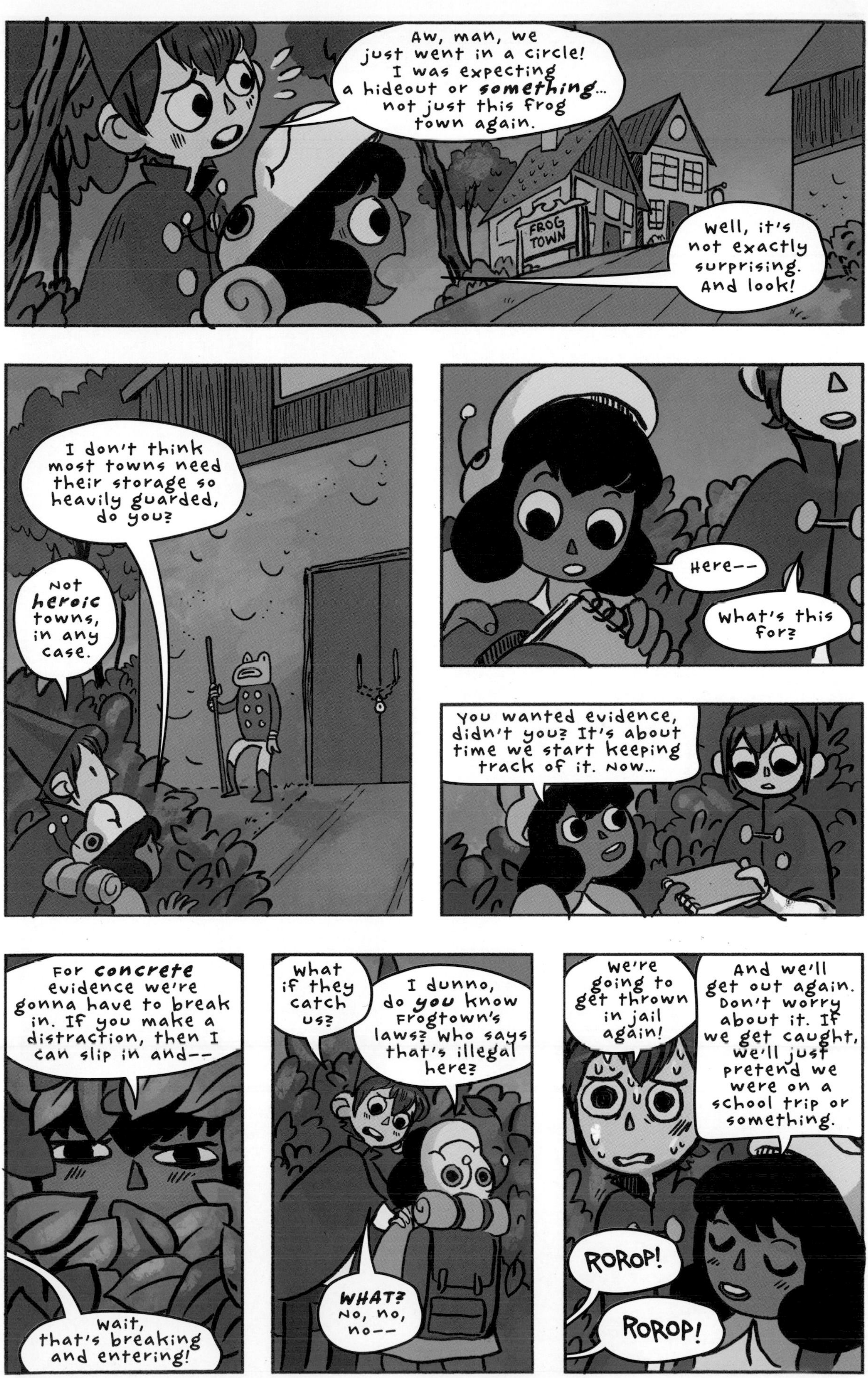

Aw, man, we just went in a circle! I was expecting a hideout or *something*... not just this frog town again.
FROG TOWN
Well, it's not exactly surprising. And look!
I don't think most towns need their storage so heavily guarded, do you?
Not *heroic* towns, in any case.
Here--
What's this for?
You wanted evidence, didn't you? It's about time we start keeping track of it. Now...
For *concrete* evidence we're gonna have to break in. If you make a distraction, then I can slip in and--
Wait, that's breaking and entering!
What if they catch us?
I dunno, do *you* know Frogtown's laws? Who says that's illegal here?
WHAT? No, no, no--
We're going to get thrown in jail again!
And we'll get out again. Don't worry about it. If we get caught, we'll just pretend we were on a school trip or something.
ROROP!
ROROP!

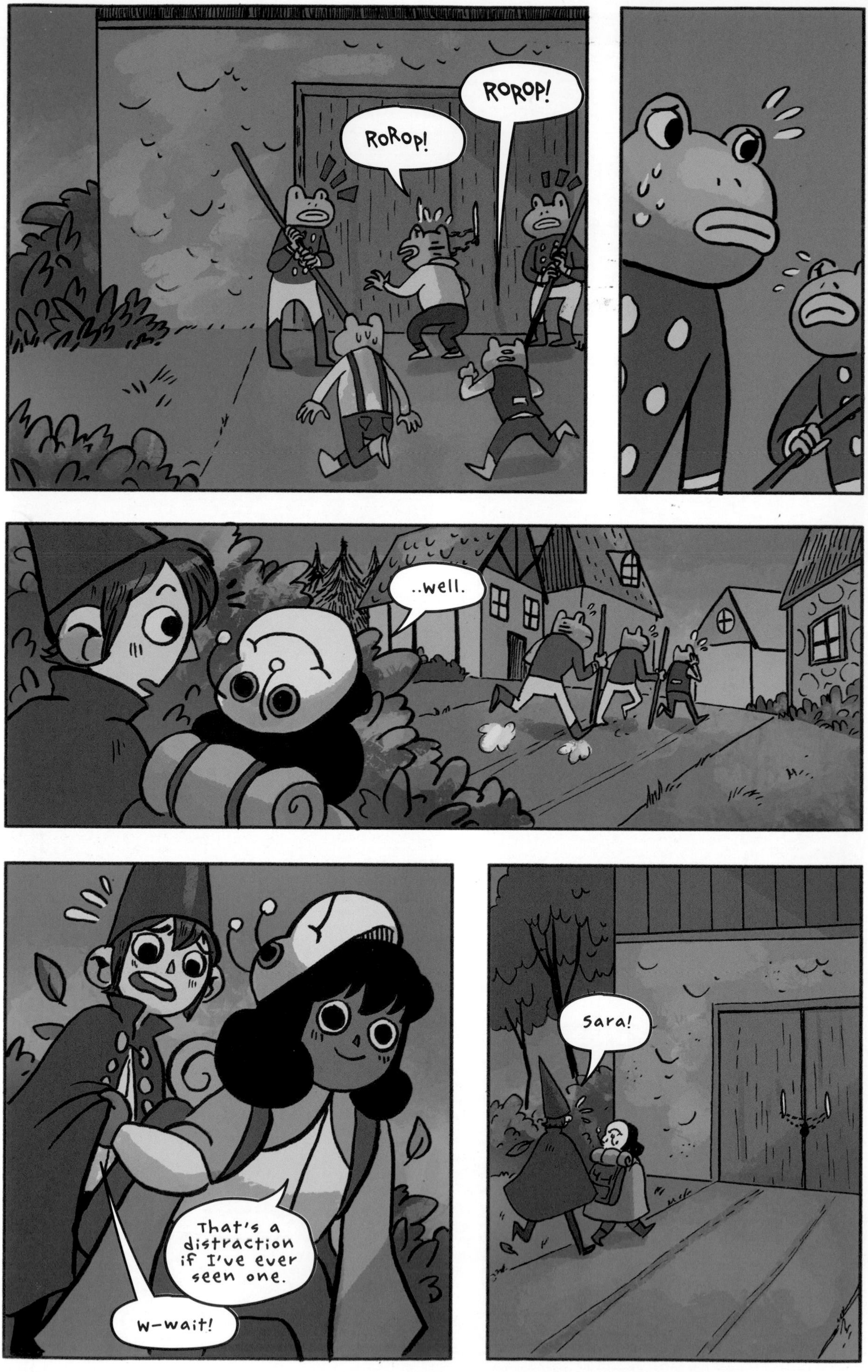
RoRop!
ROROP!
..well.
That's a distraction if I've ever seen one.
W-wait!
Sara!

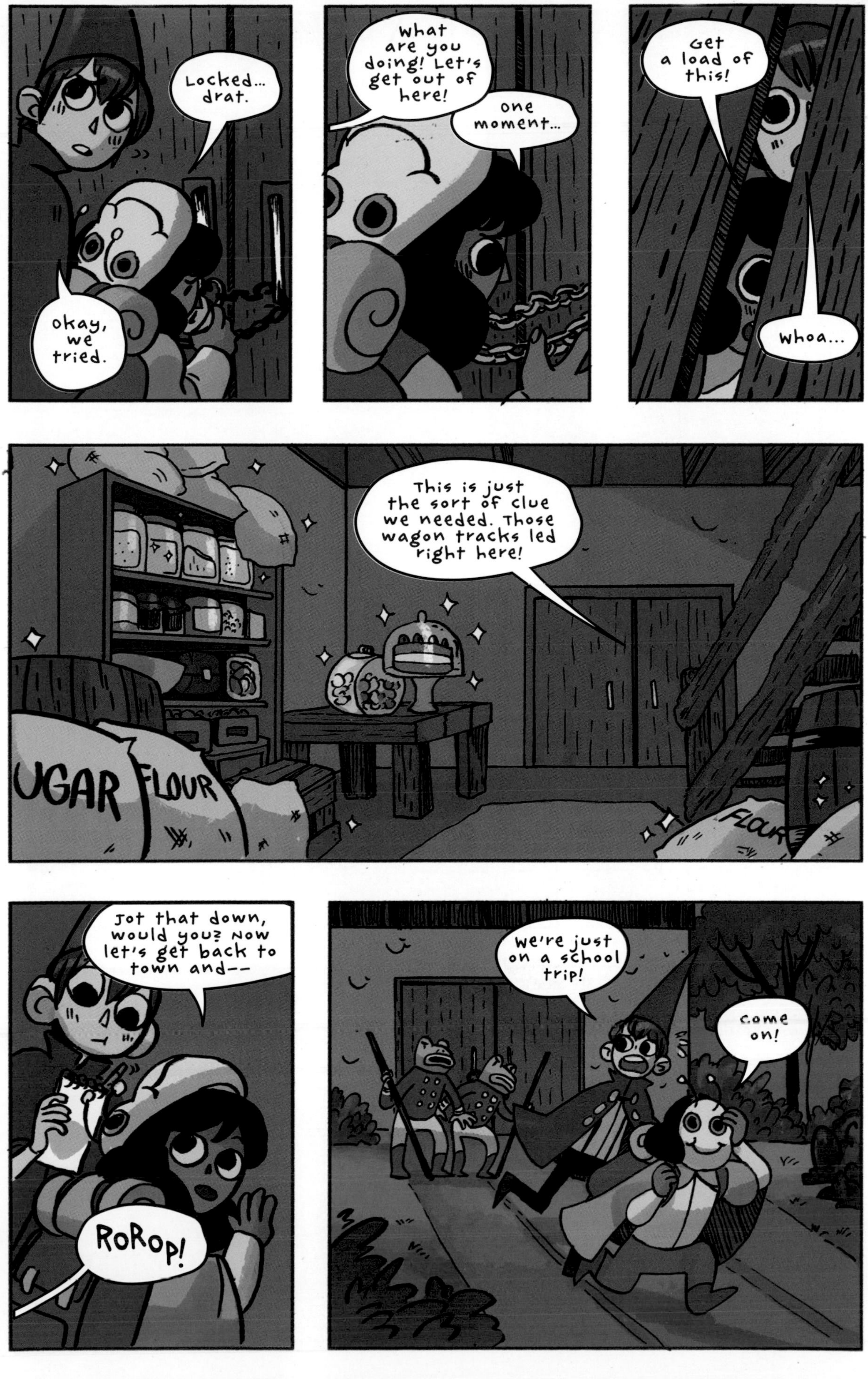
Locked... drat.
okay, we tried.
What are you doing! Let's get out of here!
one moment...
Get a load of this!
Whoa...
This is just the sort of clue we needed. Those wagon tracks led right here!
UGAR
FLOUR
FLOUR
Jot that down, would you? Now let's get back to town and--
ROROP!
We're just on a school trip!
Come on!

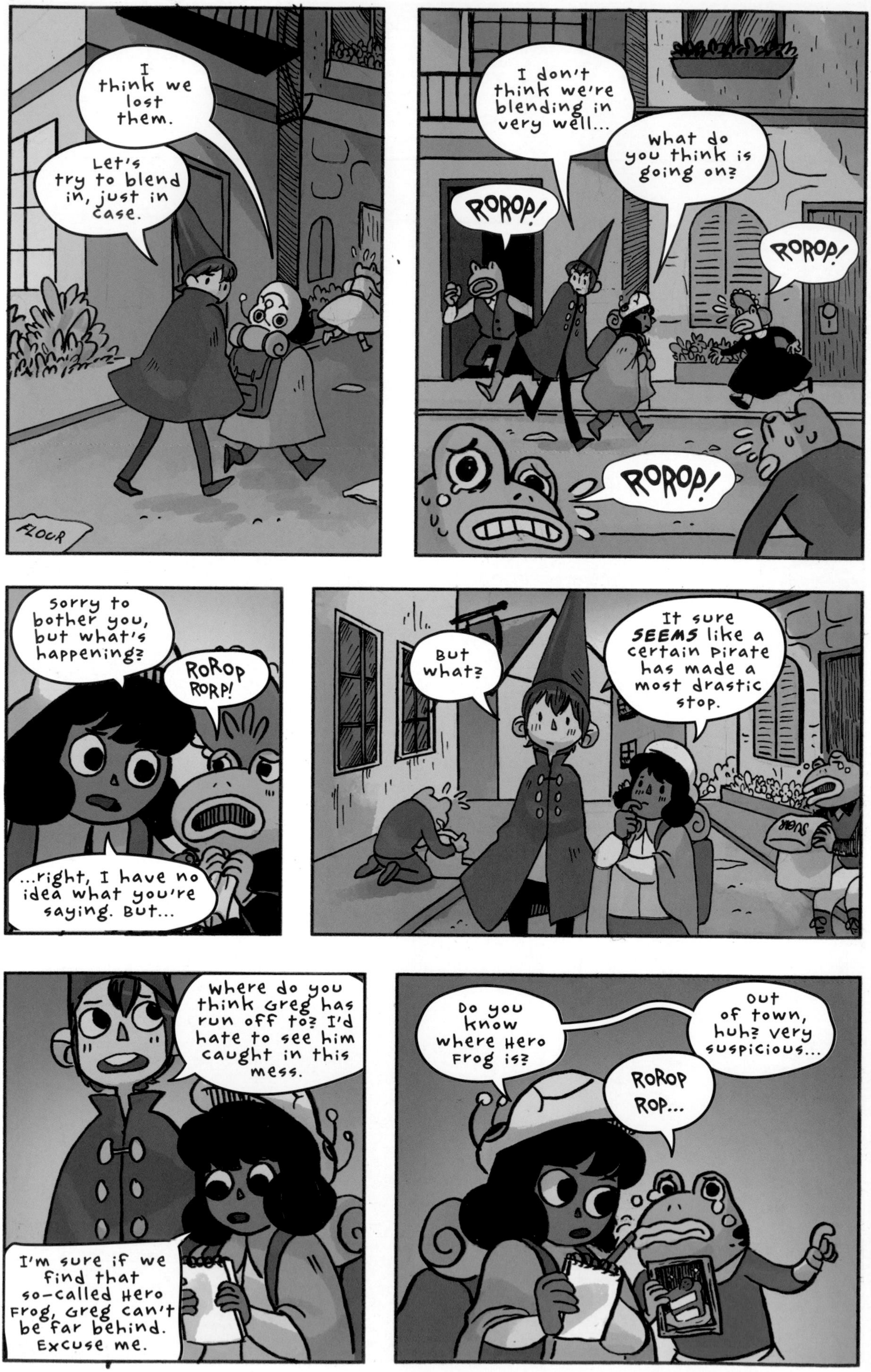
I think we lost them.
Let's try to blend in, just in case.
FLOUR
I don't think we're blending in very well...
What do you think is going on?
ROROP!
ROROP!
ROROP!
Sorry to bother you, but what's happening?
RoRop RorP!
...right, I have no idea what you're saying. But...
But what?
It sure SEEMS like a certain pirate has made a most drastic stop.
Where do you think Greg has run off to? I'd hate to see him caught in this mess.
I'm sure if we find that so-called Hero Frog, Greg can't be far behind. Excuse me.
Do you know where Hero Frog is?
RoRop Rop...
Out of town, huh? Very suspicious...

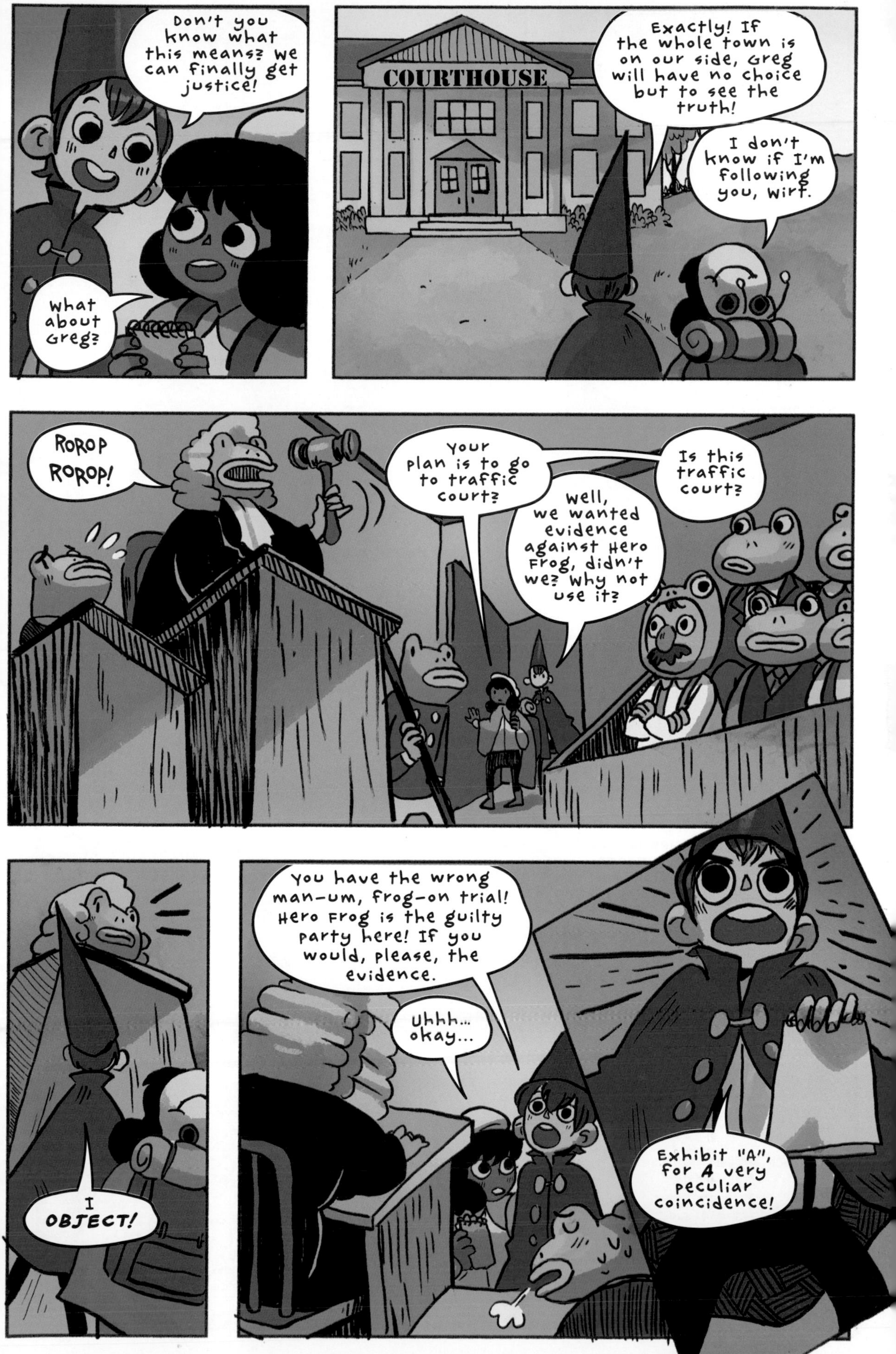
Don't you know what this means? We can finally get justice!
What about Greg?
COURTHOUSE
Exactly! If the whole town is on our side, Greg will have no choice but to see the truth!
I don't know if I'm following you, Wirt.
ROROP ROROP!
Your plan is to go to traffic court?
Is this traffic court?
Well, we wanted evidence against Hero Frog, didn't we? Why not use it?
I OBJECT!
You have the wrong man—um, frog—on trial! Hero Frog is the guilty party here! If you would, please, the evidence.
Uhhh... okay...
Exhibit "A", for A very peculiar coincidence!

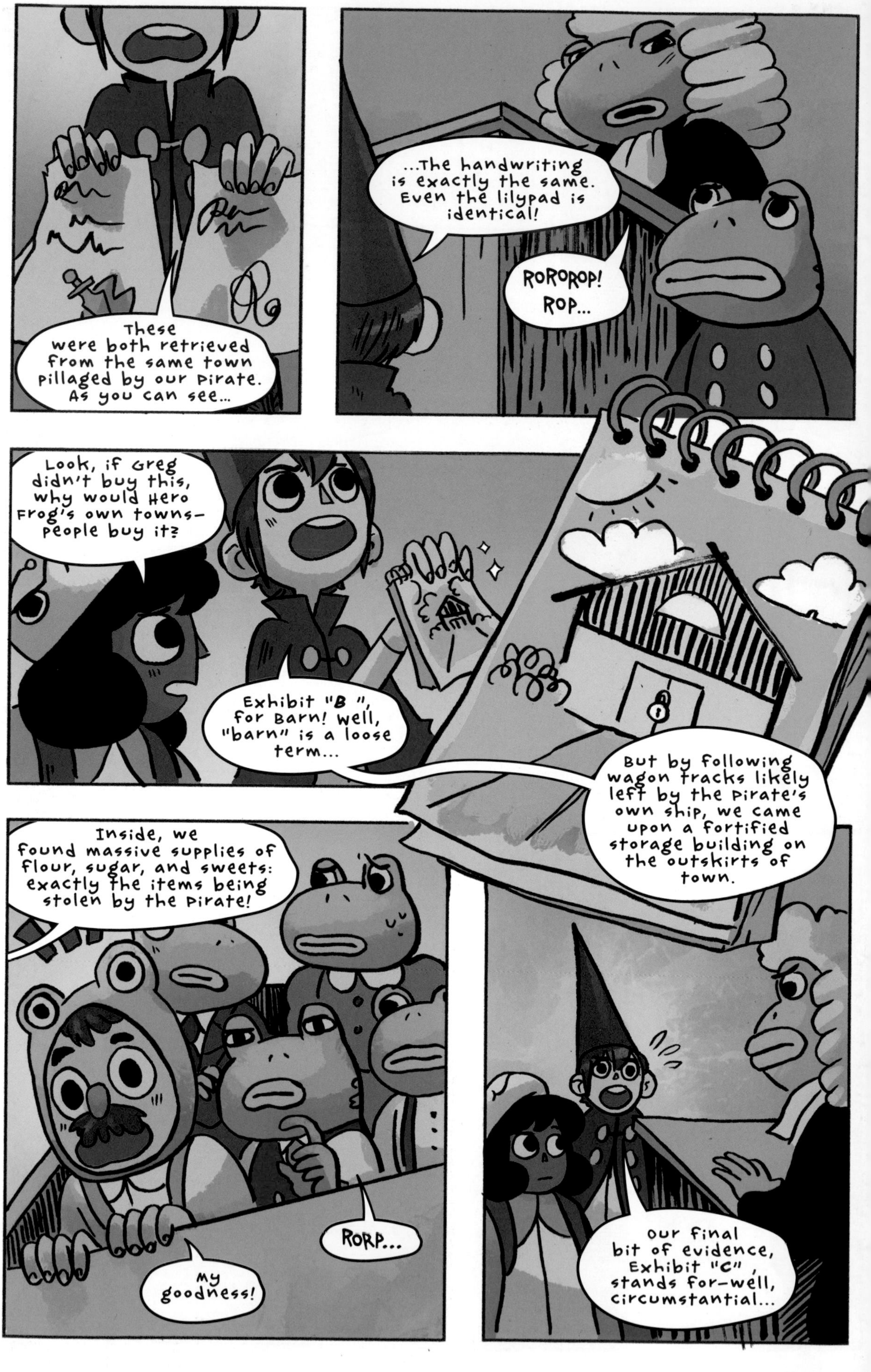
These were both retrieved from the same town pillaged by our Pirate. As you can see...
...The handwriting is exactly the same. Even the lilypad is identical!
ROROROP! ROP...
Look, if Greg didn't buy this, why would Hero Frog's own towns-people buy it?
Exhibit "B", for Barn! Well, "barn" is a loose term...
But by following wagon tracks likely left by the Pirate's own ship, we came upon a fortified storage building on the outskirts of town.
Inside, we found massive supplies of flour, sugar, and sweets: exactly the items being stolen by the Pirate!
RORP...
My goodness!
Our final bit of evidence, Exhibit "C", stands for—well, circumstantial...

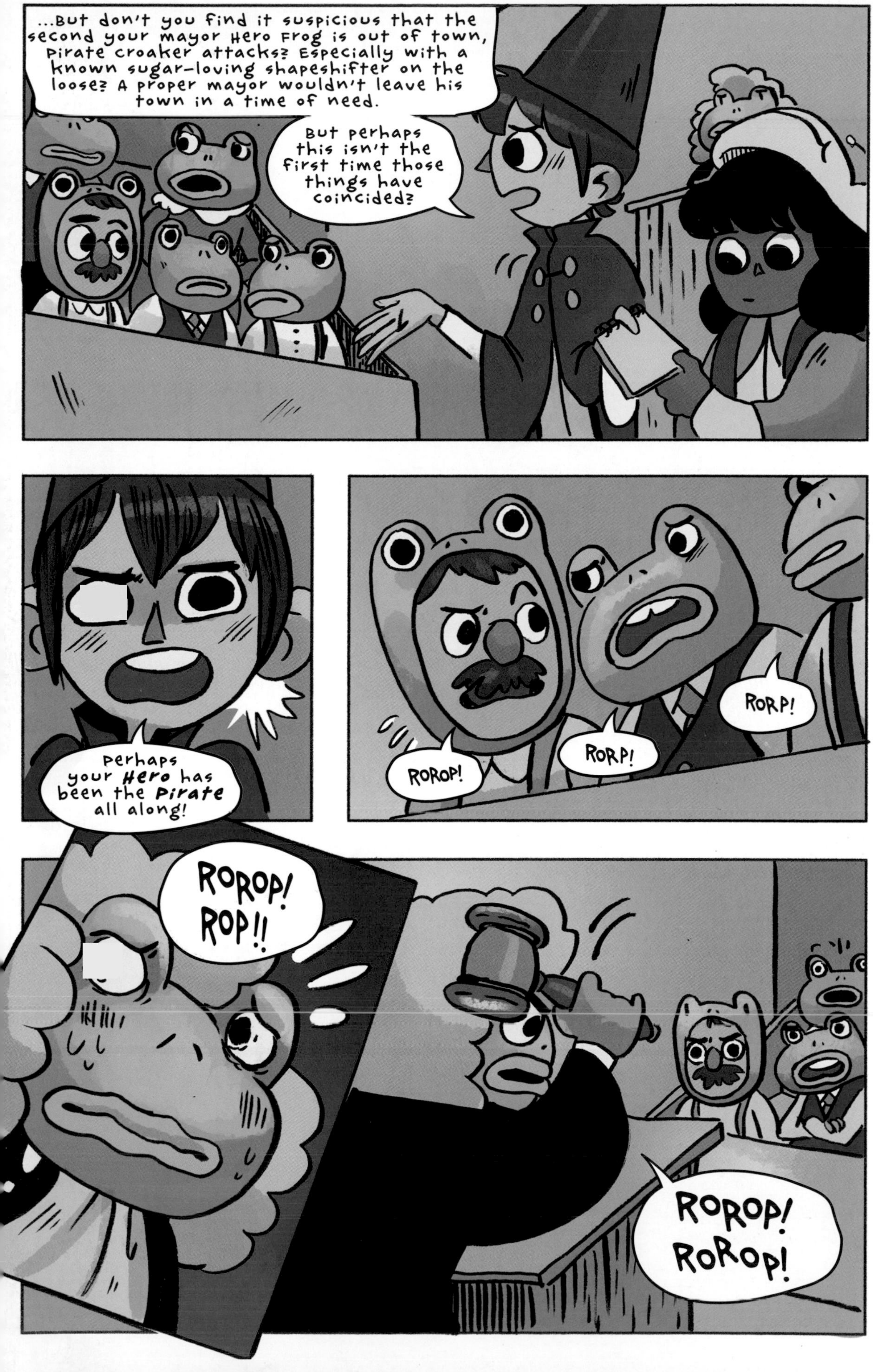
...But don't you find it suspicious that the second your mayor Hero Frog is out of town, Pirate Croaker attacks? Especially with a known sugar-loving shapeshifter on the loose? A proper mayor wouldn't leave his town in a time of need.
But perhaps this isn't the first time those things have coincided?
Perhaps your *Hero* has been the *Pirate* all along!
ROROP!
RORP!
RORP!
ROROP! ROP!!
ROROP! ROROP!

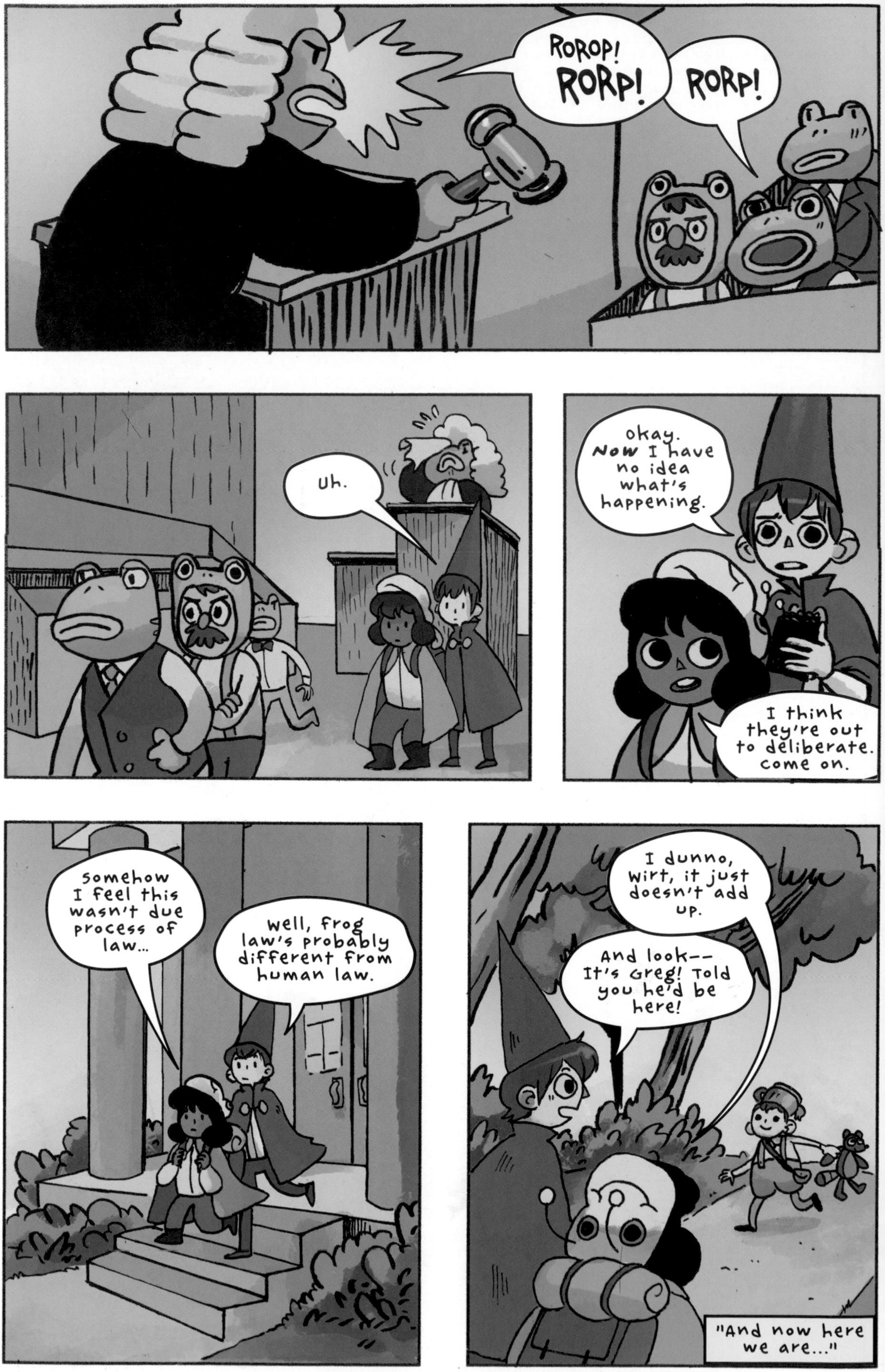
ROROP! RORP!
RORP!
Uh.
okay. Now I have no idea what's happening.
I think they're out to deliberate. come on.
Somehow I feel this wasn't due process of law...
Well, frog law's probably different from human law.
I dunno, Wirt, it just doesn't add up.
And look-- It's Greg! Told you he'd be here!
"And now here we are..."

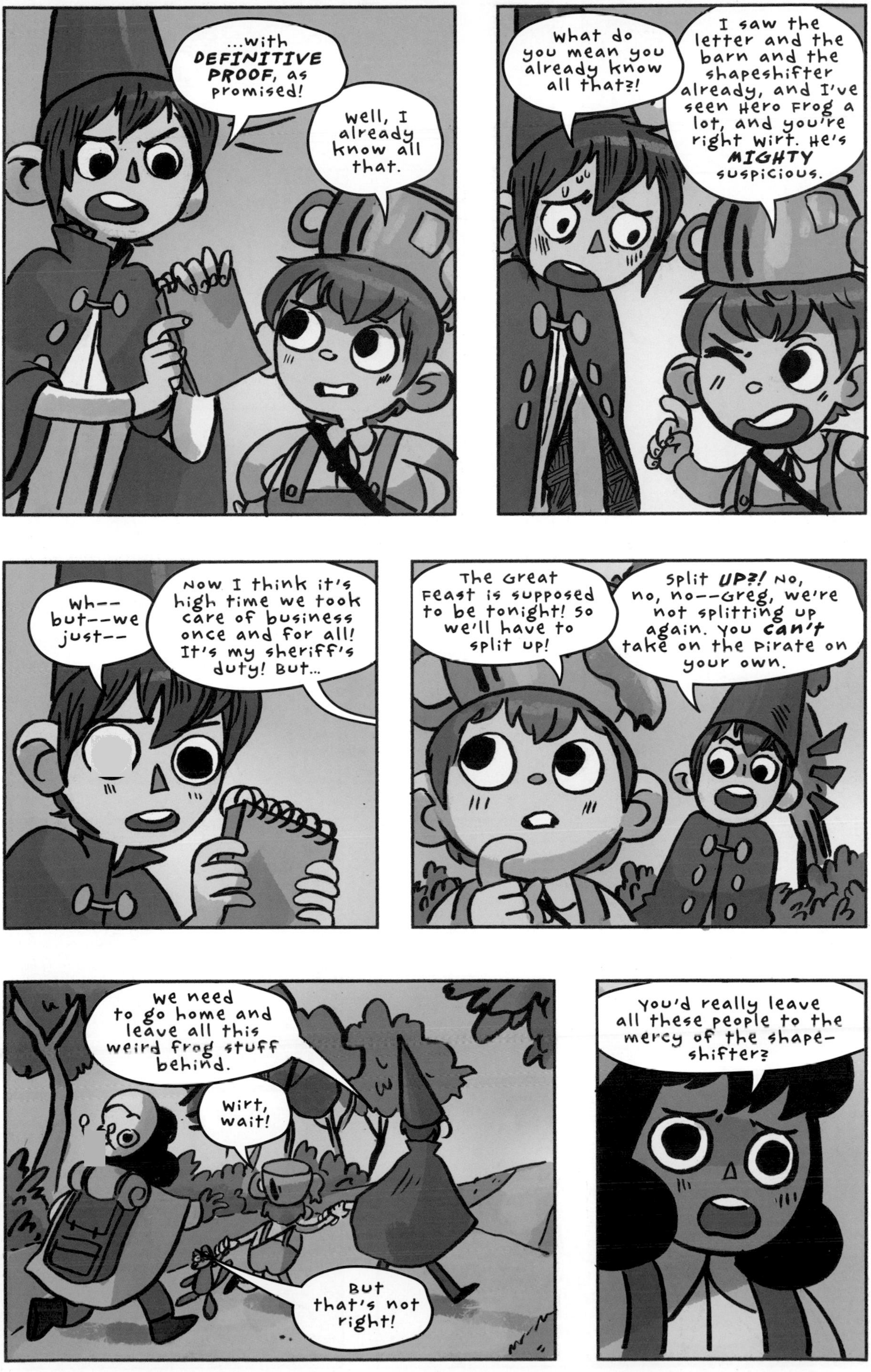
...with DEFINITIVE PROOF, as promised!
Well, I already know all that.
What do you mean you already know all that?!
I saw the letter and the barn and the shapeshifter already, and I've seen Hero Frog a lot, and you're right Wirt. He's MIGHTY suspicious.
Wh-- but--we just--
Now I think it's high time we took care of business once and for all! It's my sheriff's duty! But...
The Great Feast is supposed to be tonight! So we'll have to split up!
Split UP?! No, no, no--Greg, we're not splitting up again. You can't take on the Pirate on your own.
We need to go home and leave all this weird frog stuff behind.
Wirt, wait!
But that's not right!
You'd really leave all these people to the mercy of the shape-shifter?

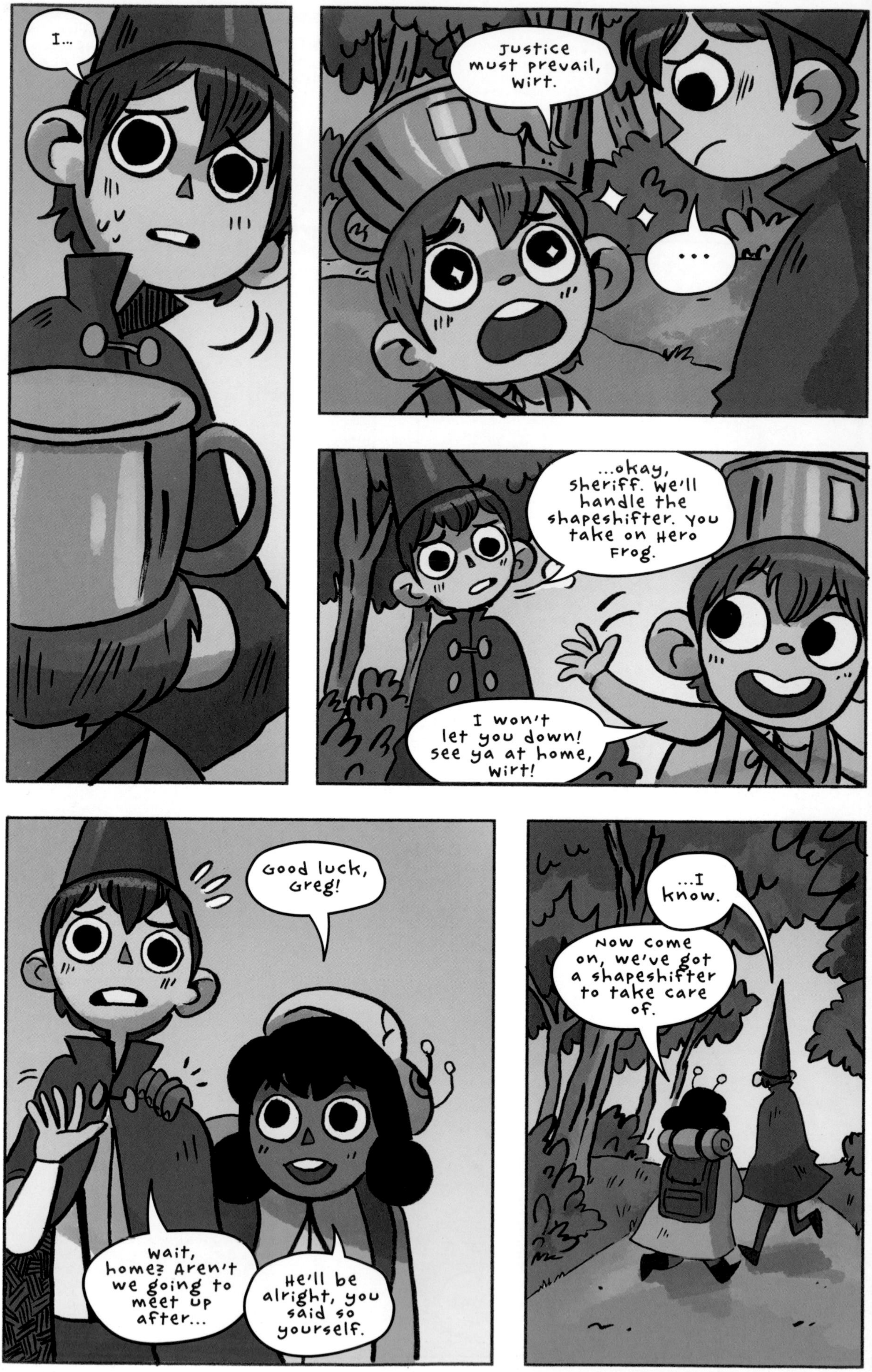
I...
Justice must prevail, Wirt.
...
...okay, sheriff. We'll handle the shapeshifter. You take on Hero Frog.
I won't let you down! See ya at home, Wirt!
Good luck, Greg!
Wait, home? Aren't we going to meet up after...
He'll be alright, you said so yourself.
...I know.
Now come on, we've got a shapeshifter to take care of.

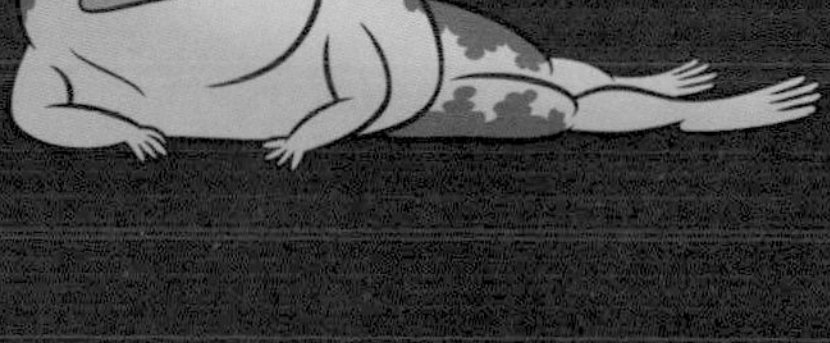

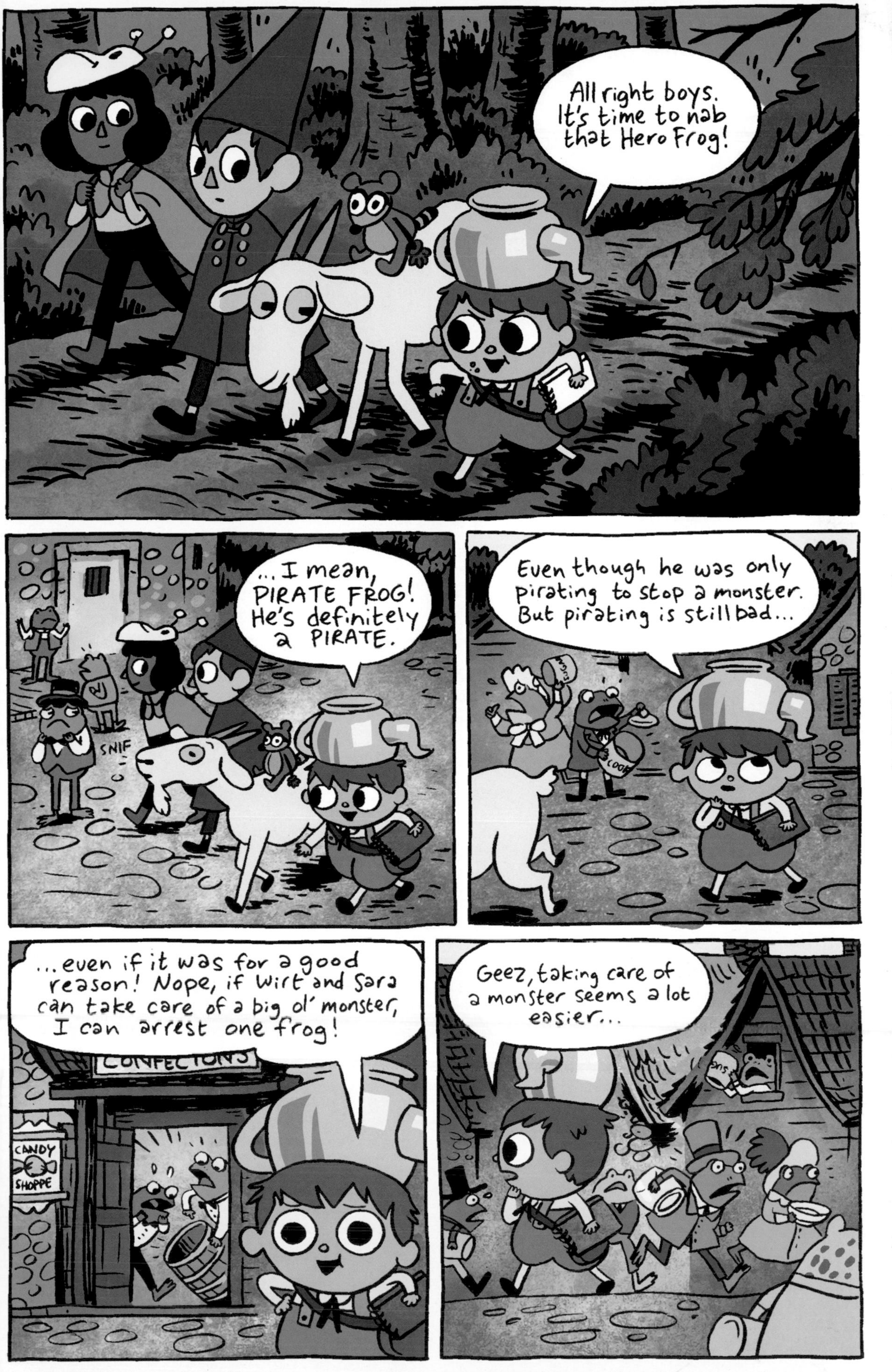
All right boys. It's time to nab that Hero Frog!
...I mean, PIRATE FROG! He's definitely a PIRATE.
SNIF
Even though he was only pirating to stop a monster. But pirating is still bad...
...even if it was for a good reason! Nope, if Wirt and Sara can take care of a big ol' monster, I can arrest one frog!
CONFECTIONS
CANDY SHOPPE
Geez, taking care of a monster seems a lot easier...

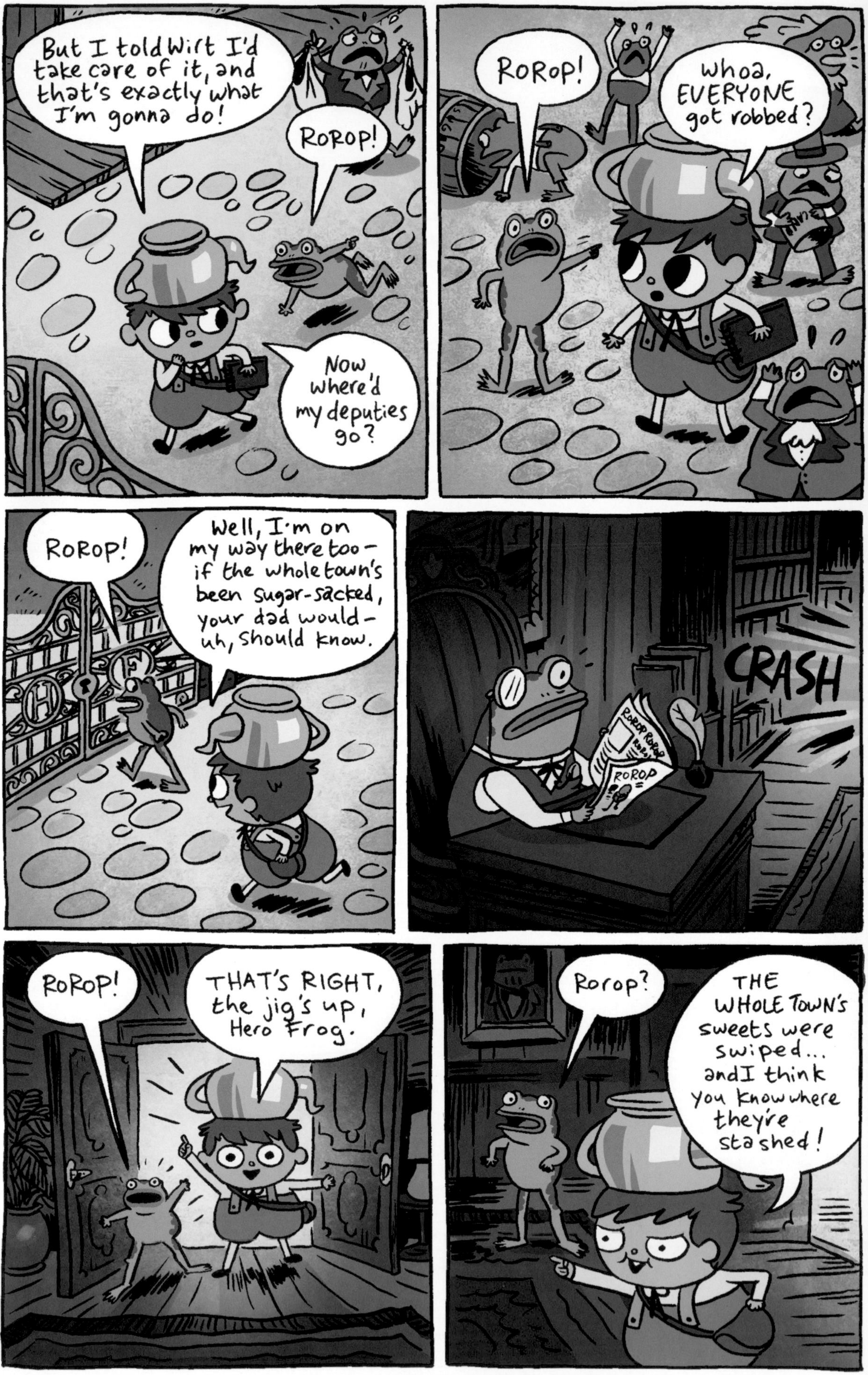
But I told Wirt I'd take care of it, and that's exactly what I'm gonna do!
ROROP!
Now where'd my deputies go?
ROROP!
Whoa, EVERYONE got robbed?
ROROP!
Well, I'm on my way there too - if the whole town's been sugar-sacked, your dad would - uh, should know.
CRASH
ROROP ROROP
ROROP
ROROP!
THAT'S RIGHT, the jig's up, Hero Frog.
Rorop?
THE WHOLE TOWN's sweets were swiped... and I think you know where they're stashed!

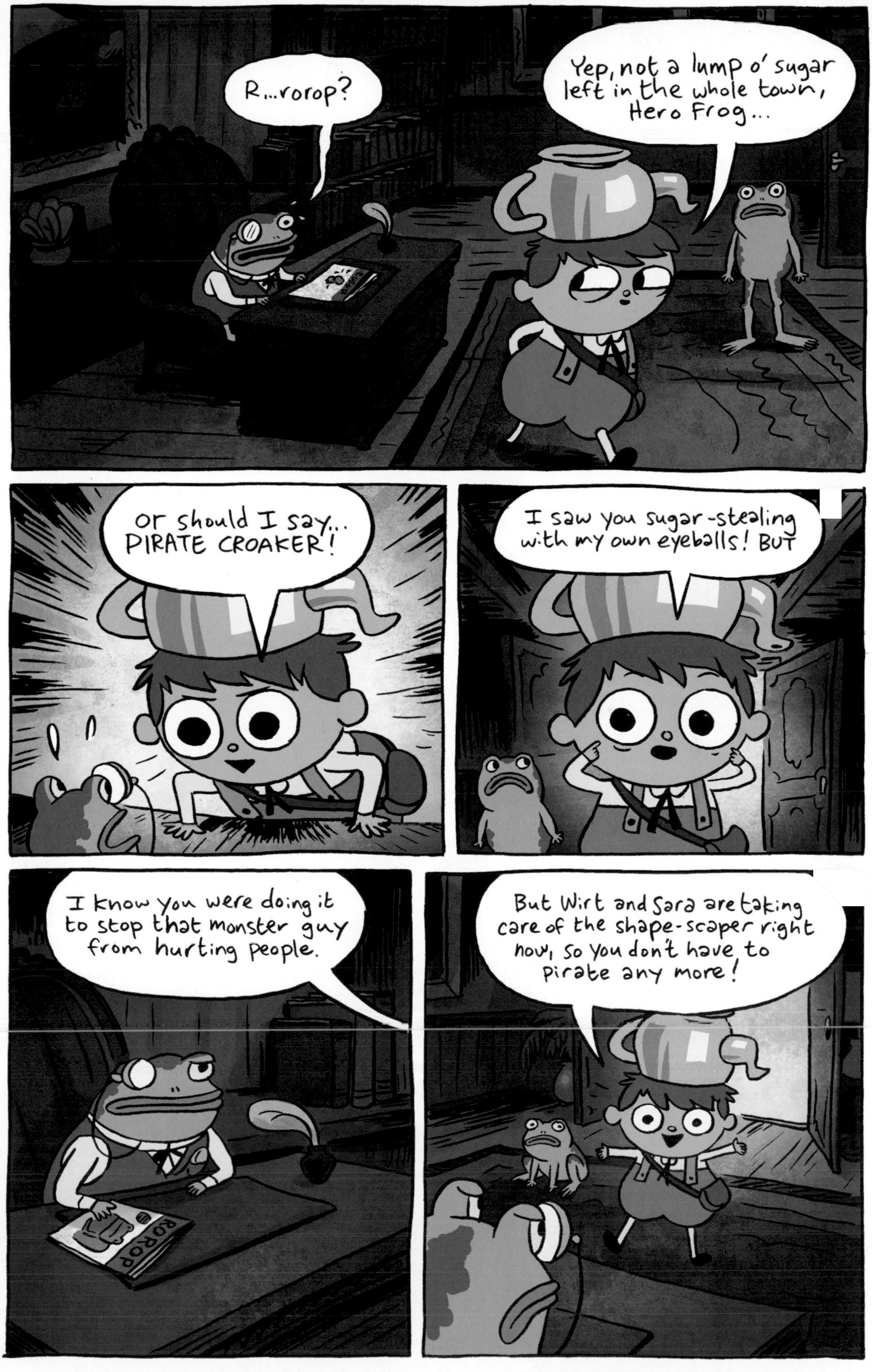
R...rorop?
Yep, not a lump o' sugar left in the whole town, Hero Frog...
Or should I say... PIRATE CROAKER!
I saw you sugar-stealing with my own eyeballs! BUT
I know you were doing it to stop that monster guy from hurting people.
RORORP
But Wirt and Sara are taking care of the shape-scaper right now, so you don't have to pirate any more!

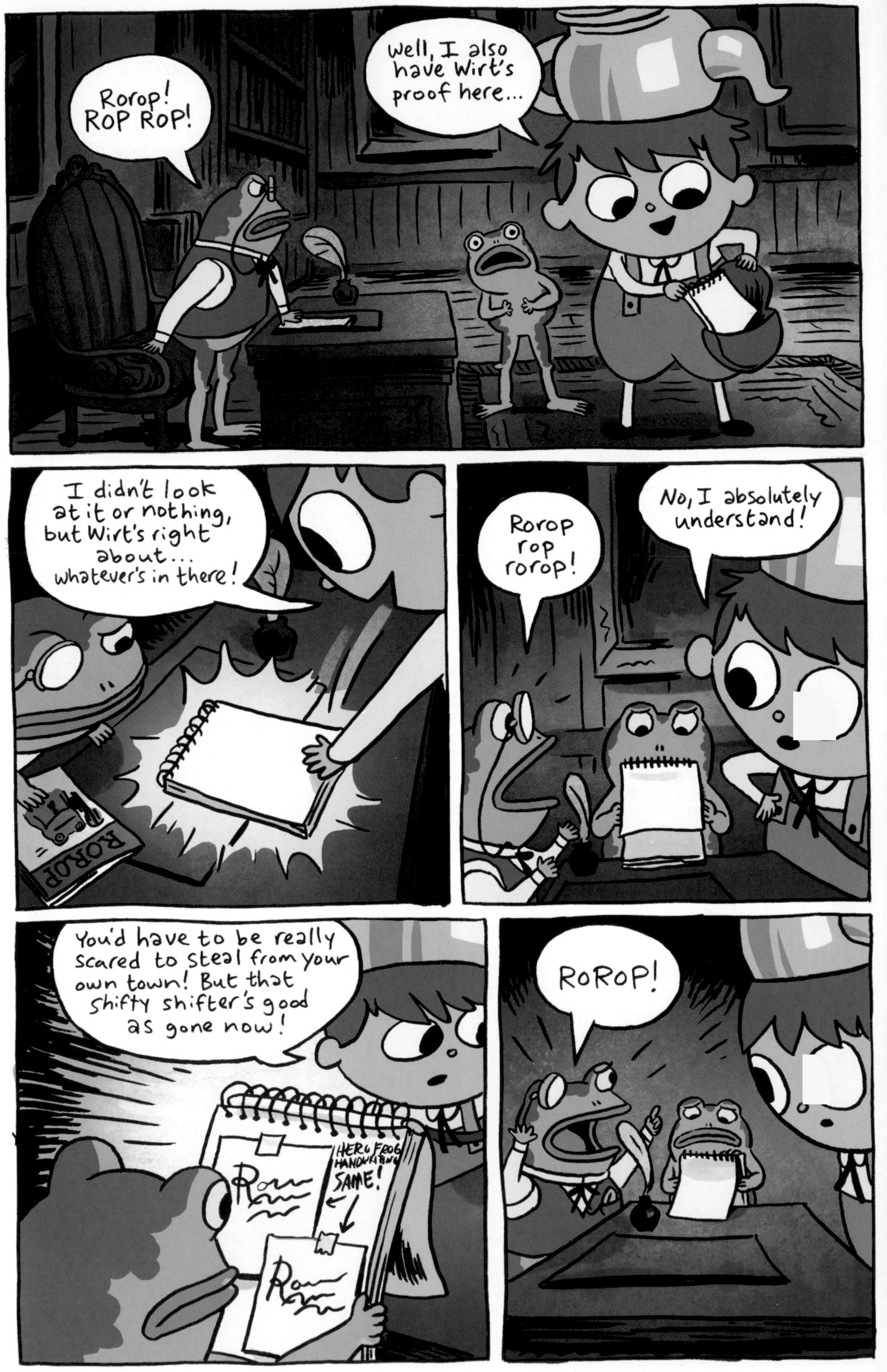
Rorop! ROP ROP!
Well, I also have Wirt's proof here...
I didn't look at it or nothing, but Wirt's right about... whatever's in there!
RORОP
Rorop rop rorop!
No, I absolutely understand!
You'd have to be really scared to steal from your own town! But that shifty shifter's good as gone now!
HERO FROG HANDWRITING SAME!
RoROP!

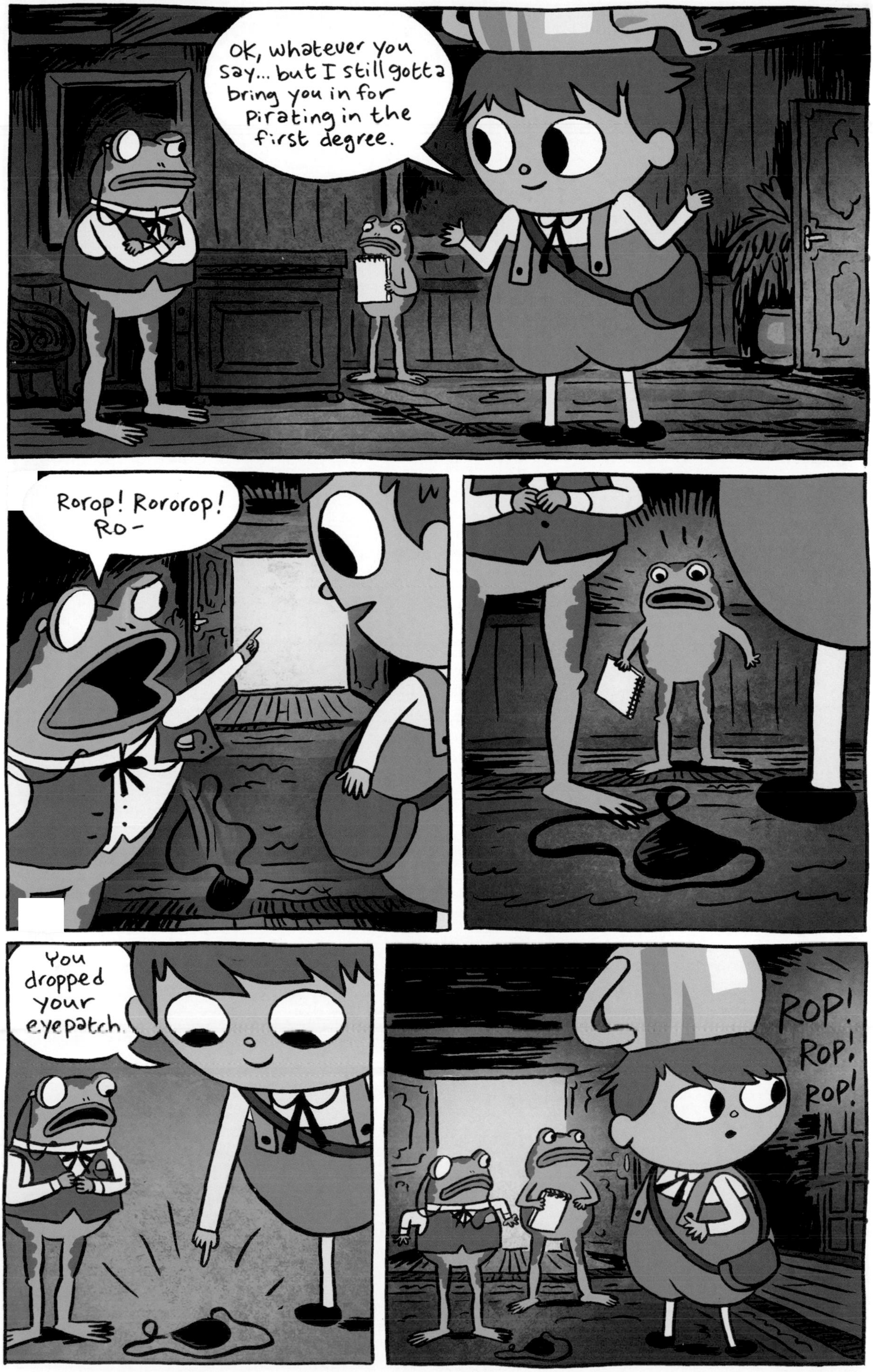

Ok, whatever you say... but I still gotta bring you in for pirating in the first degree.
Rorop! Rororop! Ro-
You dropped your eyepatch.
ROP! ROP! ROP!

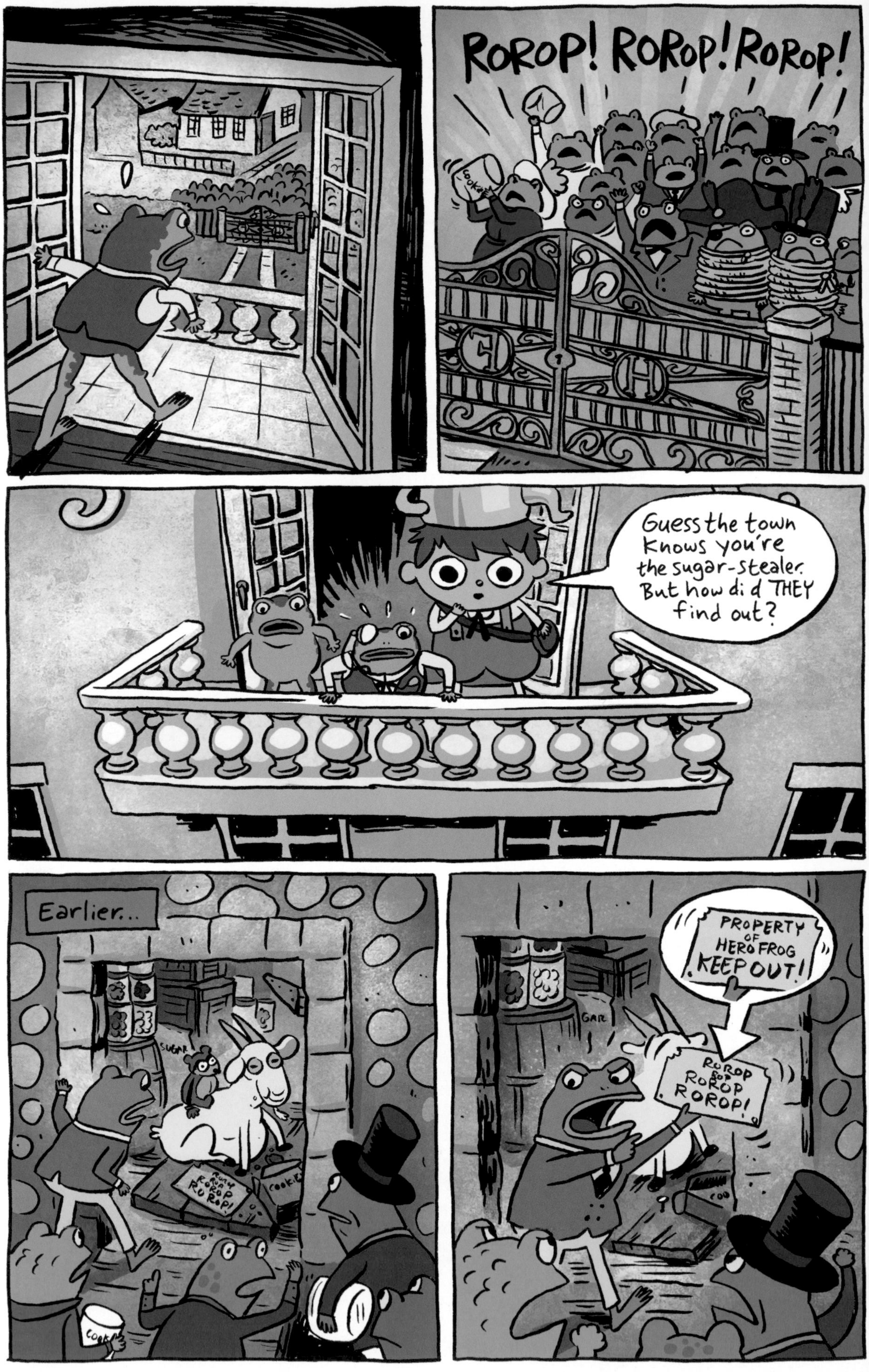
RoRoP! RoRop! RoRop!
COOKIE
Guess the town knows you're the sugar-stealer. But how did THEY find out?
Earlier...
SUGAR
RoRoP RoP RoRoP RoRoP!
COOKIE
PROPERTY OF HERO FROG KEEP OUT!
GAR
RoRoP RoP RoRoP RoRoP!

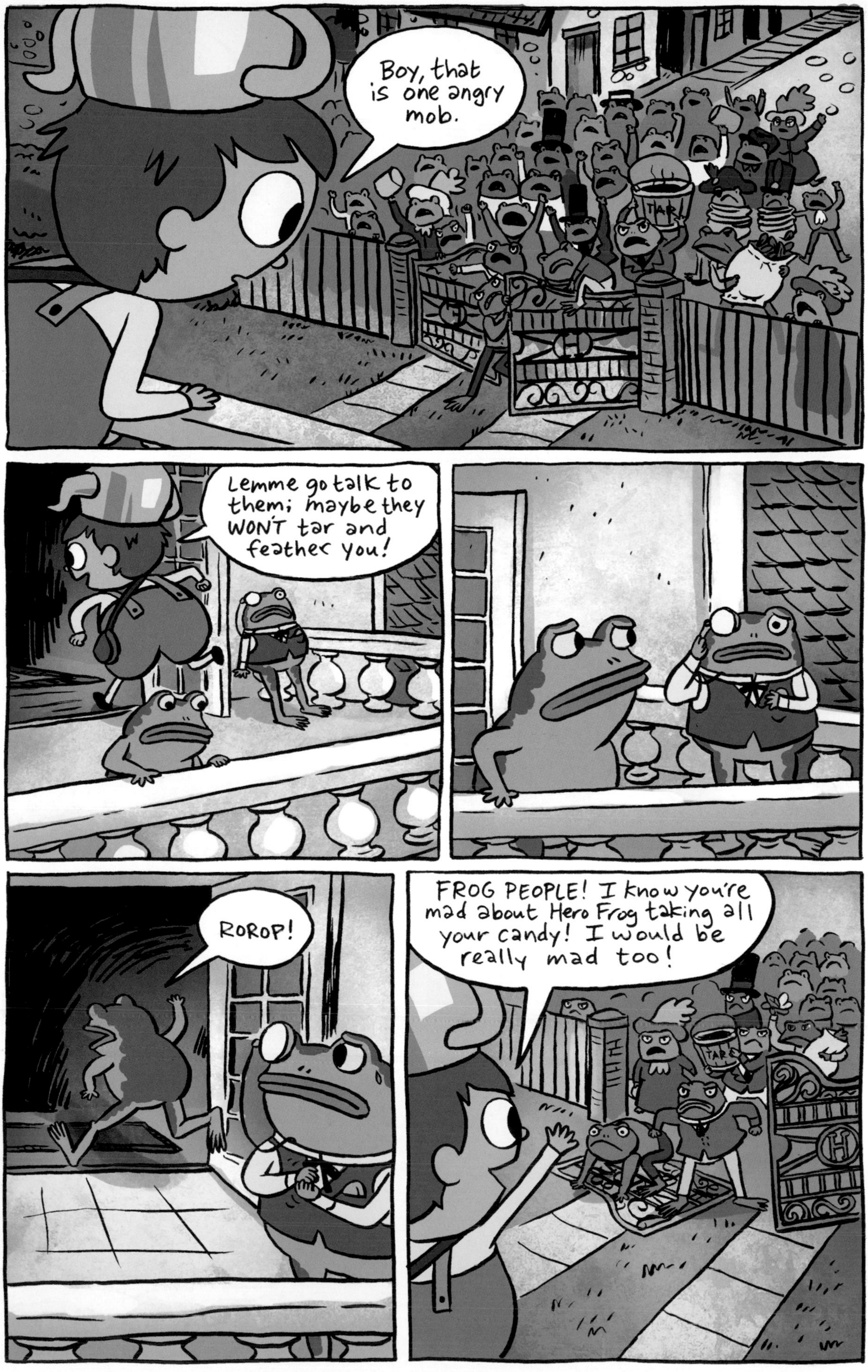
Boy, that is one angry mob.
TAR
Lemme go talk to them; maybe they WON'T tar and feather you!
ROROP!
FROG PEOPLE! I know you're mad about Hero Frog taking all your candy! I would be really mad too!
TAR

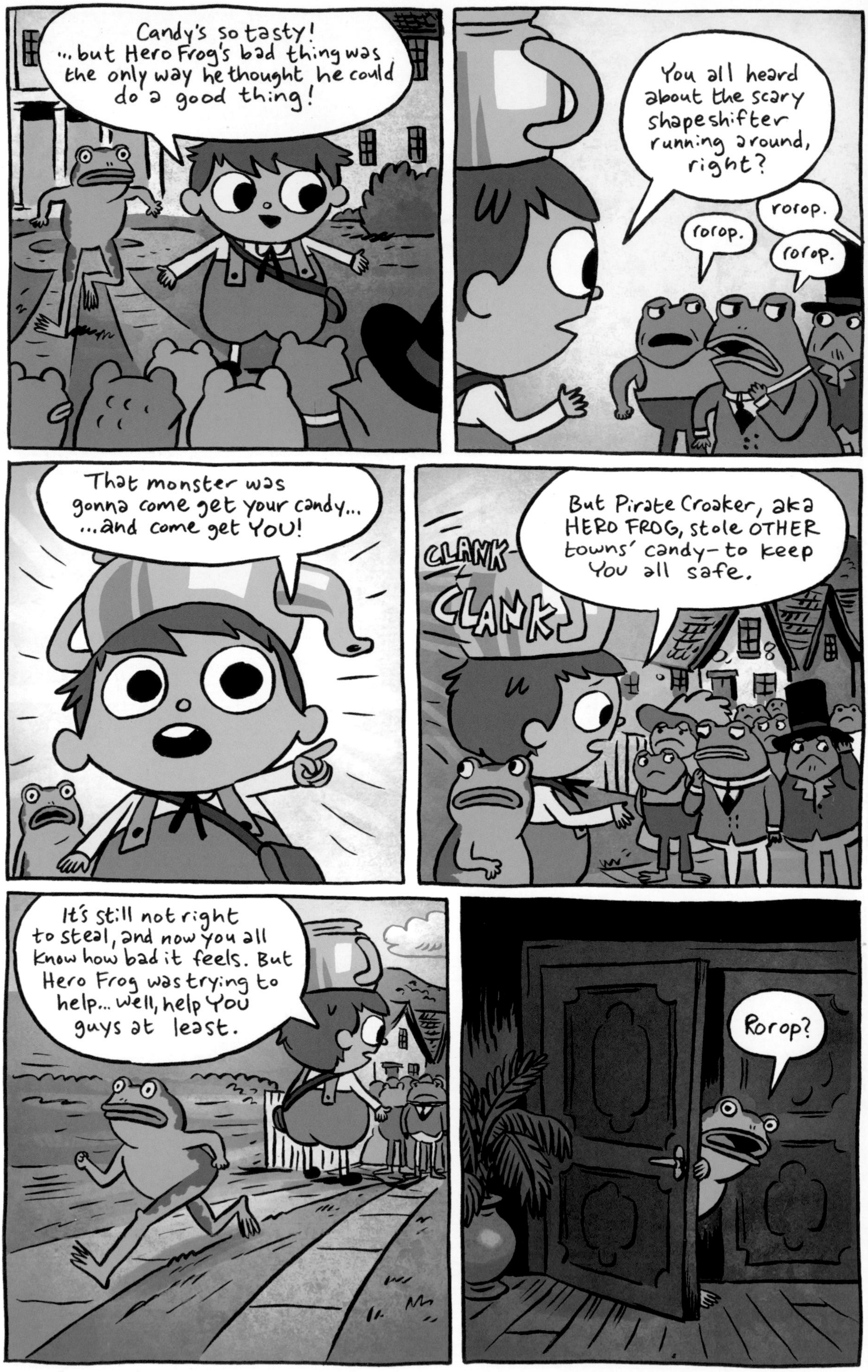
Candy's so tasty! ...but Hero Frog's bad thing was the only way he thought he could do a good thing!
You all heard about the scary shapeshifter running around, right?
rorop.
rorop.
rorop.
That monster was gonna come get your candy... ...and come get YOU!
CLANK-
CLANK
But Pirate Croaker, aka HERO FROG, stole OTHER towns' candy— to keep You all safe.
It's still not right to steal, and now you all know how bad it feels. But Hero Frog was trying to help... well, help YOU guys at least.
Rorop?

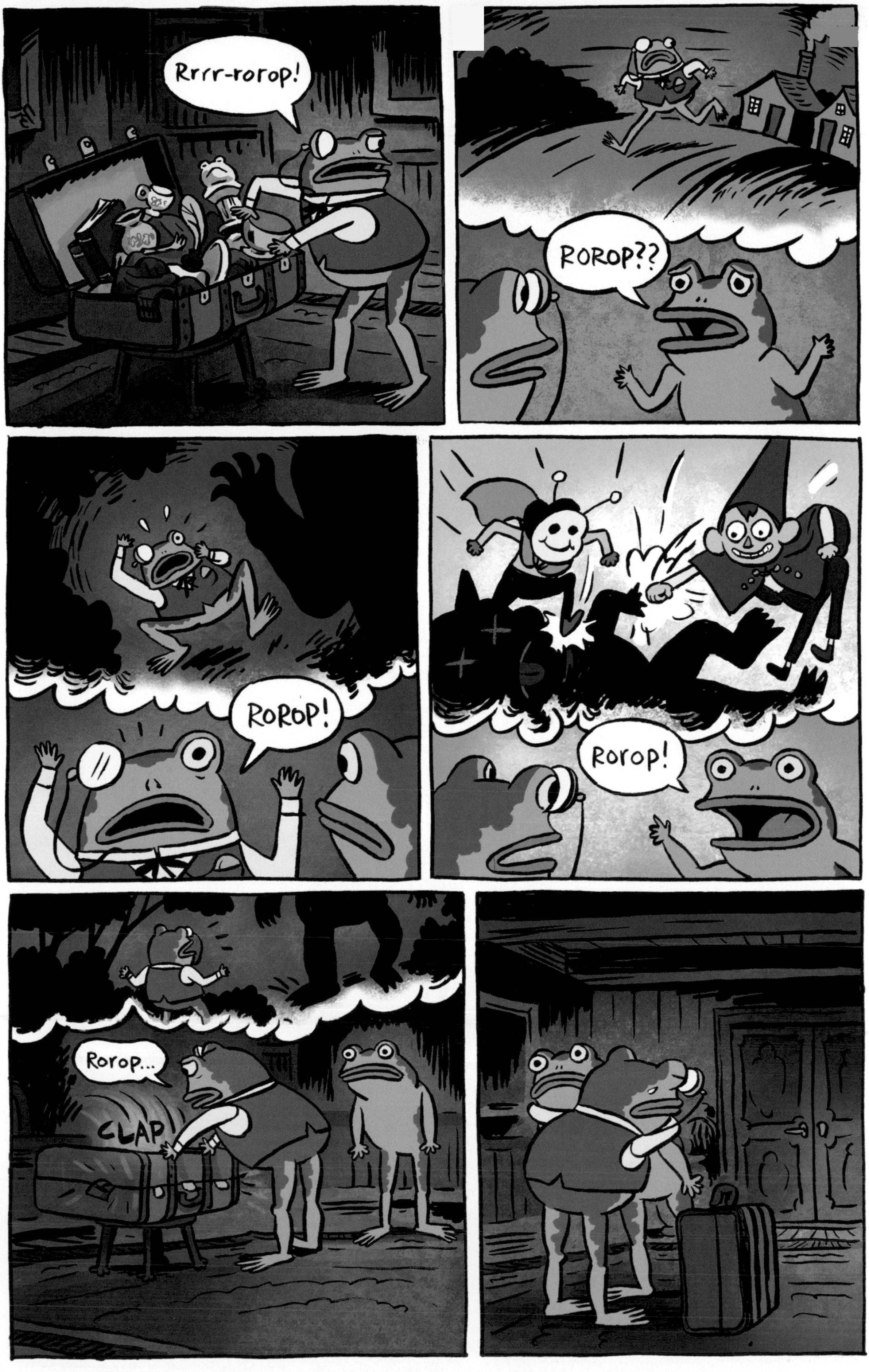
Rrrr-rorop!
ROROP??
ROROP!
Rorop!
Rorop...
CLAP

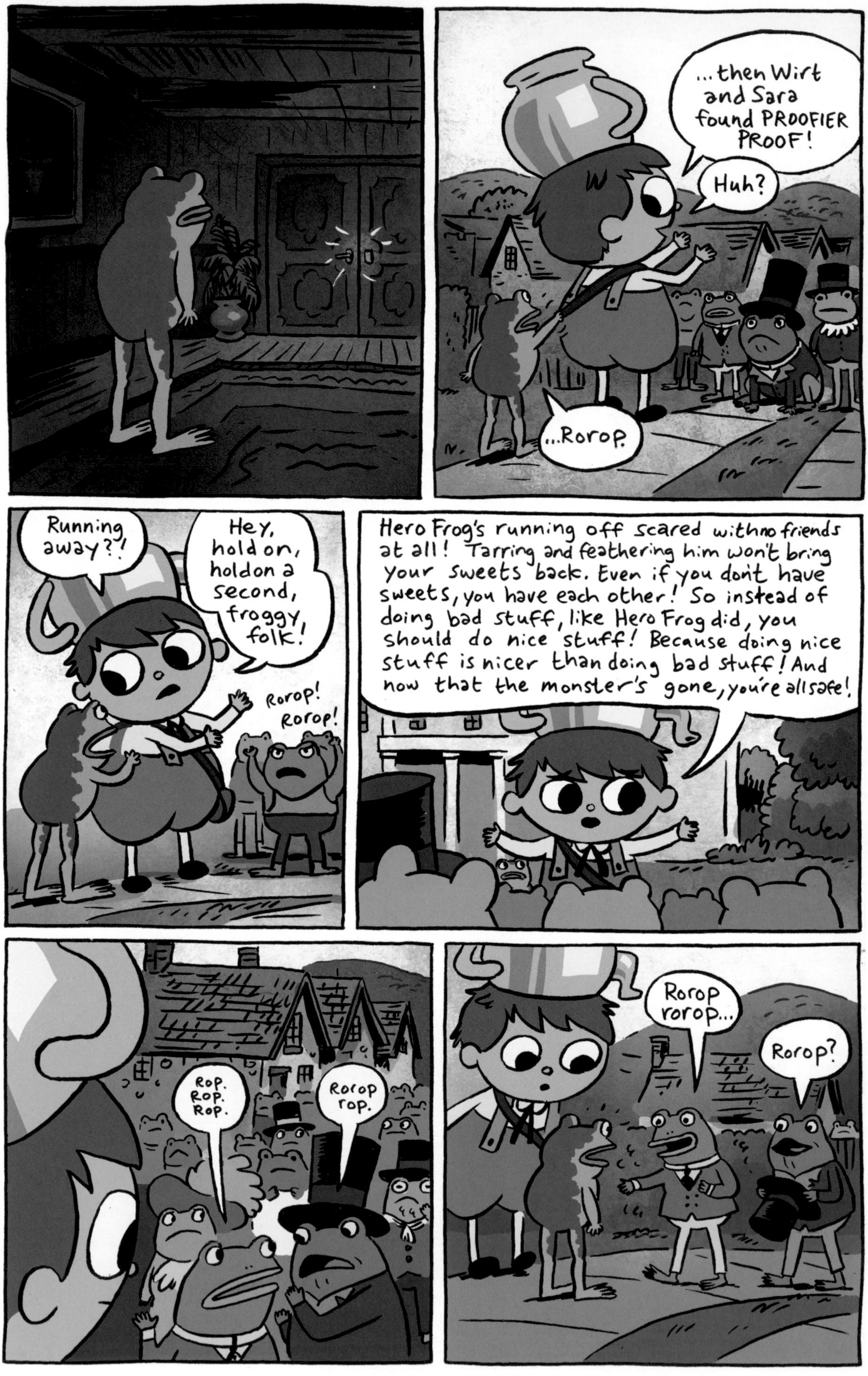
...then Wirt and Sara found PROOFIER PROOF!
Huh?
...Rorop.
Running away?!
Hey, hold on, holdon a second, froggy folk!
Rorop! Rorop!
Hero Frog's running off scared withno friends at all! Tarring and feathering him won't bring your sweets back. Even if you don't have sweets, you have each other! So instead of doing bad stuff, like Hero Frog did, you should do nice stuff! Because doing nice stuff is nicer than doing bad stuff! And now that the monster's gone, you're allsafe!
Rop. Rop. Rop.
Rorop rop.
Rorop rorop...
Rorop?

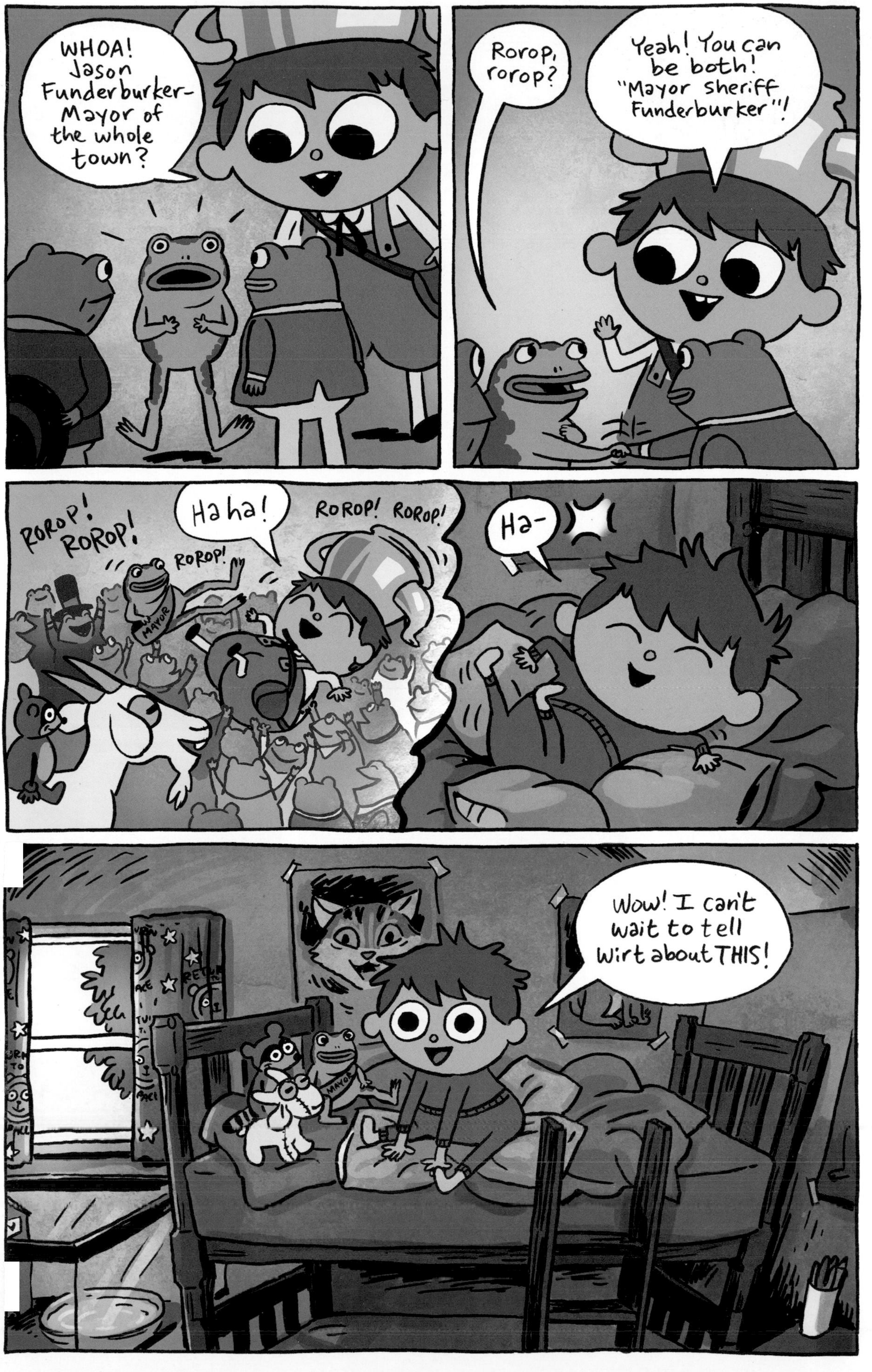
WHOA! Jason Funderburker- Mayor of the whole town?
Rorop, rorop?
Yeah! You can be both! "Mayor sheriff Funderburker"!
RoRoP! RoRoP!
RoRoP!
MAYOR
Ha ha!
RoRoP! RoRoP!
Ha-
MAYOR
Wow! I can't wait to tell Wirt about THIS!

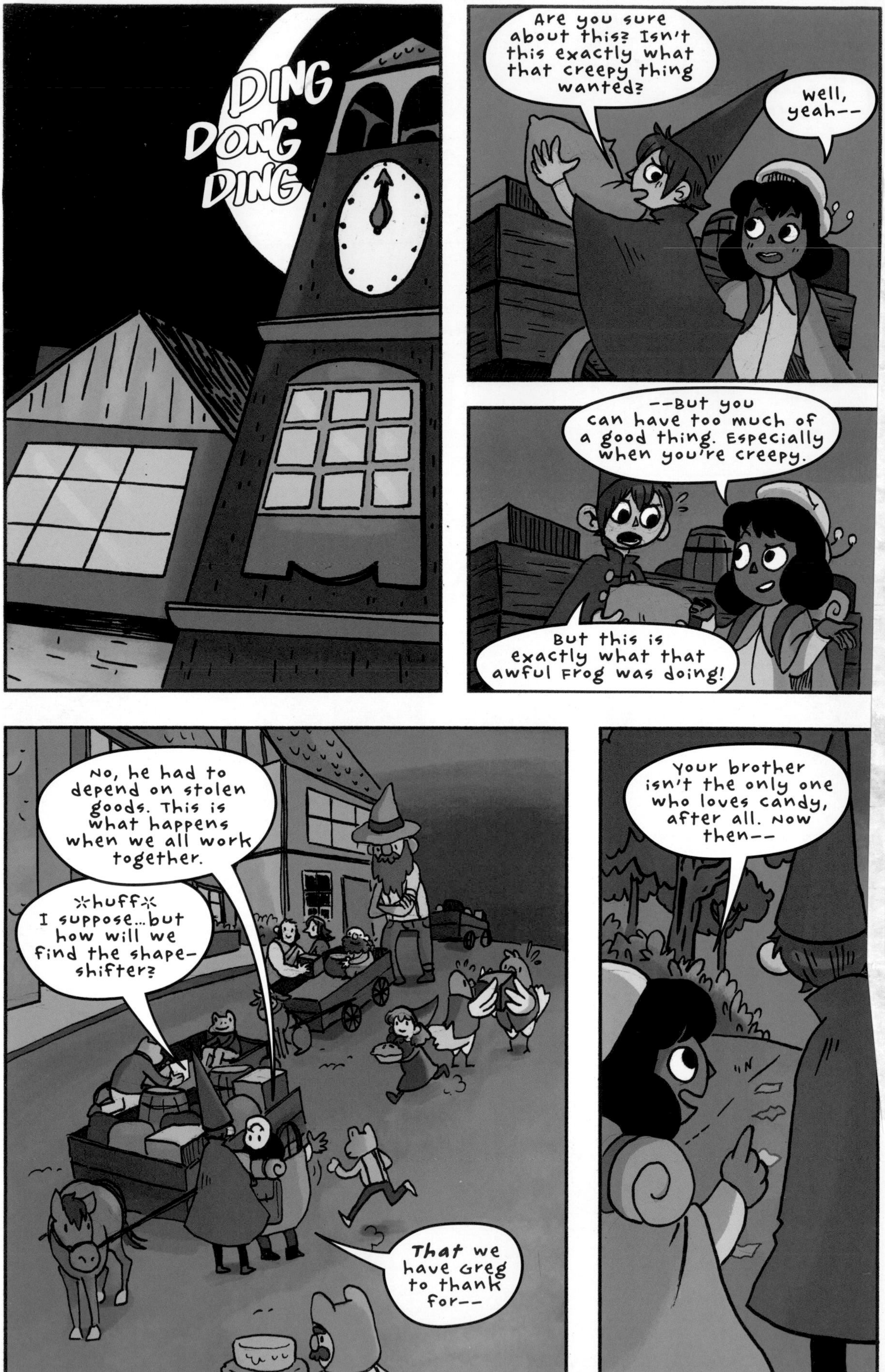
DING DONG DING
Are you sure about this? Isn't this exactly what that creepy thing wanted?
Well, yeah--
--But you can have too much of a good thing. Especially when you're creepy.
But this is exactly what that awful Frog was doing!
No, he had to depend on stolen goods. This is what happens when we all work together.
huff I suppose...but how will we find the shape-shifter?
That we have Greg to thank for--
Your brother isn't the only one who loves candy, after all. Now then--

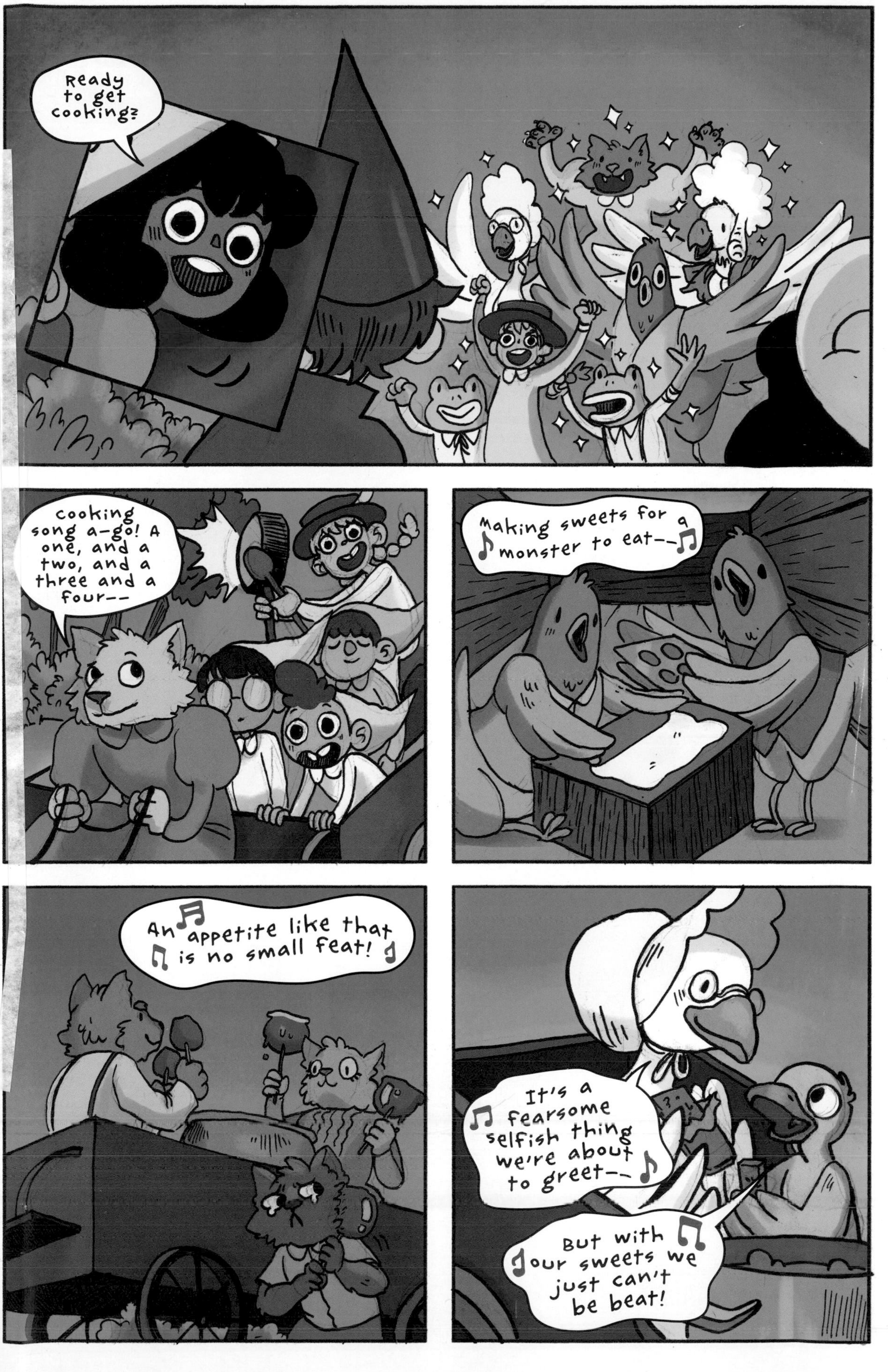
Ready to get cooking?
Cooking song a-go! A one, and a two, and a three and a four--
Making sweets for a monster to eat--
An appetite like that is no small feat!
It's a fearsome selfish thing we're about to greet--
But with our sweets we just can't be beat!

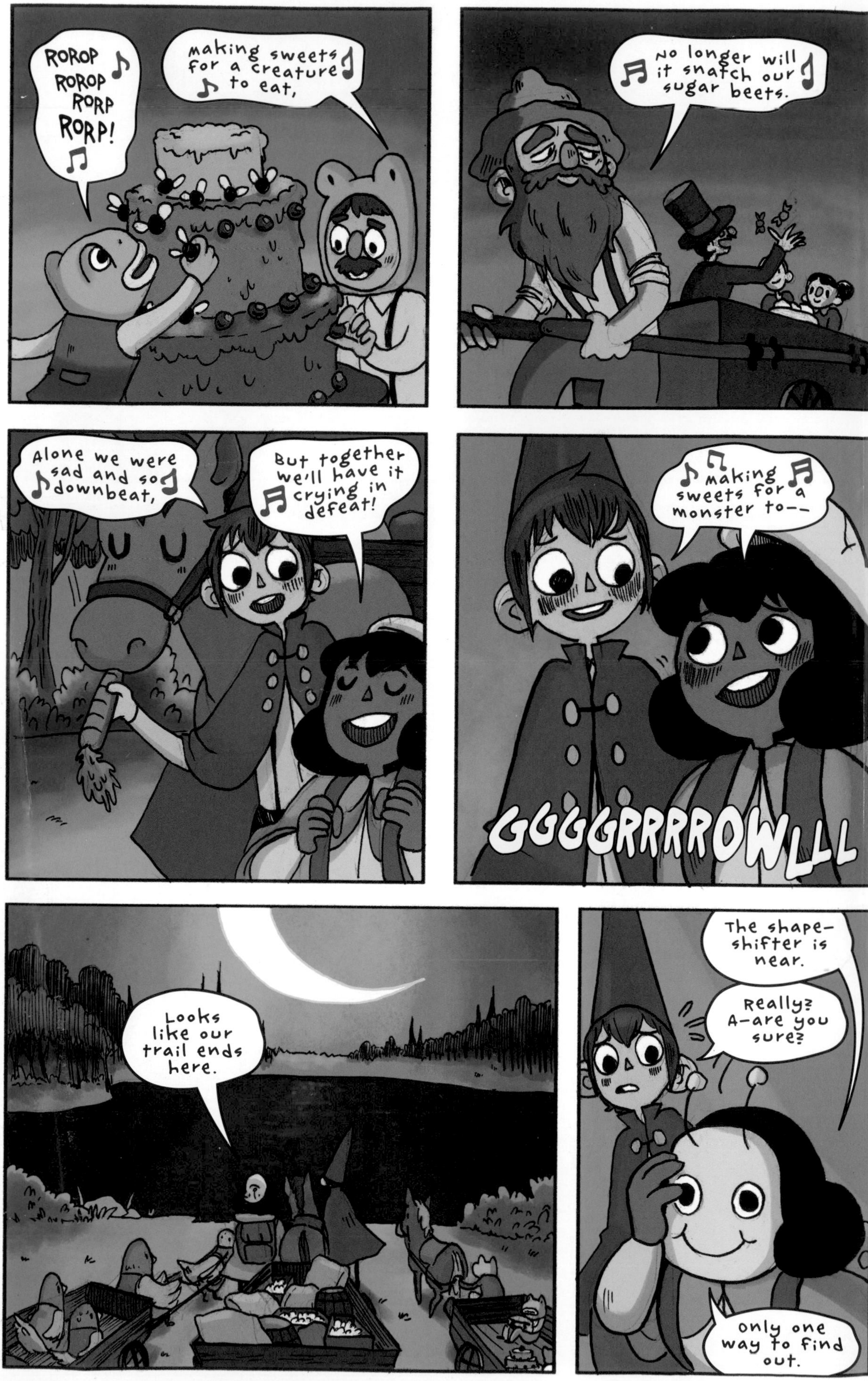
RORP RORP RORP RORP!
making sweets for a creature to eat,
No longer will it snatch our sugar beets.
Alone we were sad and so downbeat,
But together we'll have it crying in defeat!
making sweets for a monster to--
GGGGRRRROWLLL
Looks like our trail ends here.
The shape-shifter is near.
Really? A-are you sure?
Only one way to find out.

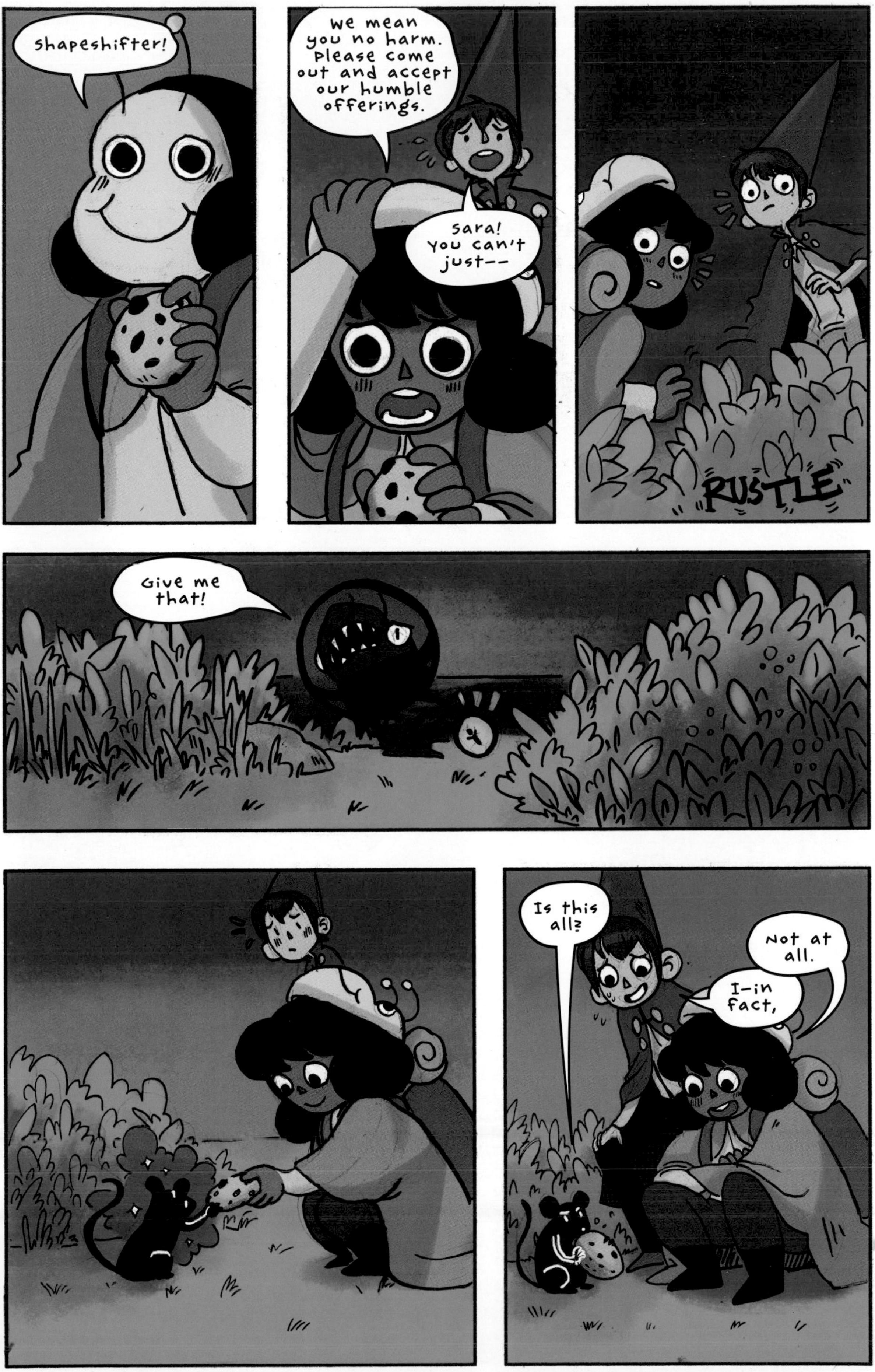
Shapeshifter!
We mean you no harm. Please come out and accept our humble offerings.
Sara! You can't just--
RUSTLE
Give me that!
Is this all?
I-in fact,
Not at all.

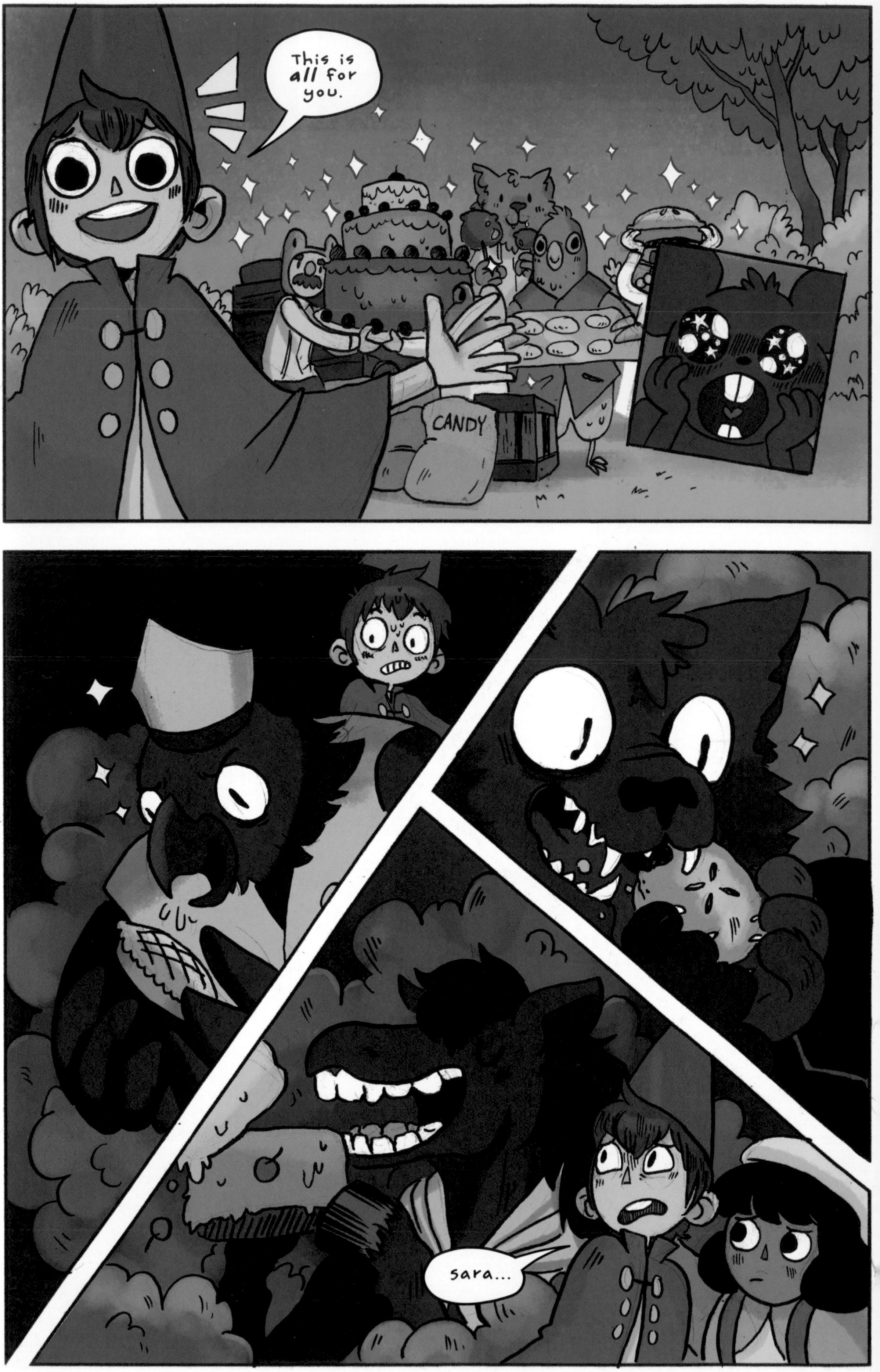
This is all for you.
CANDY
sara...

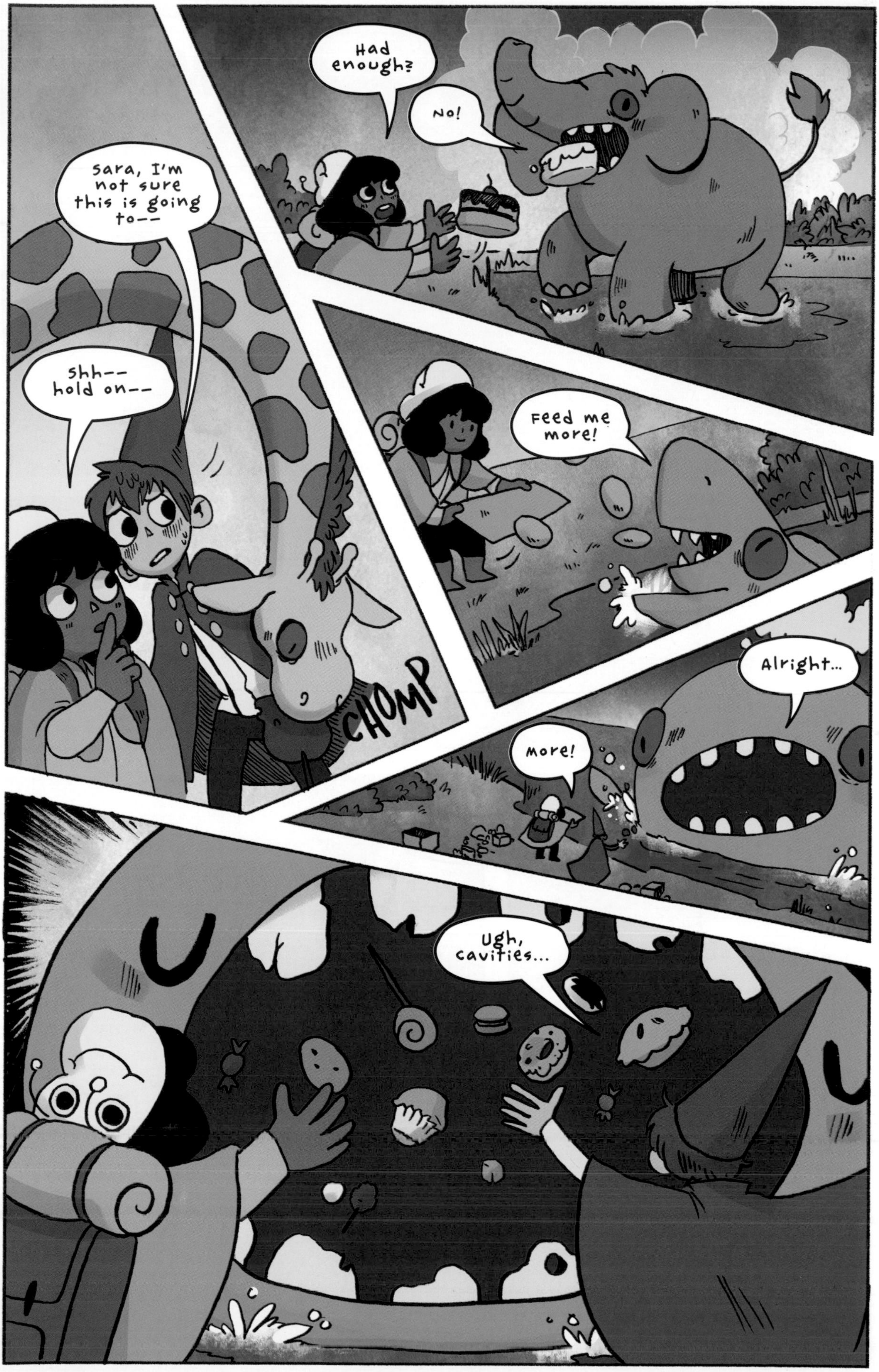
Had enough?
No!
Sara, I'm not sure this is going to--
Shh-- hold on--
CHOMP
Feed me more!
Alright...
more!
Ugh, cavities...

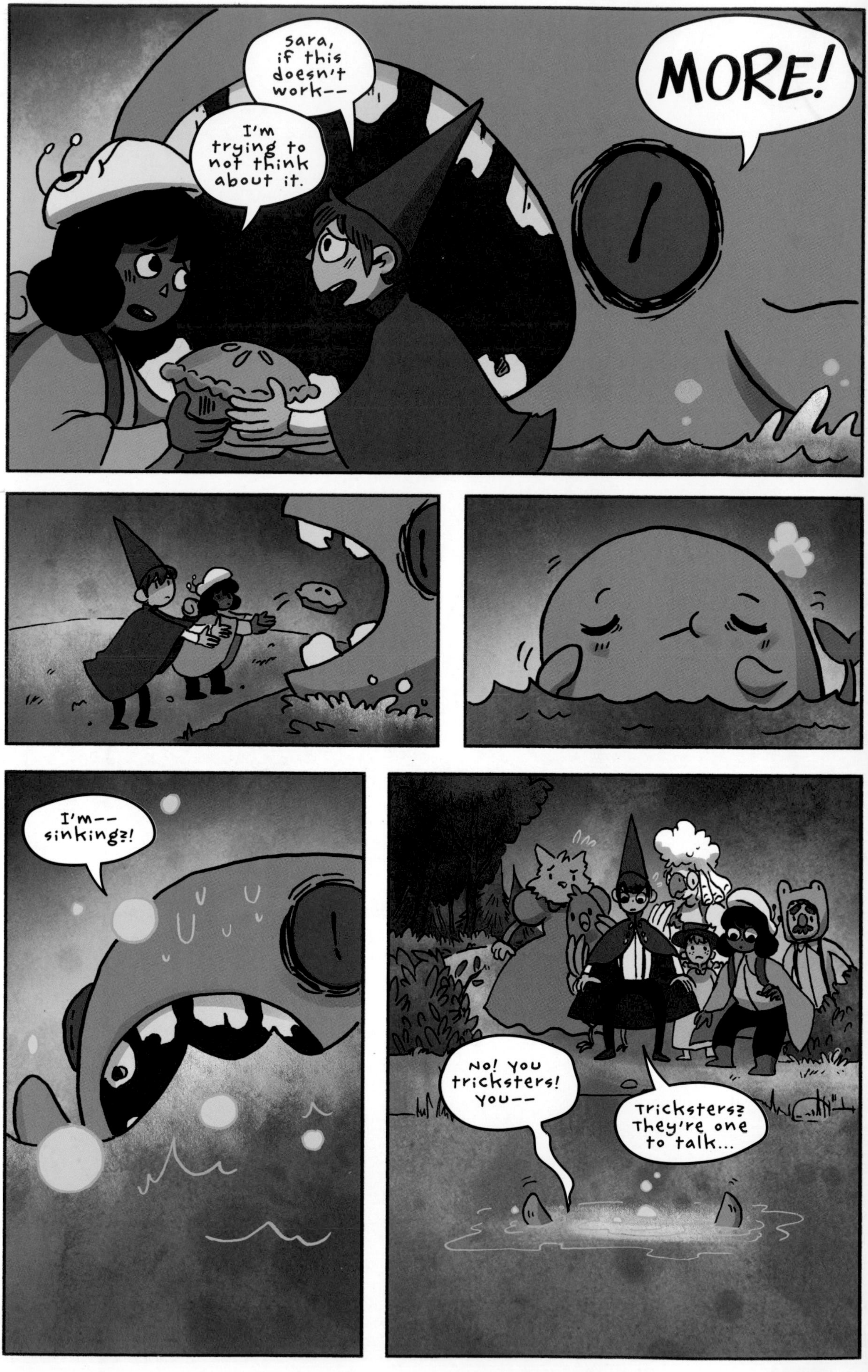
Sara, if this doesn't work--
I'm trying to not think about it.
MORE!
I'm-- sinking?!
No! You tricksters! You--
Tricksters? They're one to talk...

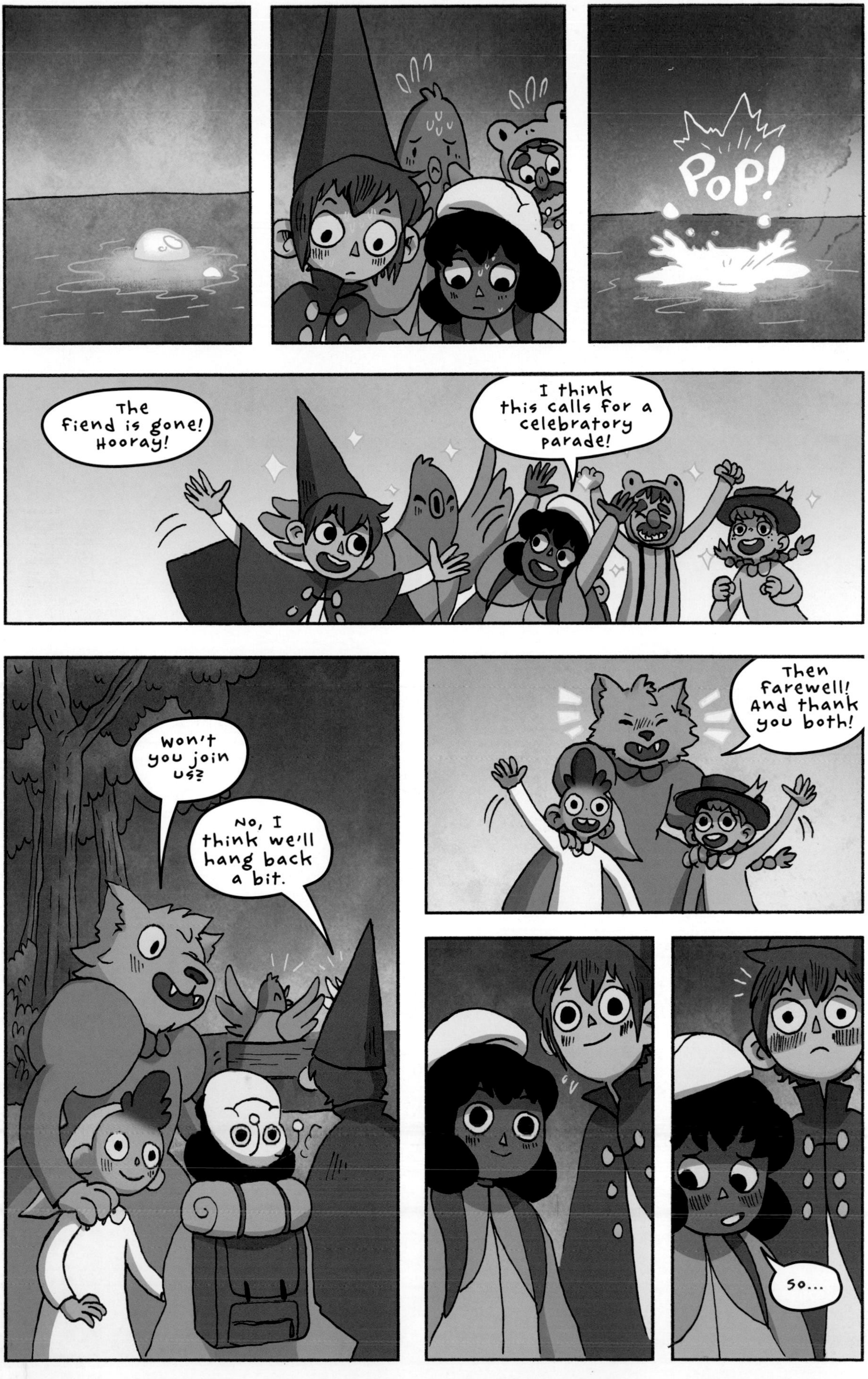
POP!
The fiend is gone! Hooray!
I think this calls for a celebratory parade!
Won't you join us?
No, I think we'll hang back a bit.
Then farewell! And thank you both!
So...

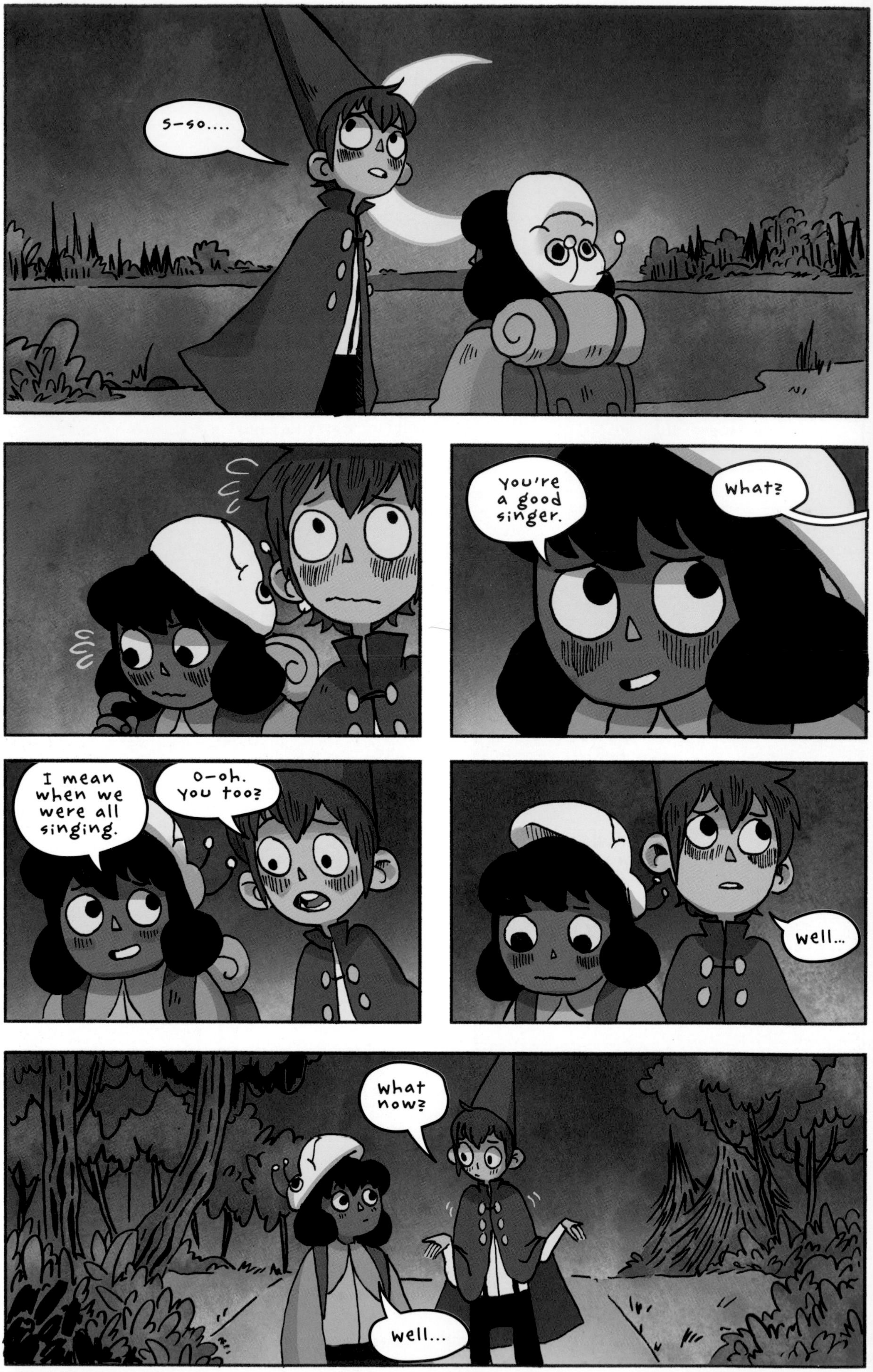
S-so....
What?
You're a good singer.
I mean when we were all singing.
O-oh. You too?
Well...
What now?
Well...

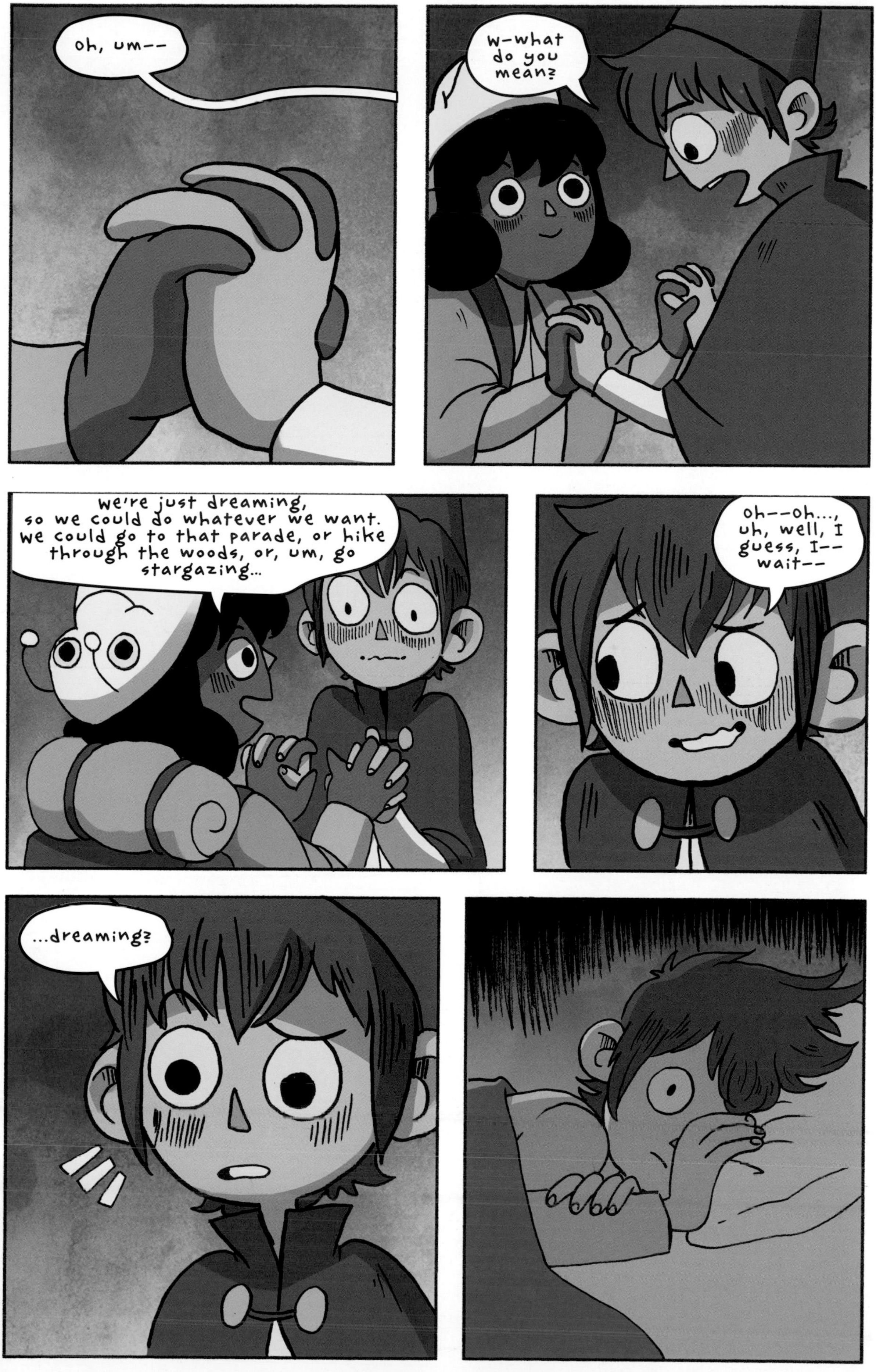
oh, um--
w-what do you mean?
we're just dreaming, so we could do whatever we want. we could go to that parade, or hike through the woods, or, um, go stargazing...
oh--oh..., uh, well, I guess, I-- wait--
...dreaming?

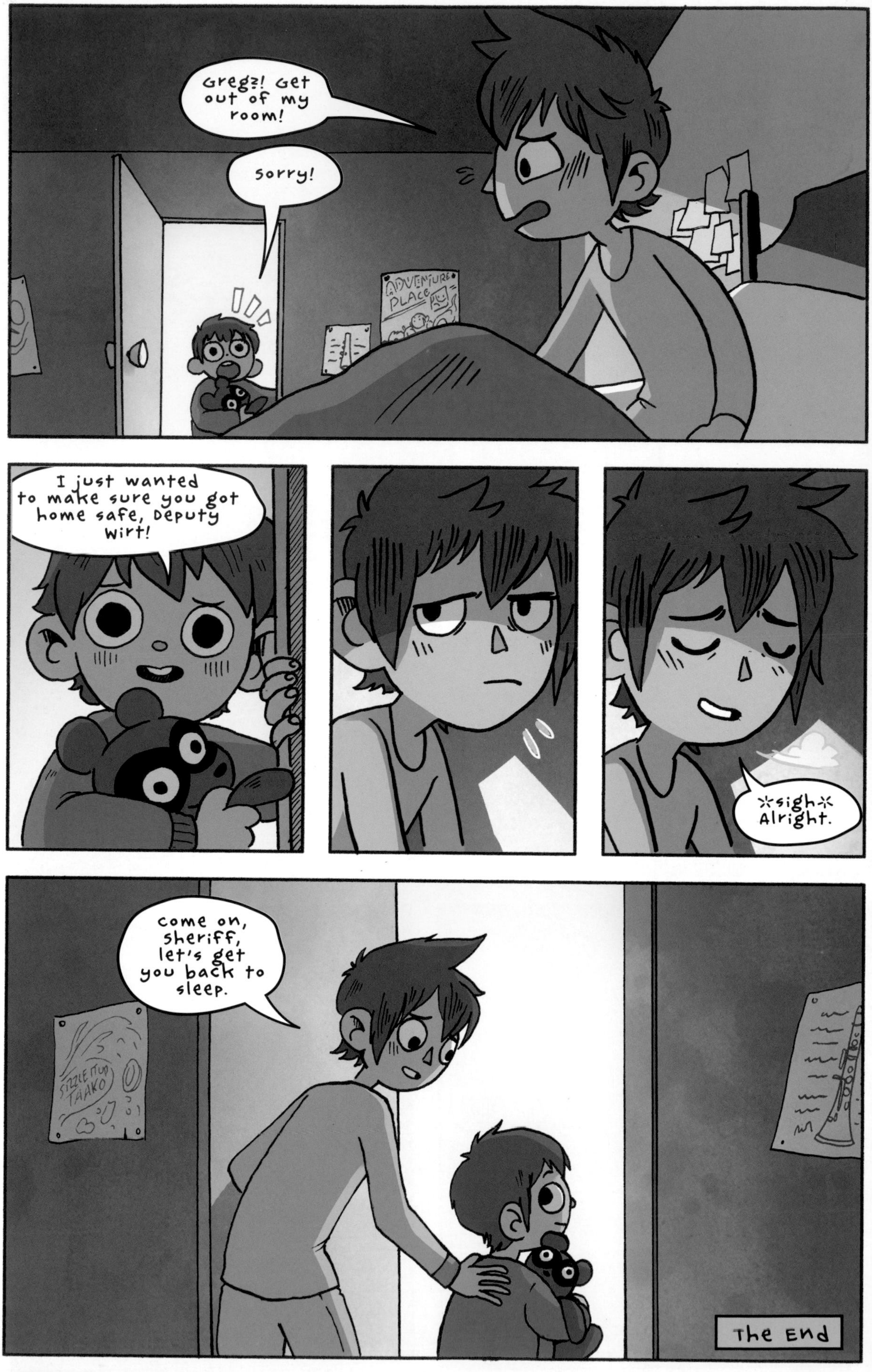
Greg?! Get out of my room!
Sorry!
ADVENTURE PLACE
I just wanted to make sure you got home safe, Deputy Wirt!
sigh Alright.
Come on, Sheriff, let's get you back to sleep.
SIZZLE IT UP TAAKO
The End

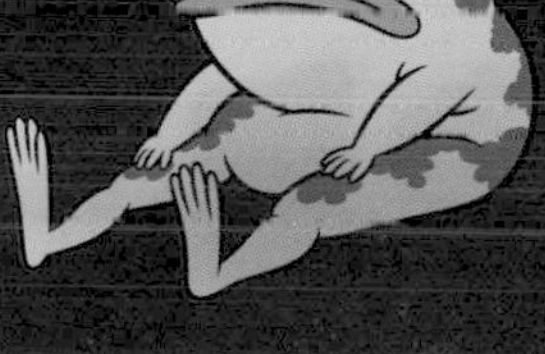

THREE WISE MEN

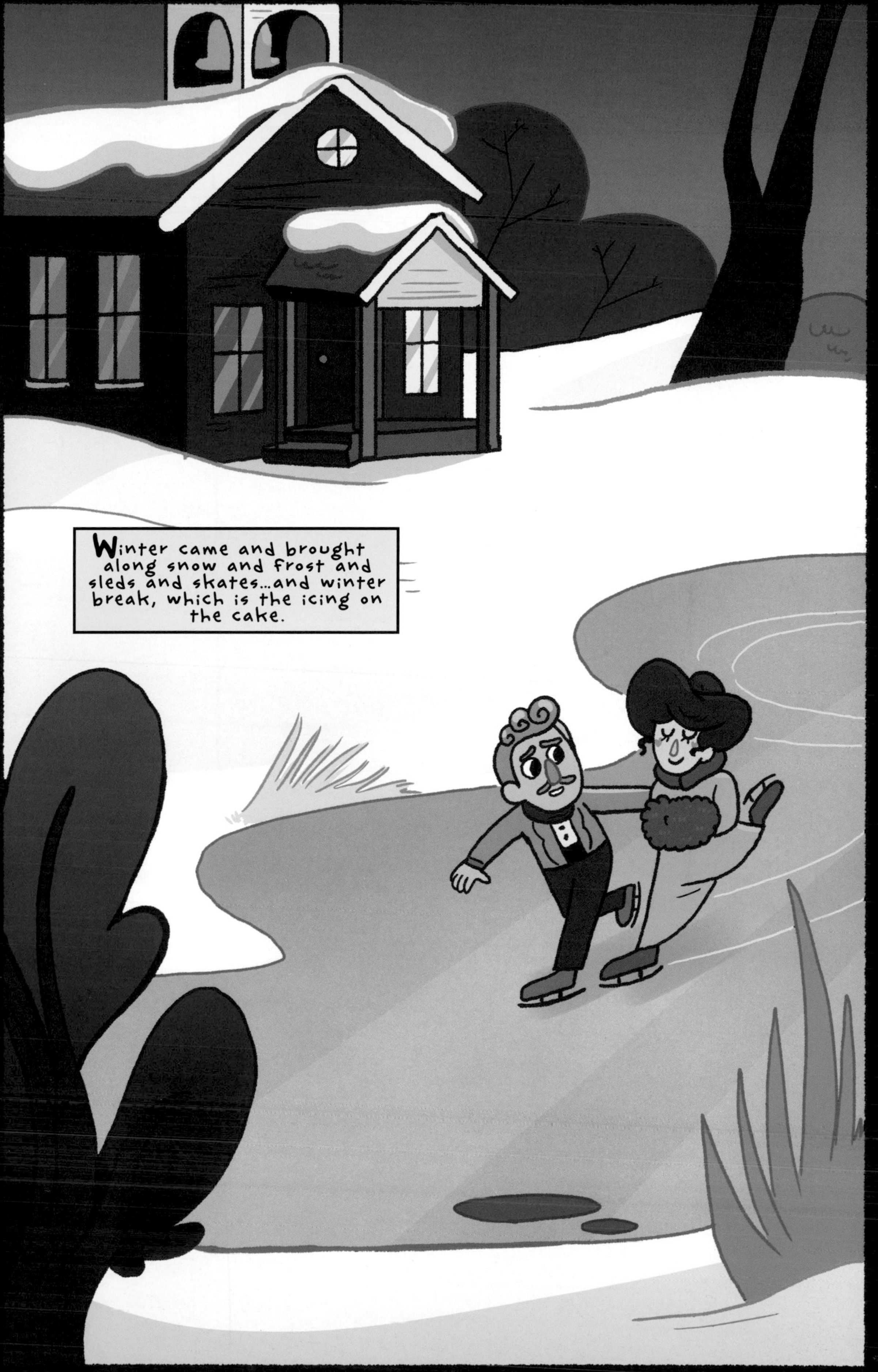
Winter came and brought along snow and frost and sleds and skates...and winter break, which is the icing on the cake.

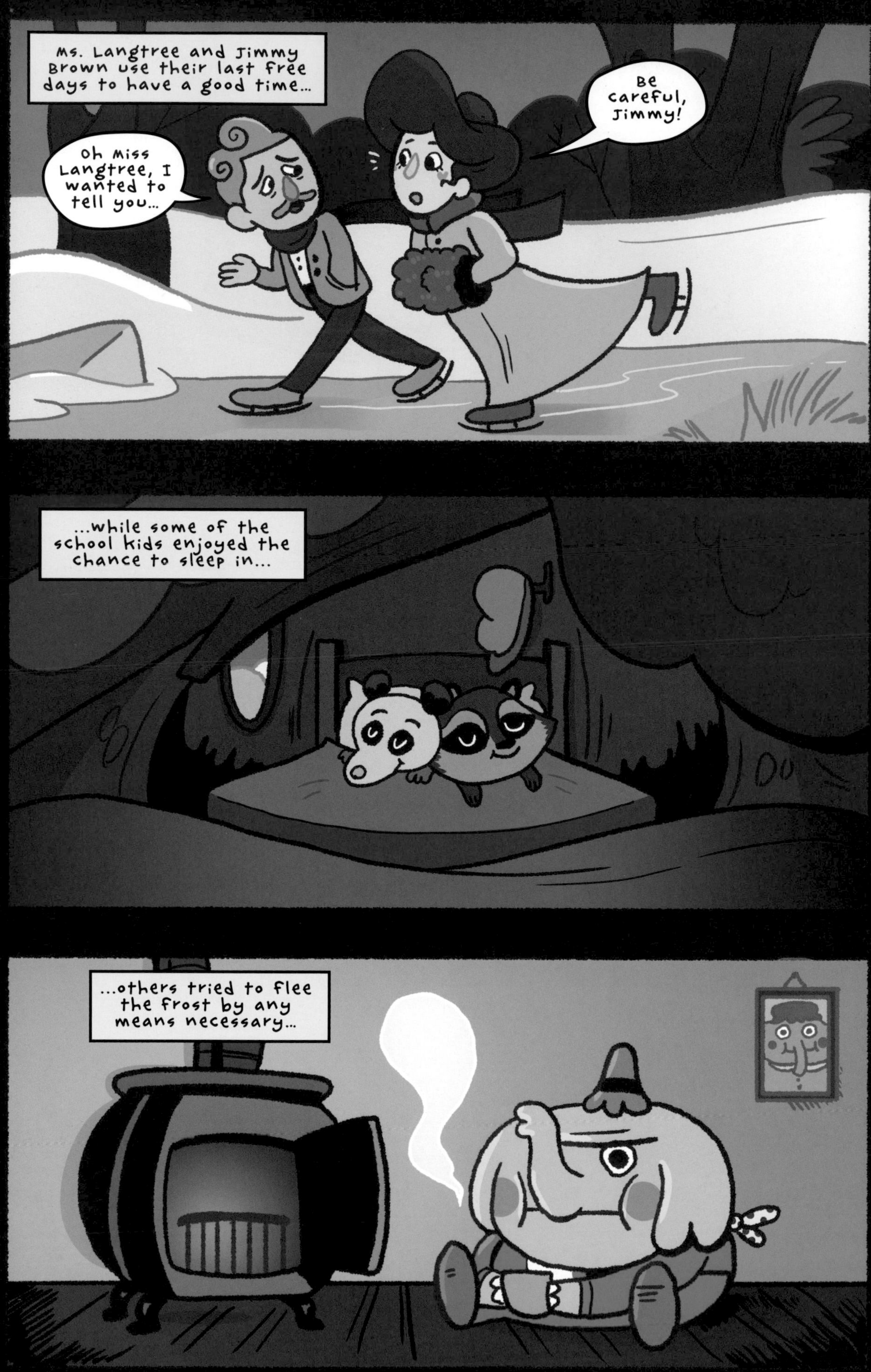

Ms. Langtree and Jimmy Brown use their last free days to have a good time...
Oh Miss Langtree, I wanted to tell you...
Be careful, Jimmy!
...while some of the school kids enjoyed the chance to sleep in...
...others tried to flee the frost by any means necessary...

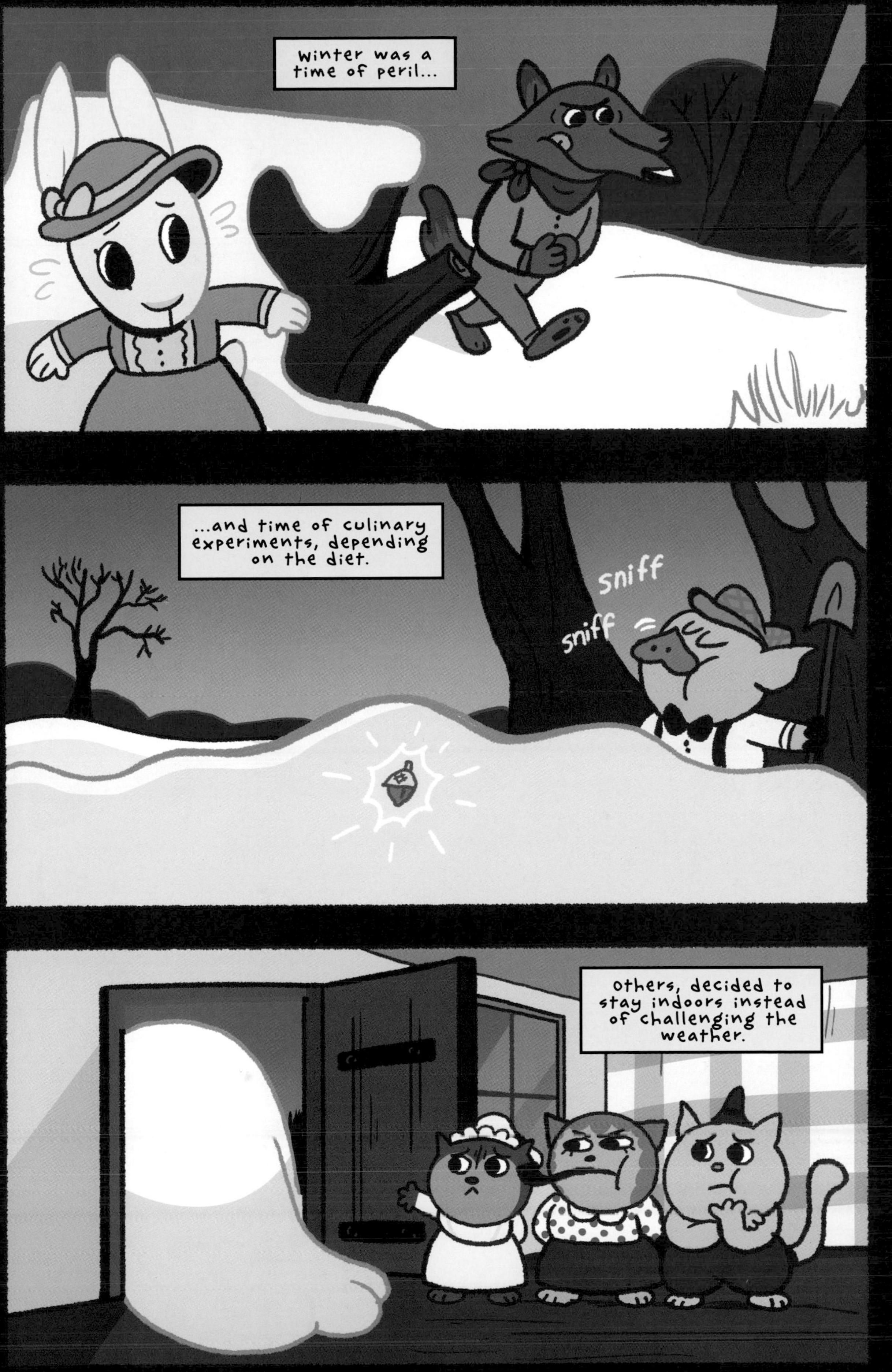
Winter was a time of peril...
...and time of culinary experiments, depending on the diet.
sniff
sniff
Others, decided to stay indoors instead of challenging the weather.

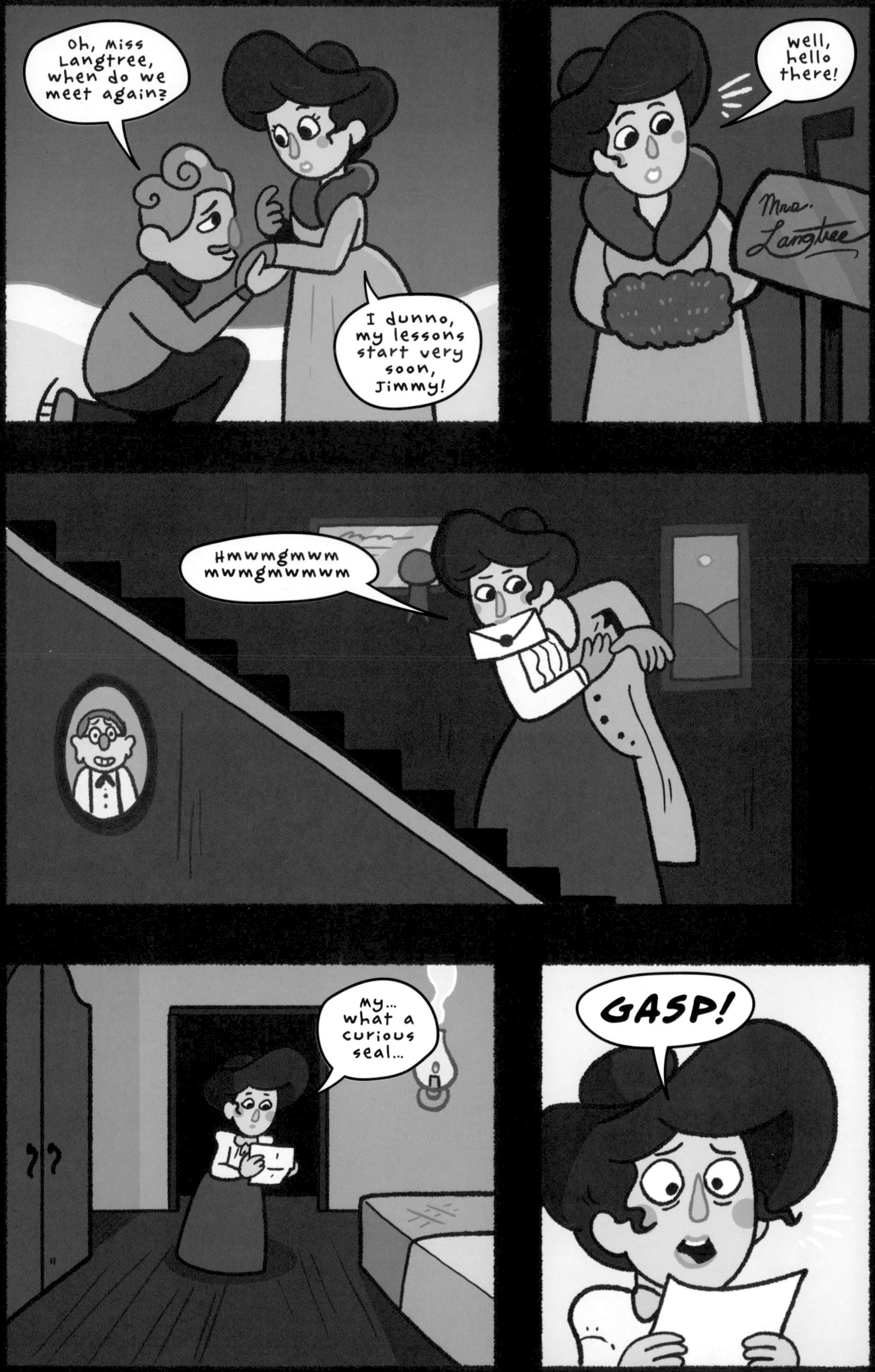
Oh, Miss Langtree, when do we meet again?
I dunno, my lessons start very soon, Jimmy!
Well, hello there!
Mrs. Langtree
Hmwmgmwm mwmgmwmwm
My... what a curious seal...
GASP!

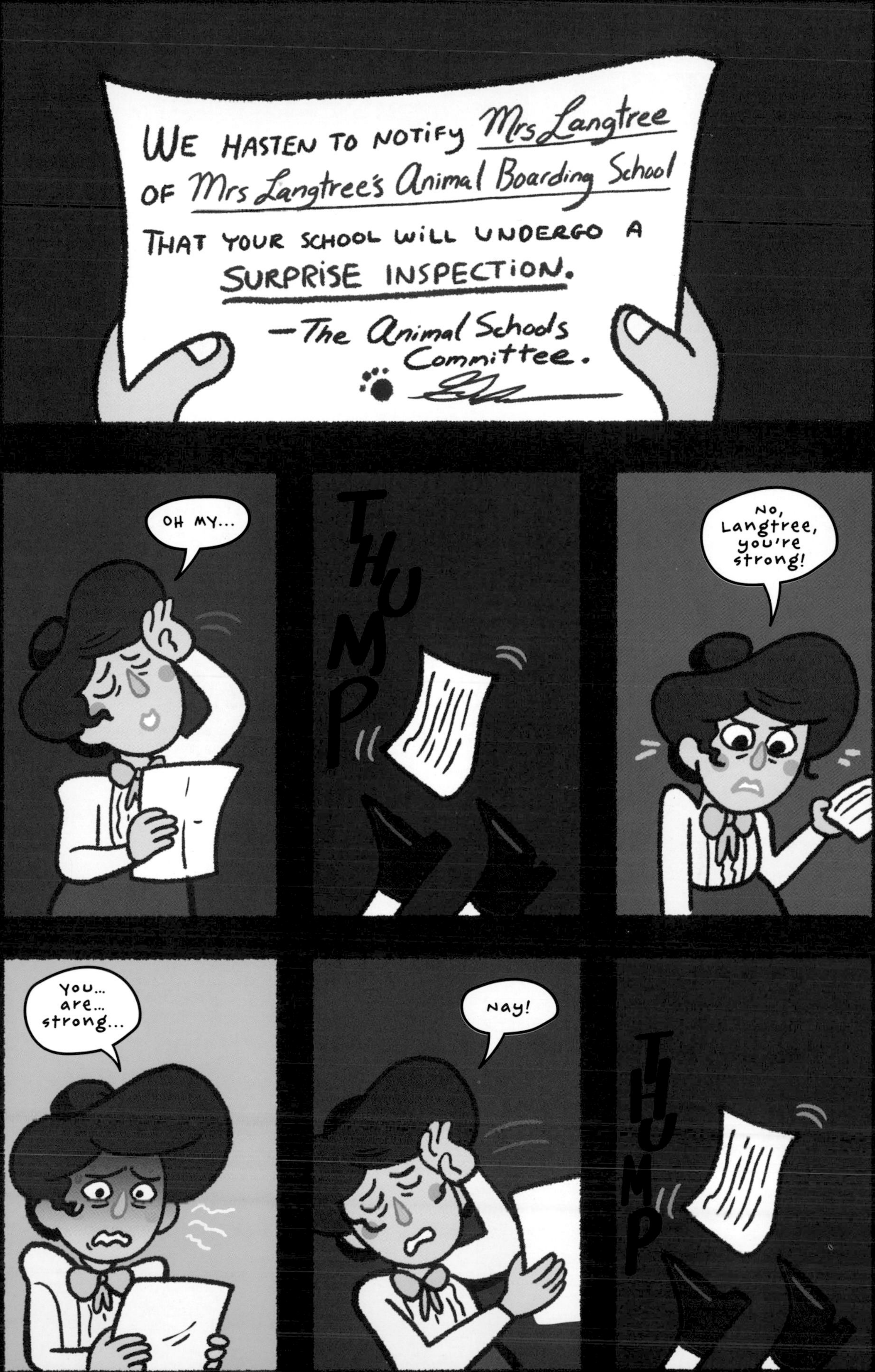
WE HASTEN TO NOTIFY Mrs Langtree
OF Mrs Langtree's Animal Boarding School
THAT YOUR SCHOOL WILL UNDERGO A
SURPRISE INSPECTION.
—The Animal Schools Committee.
OH MY...
THUMP
No, Langtree, you're strong!
You... are... strong...
Nay!
THUMP

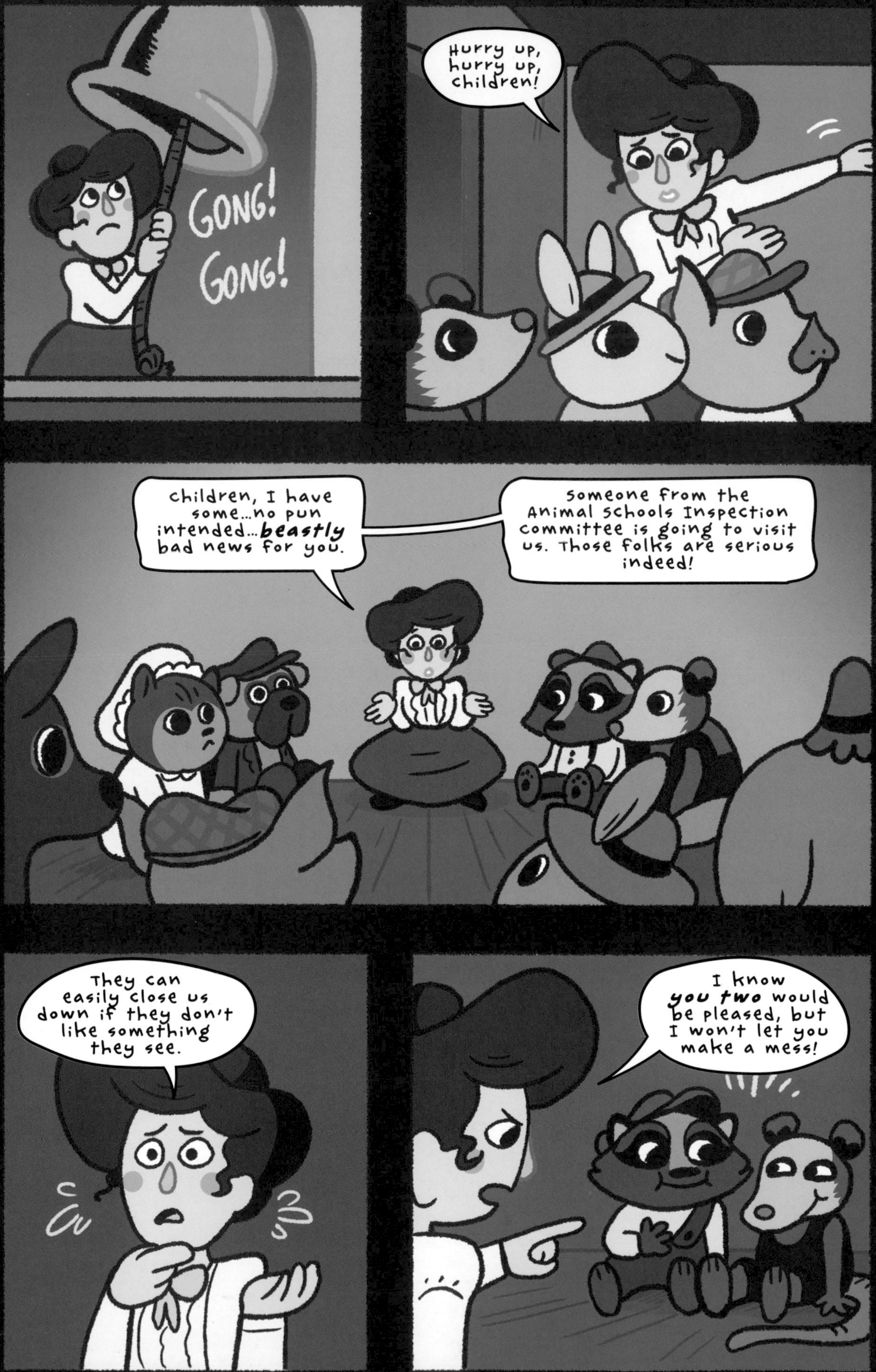
GONG!
GONG!
Hurry up, hurry up, children!
Children, I have some...no pun intended...beastly bad news for you.
Someone from the Animal Schools Inspection committee is going to visit us. Those folks are serious indeed!
They can easily close us down if they don't like something they see.
I know you two would be pleased, but I won't let you make a mess!

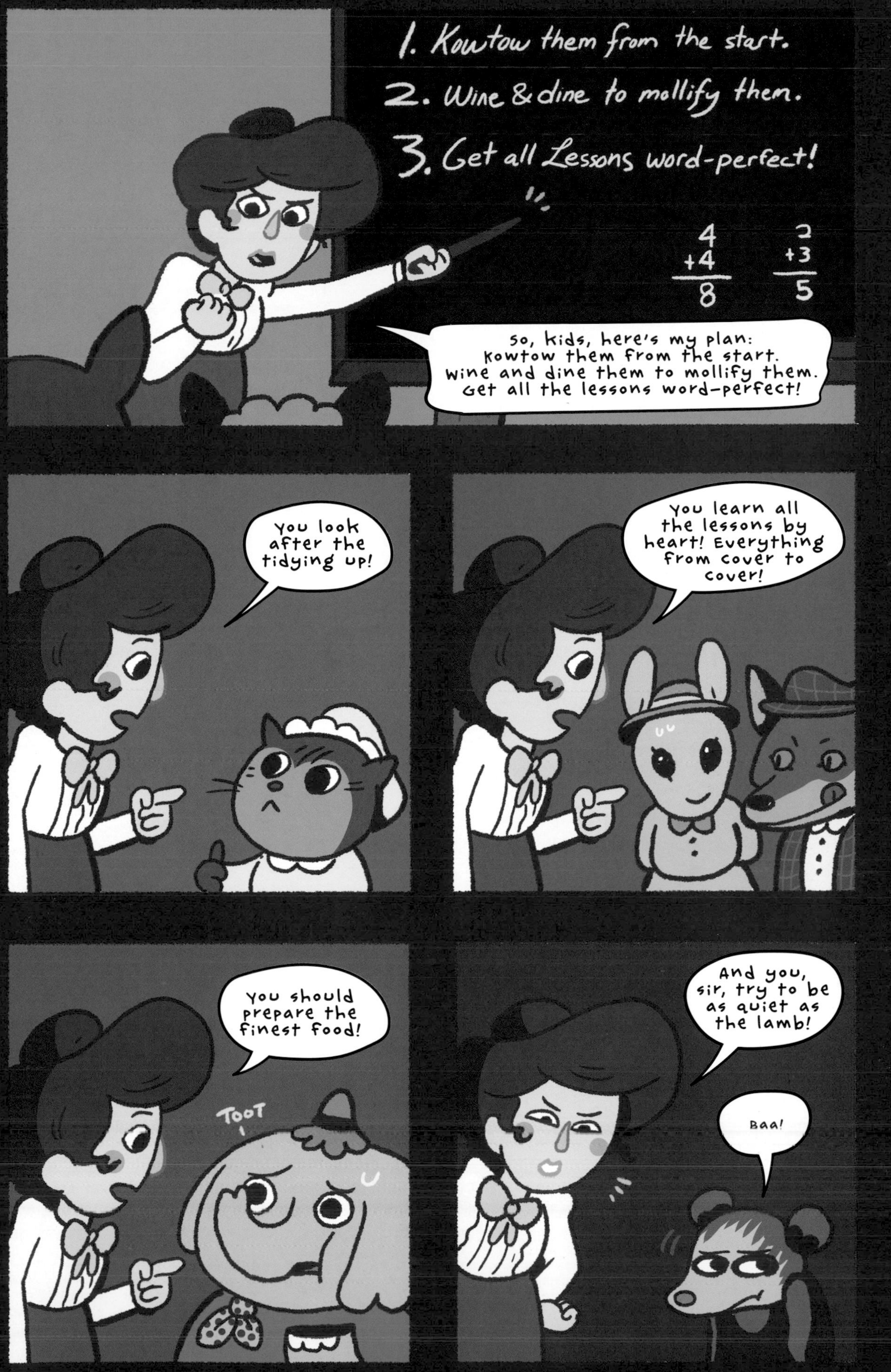

1. Kowtow them from the start.
2. Wine & dine to mollify them.
3. Get all Lessons word-perfect!
4 +4 8
2 +3 5
So, kids, here's my plan: Kowtow them from the start. Wine and dine them to mollify them. Get all the lessons word-perfect!
You look after the tidying up!
You learn all the lessons by heart! Everything from cover to cover!
You should prepare the finest food!
TOOT
And you, sir, try to be as quiet as the lamb!
Baa!

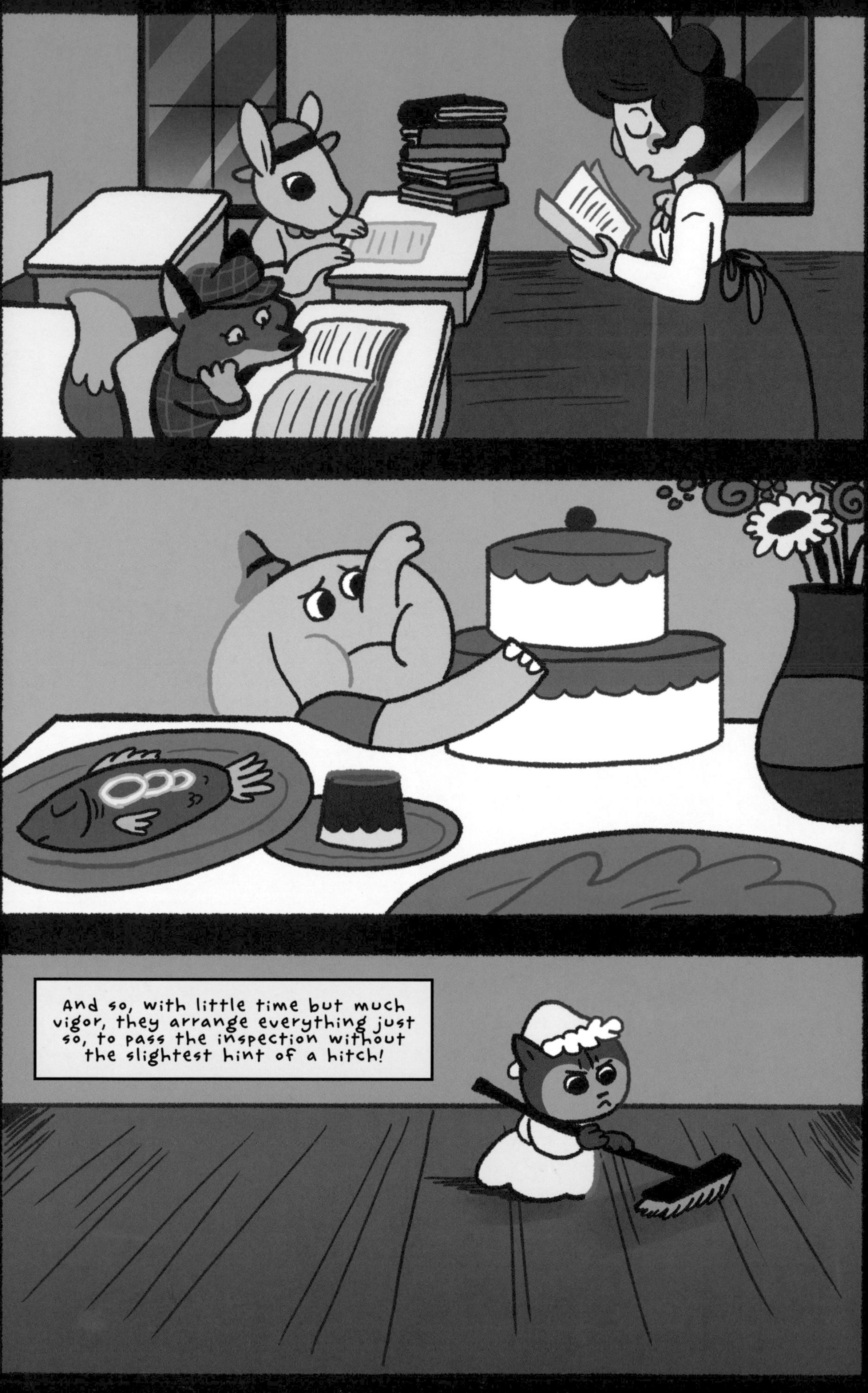
And so, with little time but much vigor, they arrange everything just so, to pass the inspection without the slightest hint of a hitch!

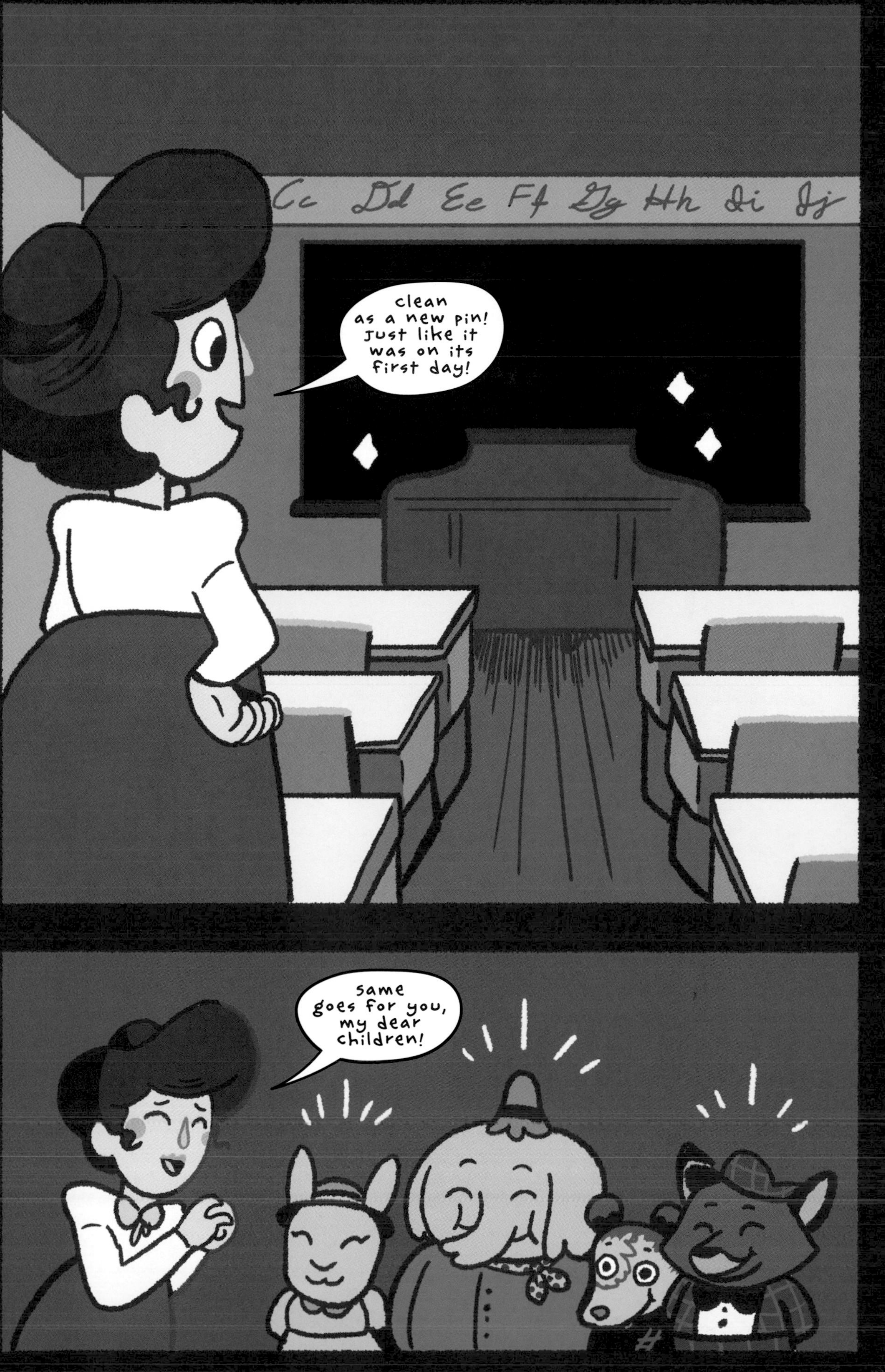
Cc Dd Ee Ff Gg Hh Ii Jj
clean as a new pin! Just like it was on its first day!
same goes for you, my dear children!

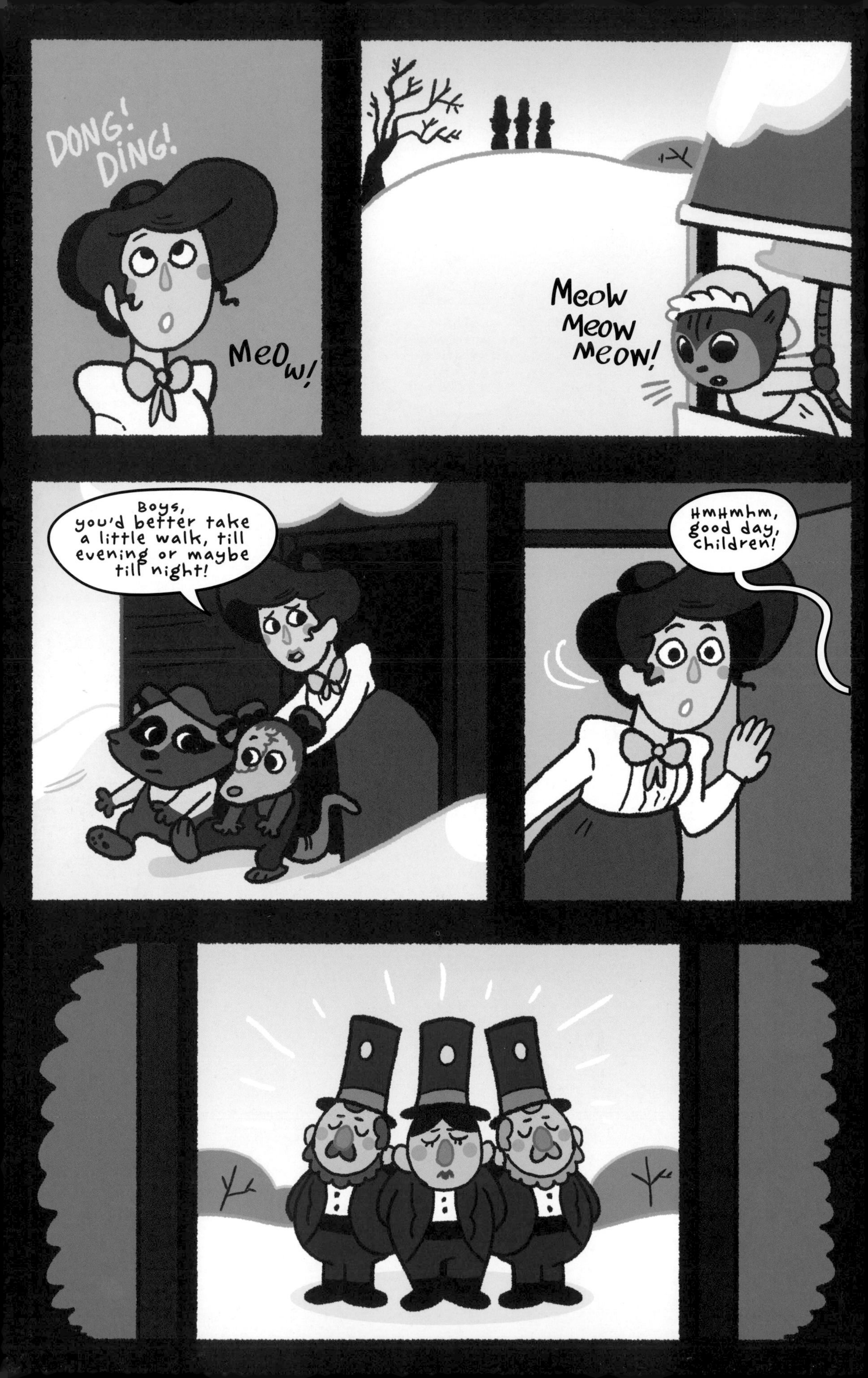
DONG!
DING!
MEOW!
Meow
Meow
meow!
Boys, you'd better take a little walk, till evening or maybe till night!
HMHMhm, good day, children!

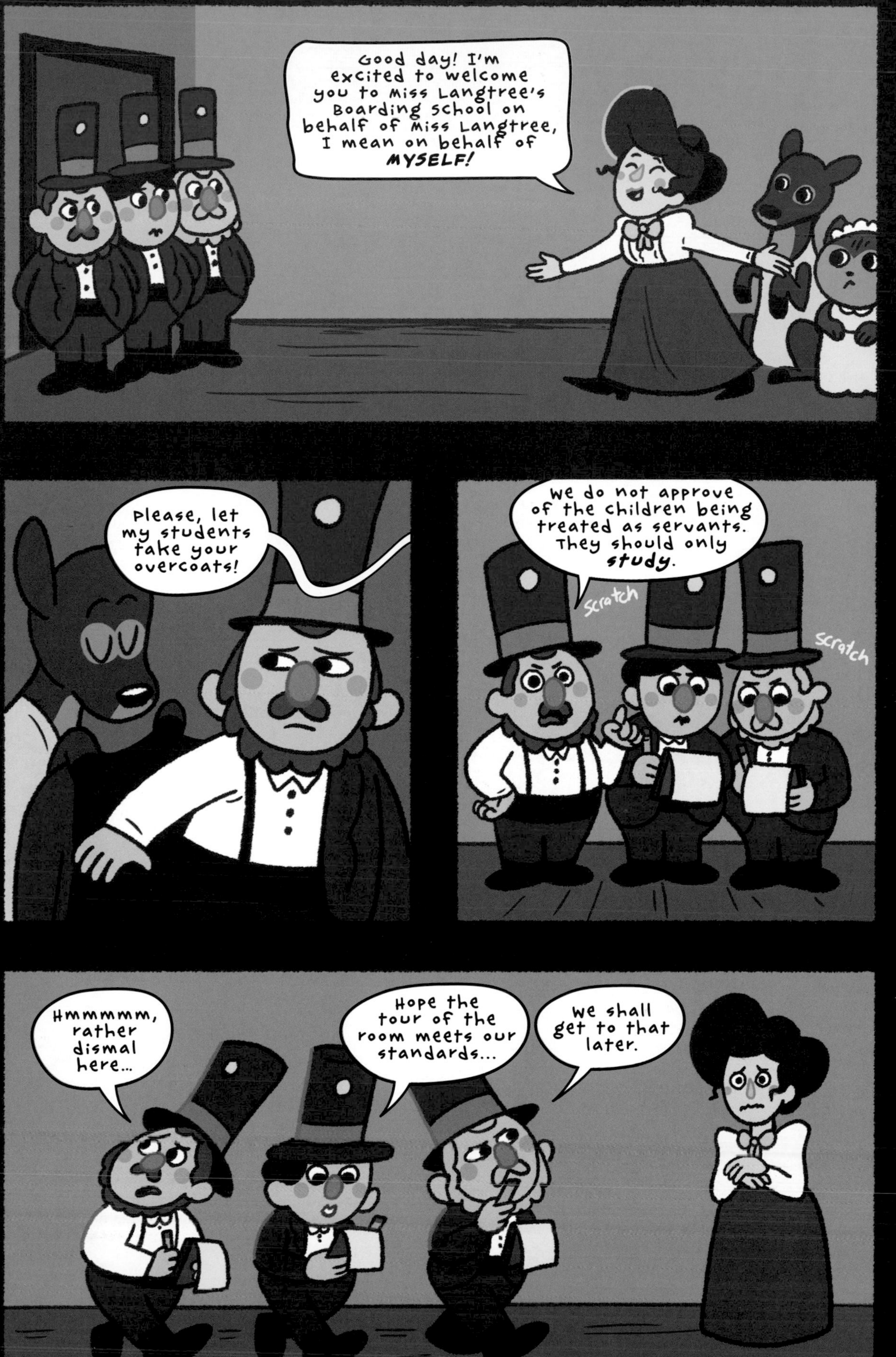

Good day! I'm excited to welcome you to Miss Langtree's Boarding school on behalf of Miss Langtree, I mean on behalf of MYSELF!
Please, let my students take your overcoats!
We do not approve of the children being treated as servants. They should only study.
scratch
scratch
Hmmmmm, rather dismal here...
Hope the tour of the room meets our standards...
We shall get to that later.

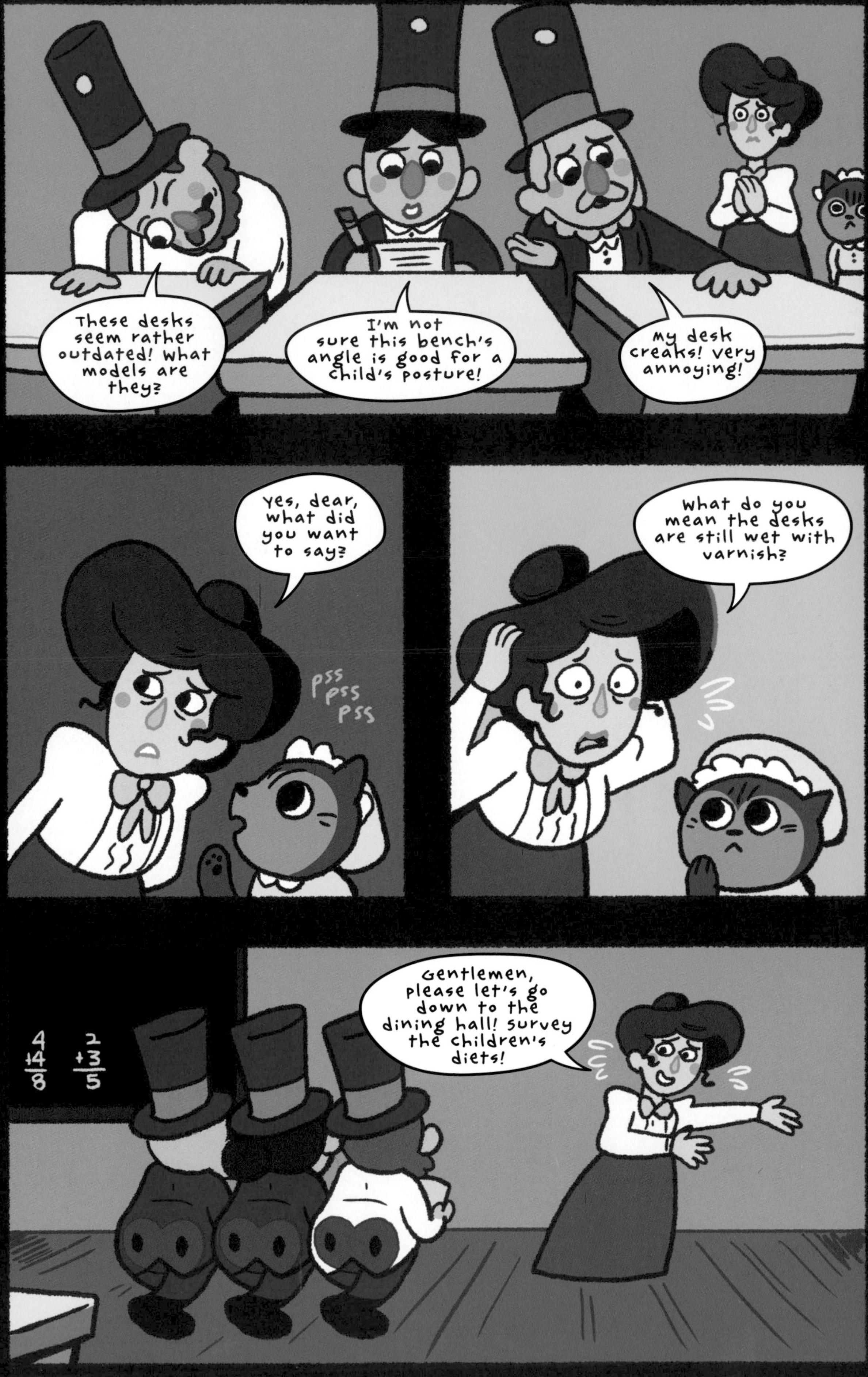
These desks seem rather outdated! What models are they?
I'm not sure this bench's angle is good for a child's posture!
My desk creaks! Very annoying!
Yes, dear, what did you want to say?
PSS PSS PSS
What do you mean the desks are still wet with varnish?
4 +4 8
2 +3 5
Gentlemen, please let's go down to the dining hall! Survey the children's diets!

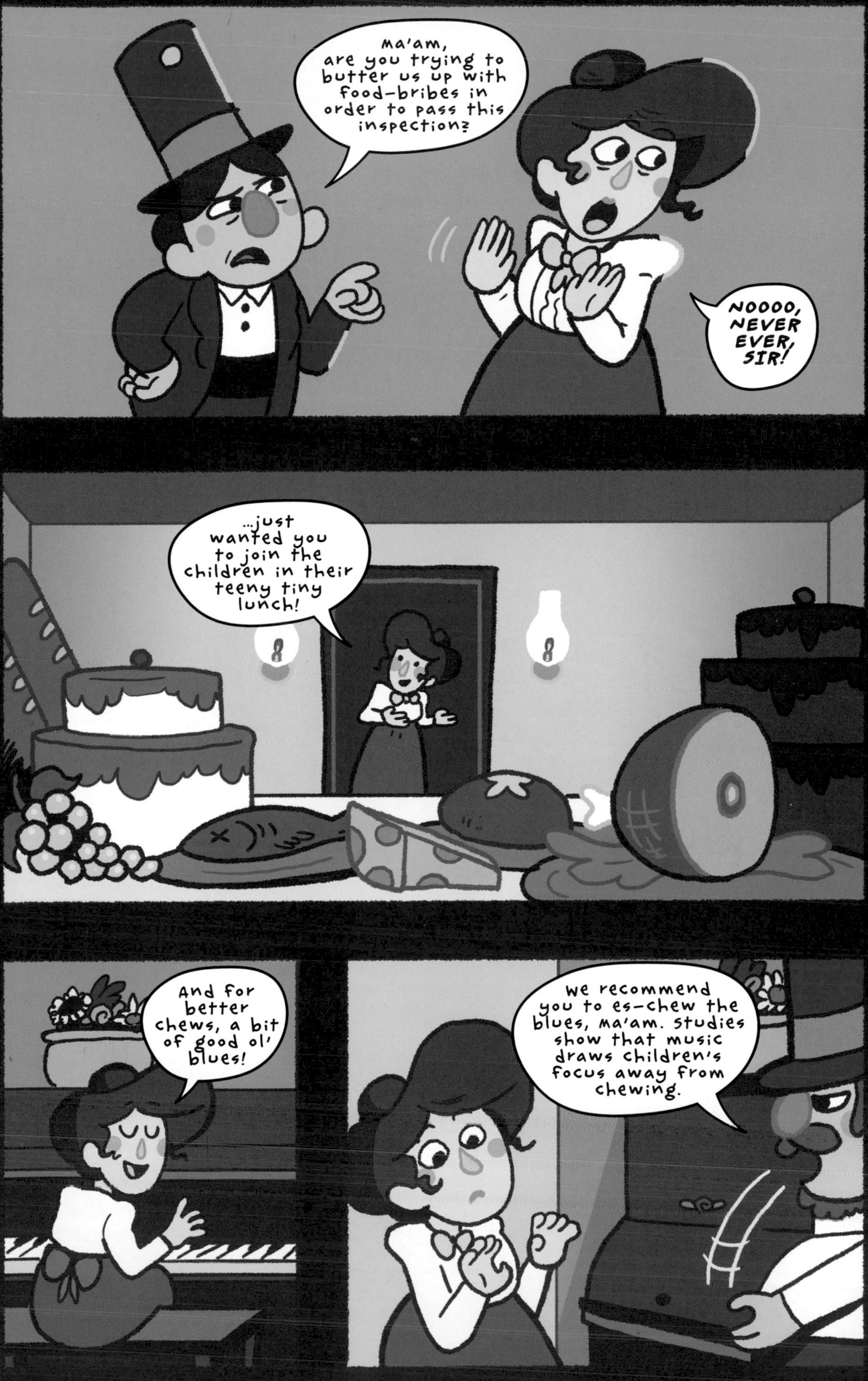
Ma'am, are you trying to butter us up with food-bribes in order to pass this inspection?
NOOOO, NEVER EVER, SIR!
...just wanted you to join the children in their teeny tiny lunch!
And for better chews, a bit of good ol' blues!
We recommend you to es-chew the blues, ma'am. Studies show that music draws children's focus away from chewing.

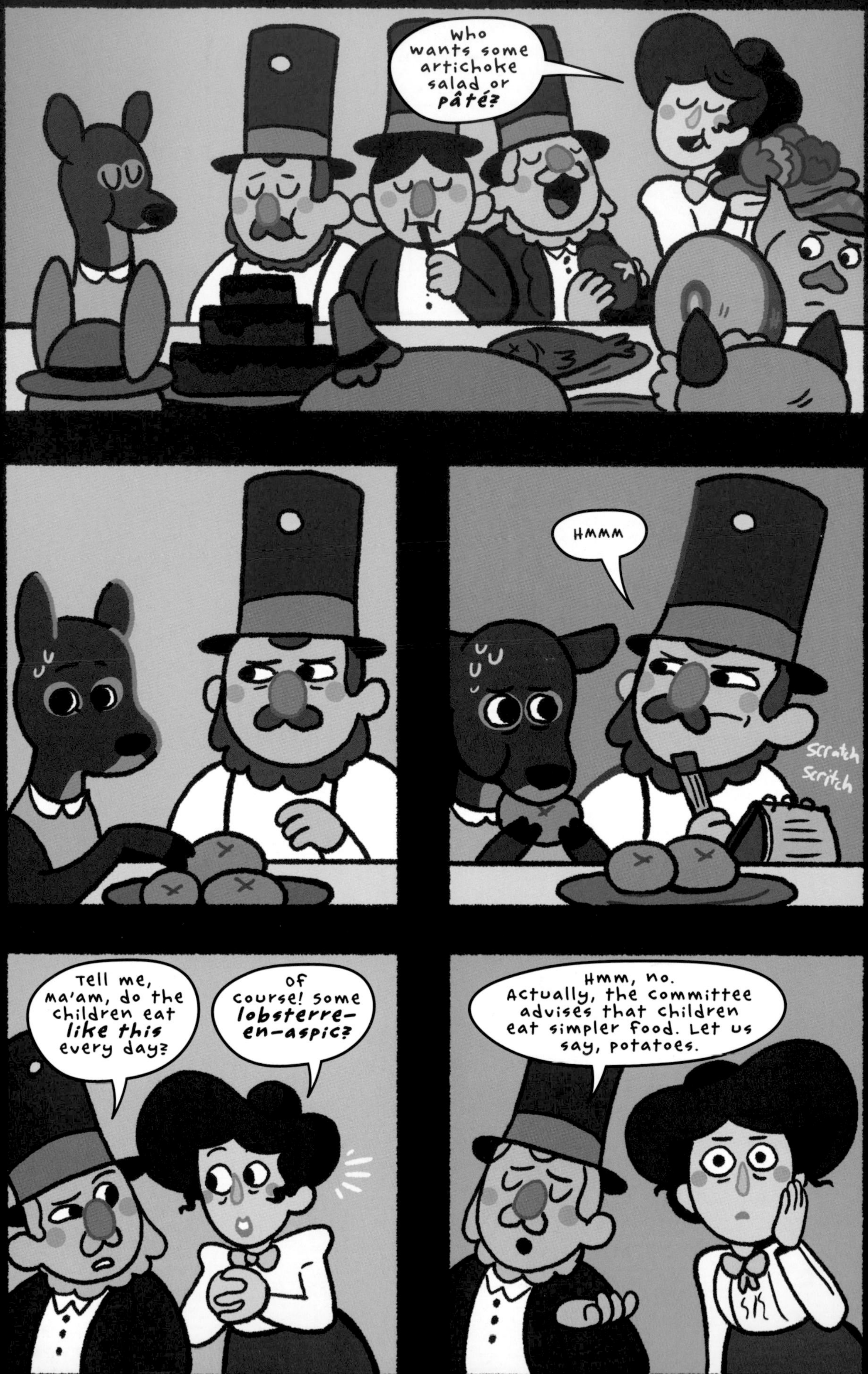
Who wants some artichoke salad or *pâté?*
HMMM
SCRATCH SCRITCH
Tell me, ma'am, do the children eat *like this* every day?
Of course! Some *lobsterre-en-aspic?*
Hmm, no. Actually, the committee advises that children eat simpler food. Let us say, potatoes.

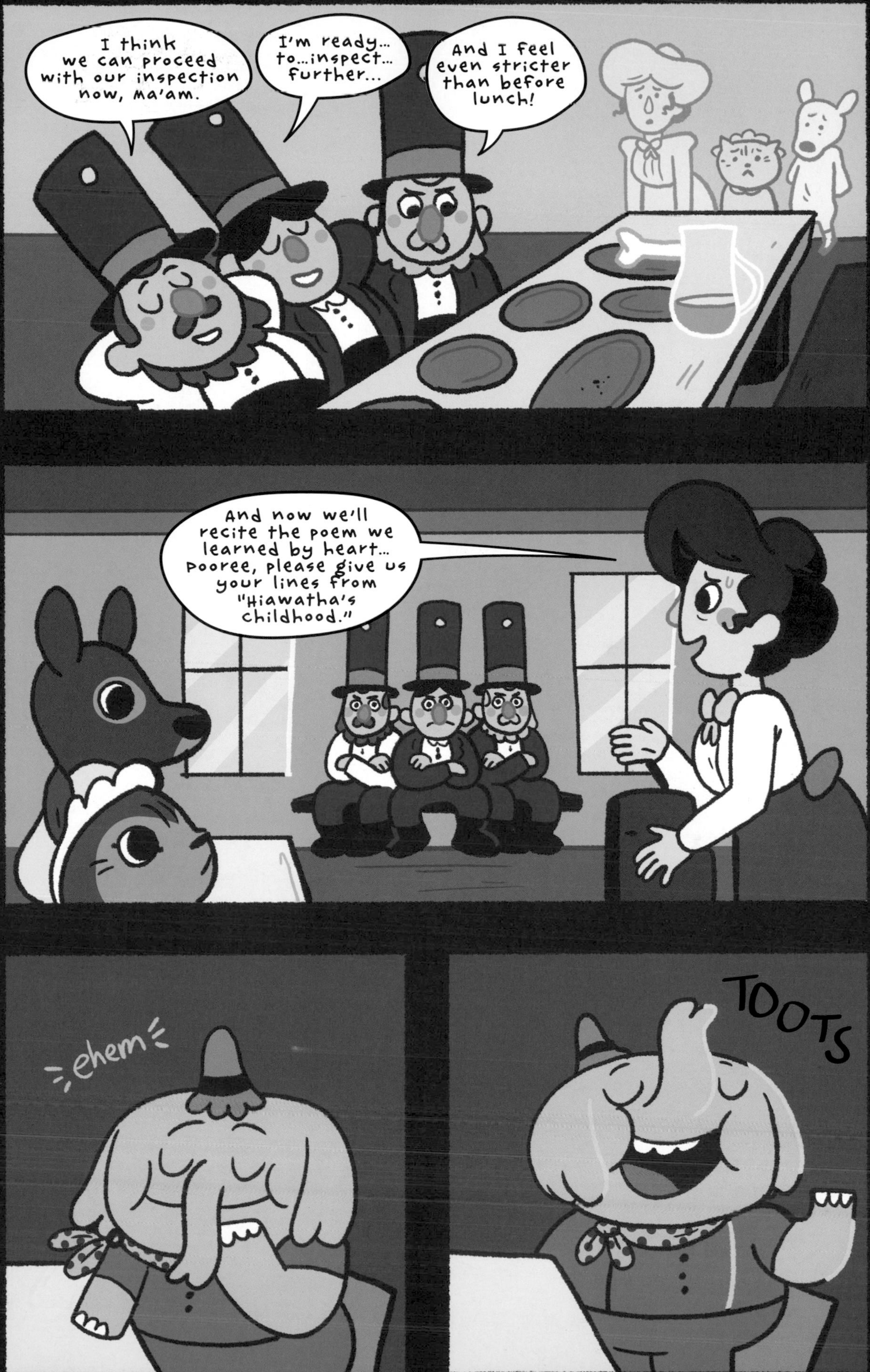
I think we can proceed with our inspection now, ma'am.
I'm ready... to...inspect... further...
And I feel even stricter than before lunch!
And now we'll recite the poem we learned by heart... Pooree, please give us your lines from "Hiawatha's childhood."
ehem
TOOTS

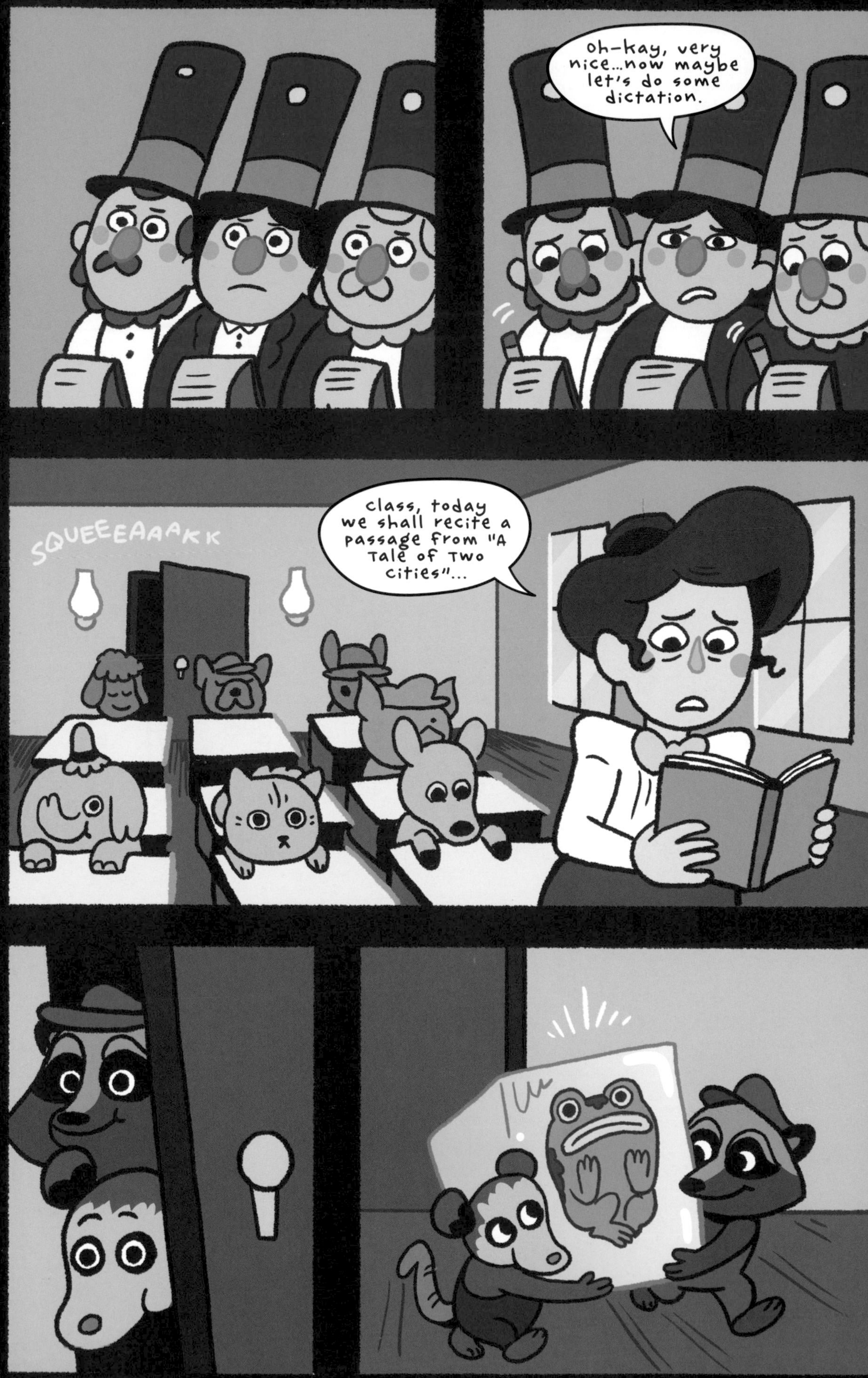
oh-kay, very nice...now maybe let's do some dictation.
SQUEEEAAAKK
class, today we shall recite a passage from "A Tale of Two cities"...

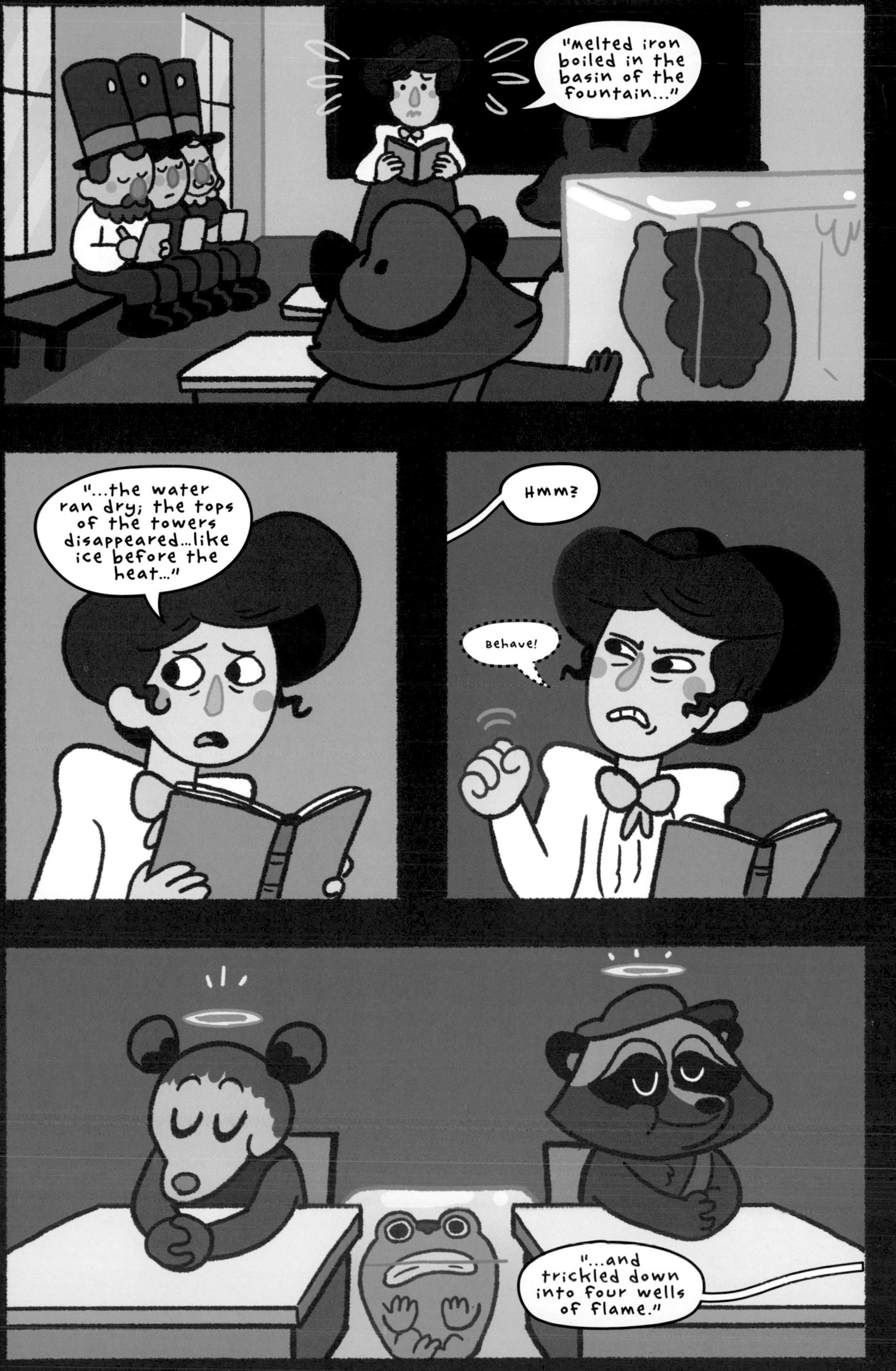
"melted iron boiled in the basin of the fountain..."
"...the water ran dry; the tops of the towers disappeared...like ice before the heat..."
Hmm?
Behave!
"...and trickled down into four wells of flame."

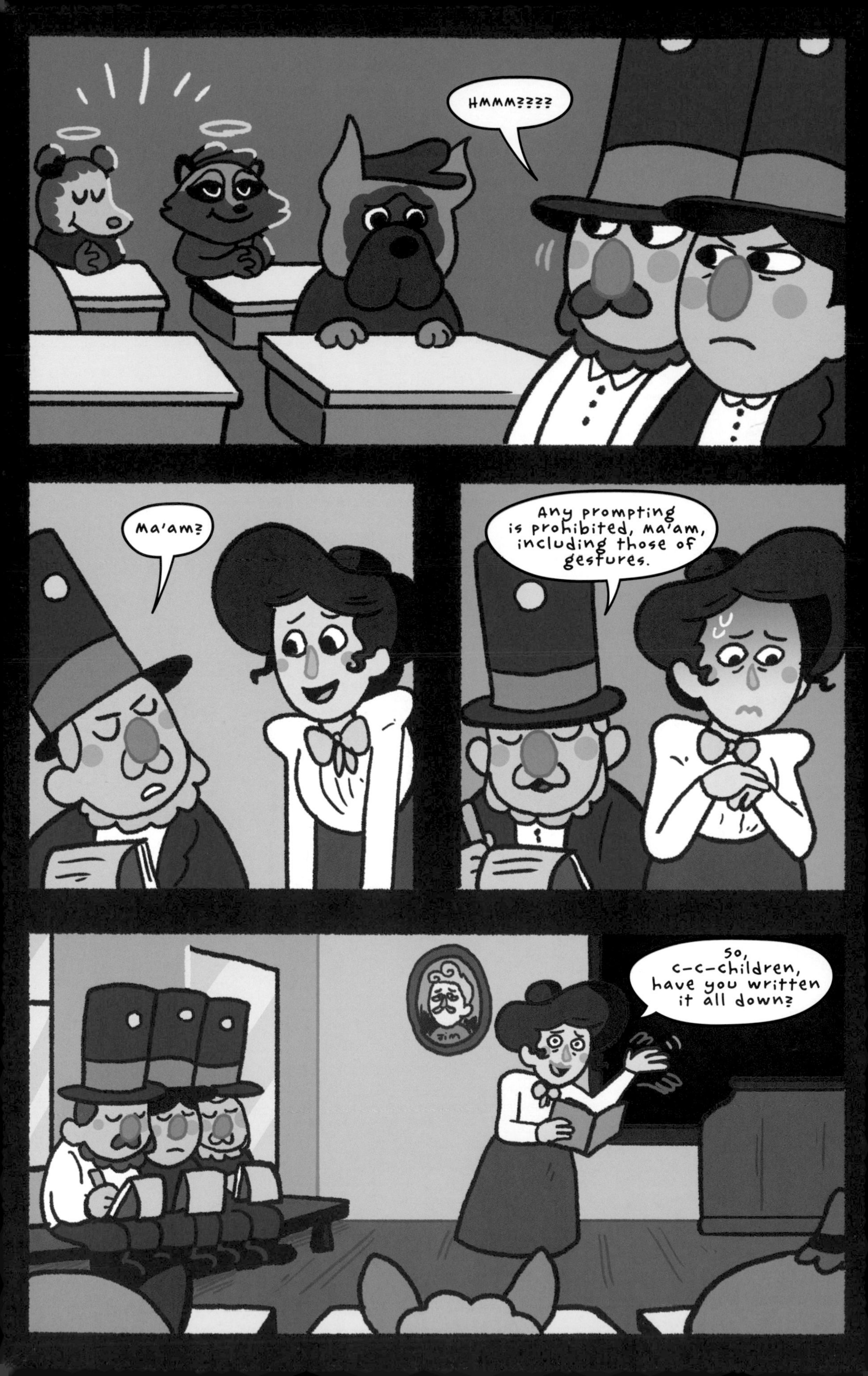
HMMM????
Ma'am?
Any prompting is prohibited, ma'am, including those of gestures.
So, c-c-children, have you written it all down?
JIM

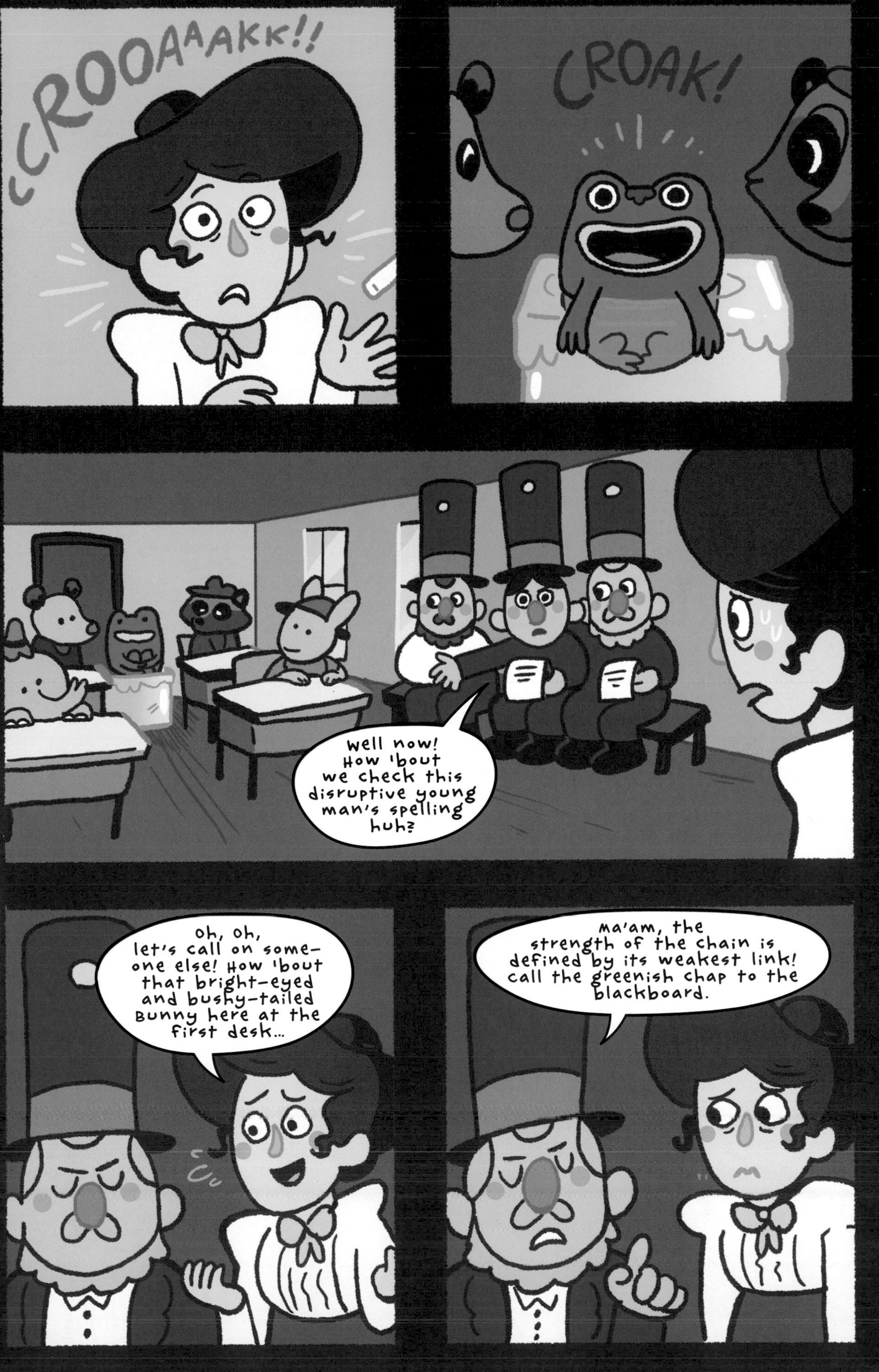
CROOAAAKK!!
CROAK!
Well now! How 'bout we check this disruptive young man's spelling huh?
Oh, oh, let's call on some-one else! How 'bout that bright-eyed and bushy-tailed Bunny here at the first desk...
Ma'am, the strength of the chain is defined by its weakest link! Call the greenish chap to the blackboard.

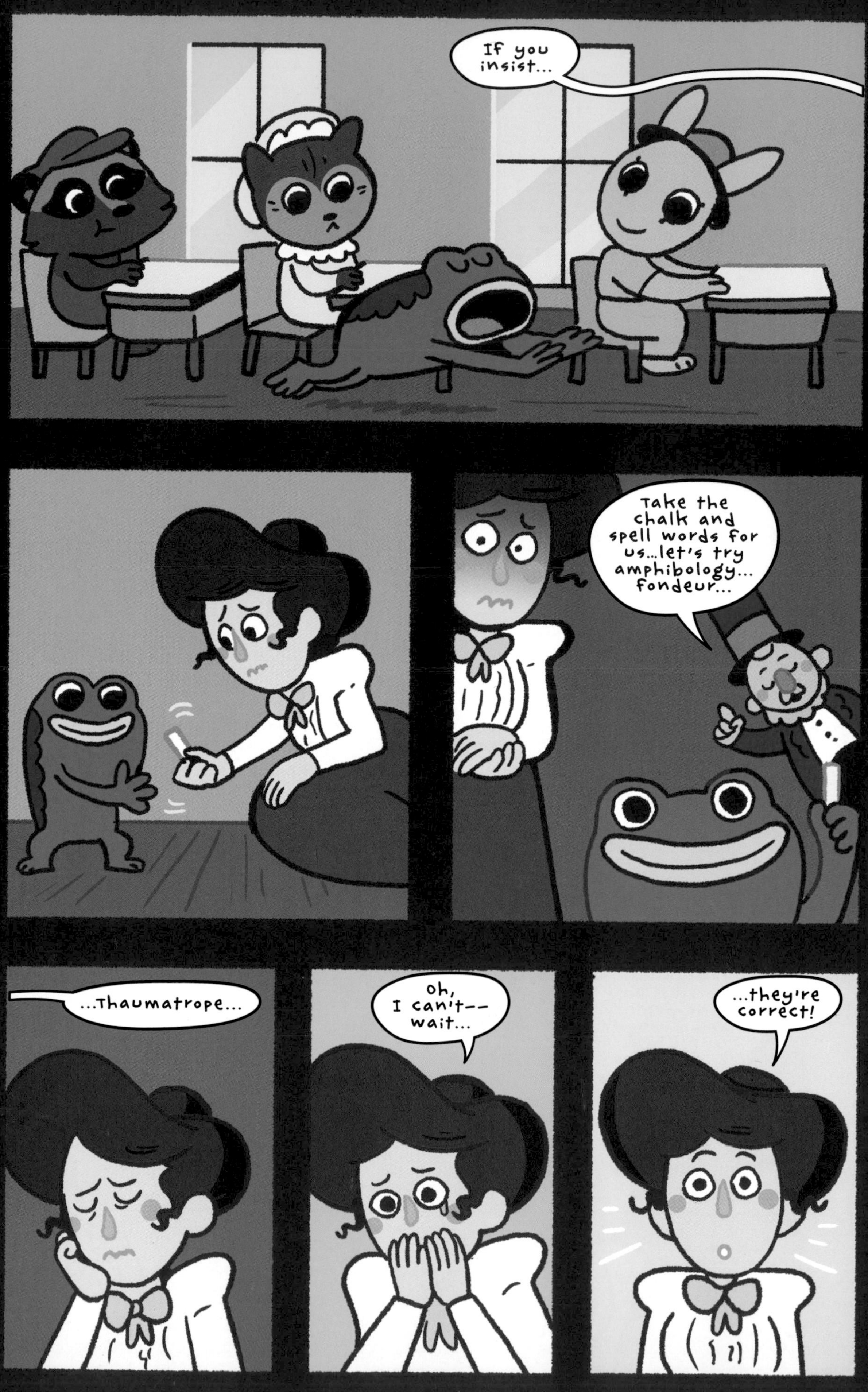
If you insist...
Take the chalk and spell words for us...let's try amphibology... fondeur...
...Thaumatrope...
Oh, I can't-- wait...
...they're correct!

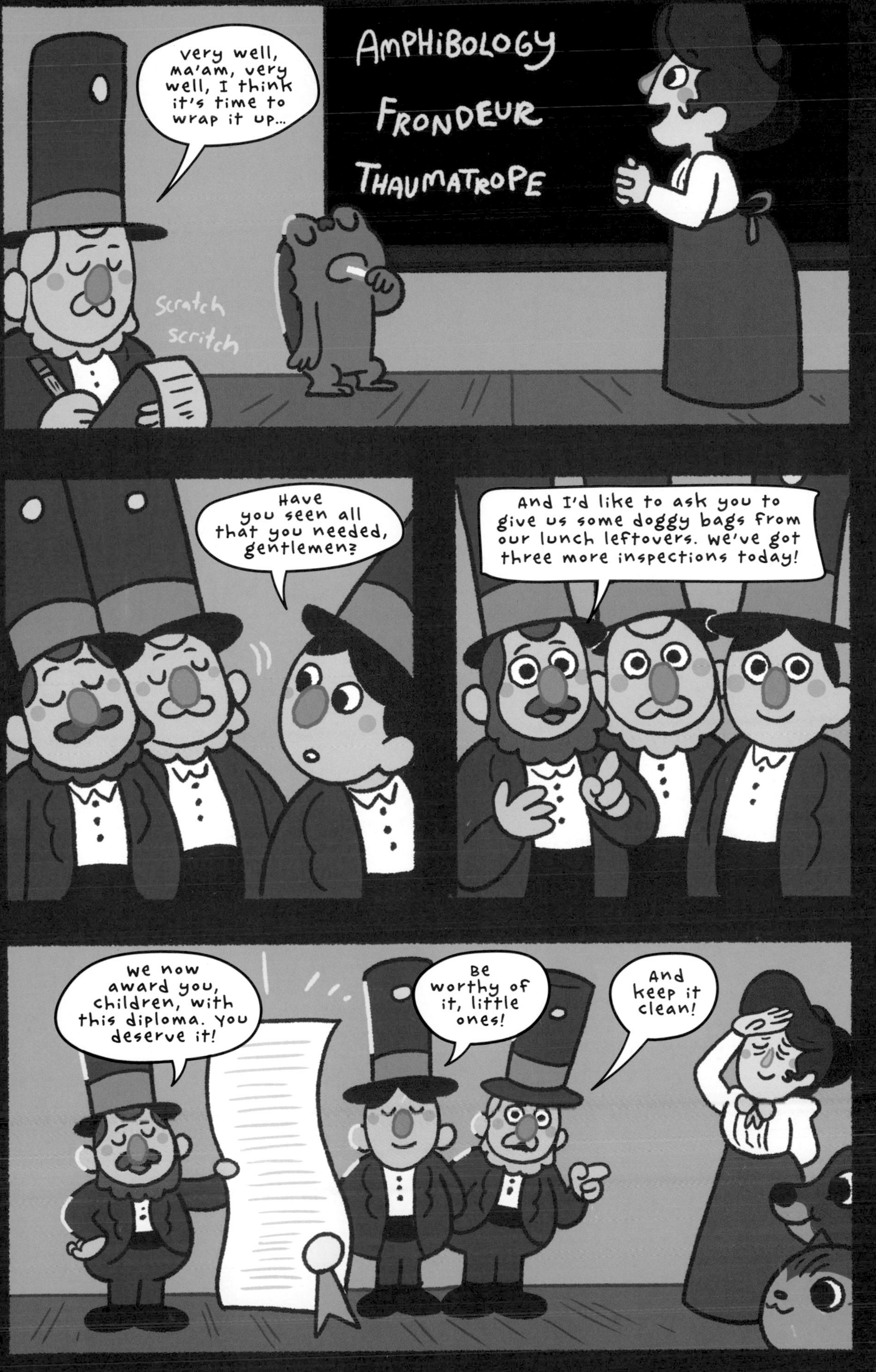
very well, ma'am, very well, I think it's time to wrap it up...
AMPHIBOLOGY
FRONDEUR
THAUMATROPE
scratch
scritch
Have you seen all that you needed, gentlemen?
And I'd like to ask you to give us some doggy bags from our lunch leftovers. We've got three more inspections today!
We now award you, children, with this diploma. You deserve it!
Be worthy of it, little ones!
And keep it clean!

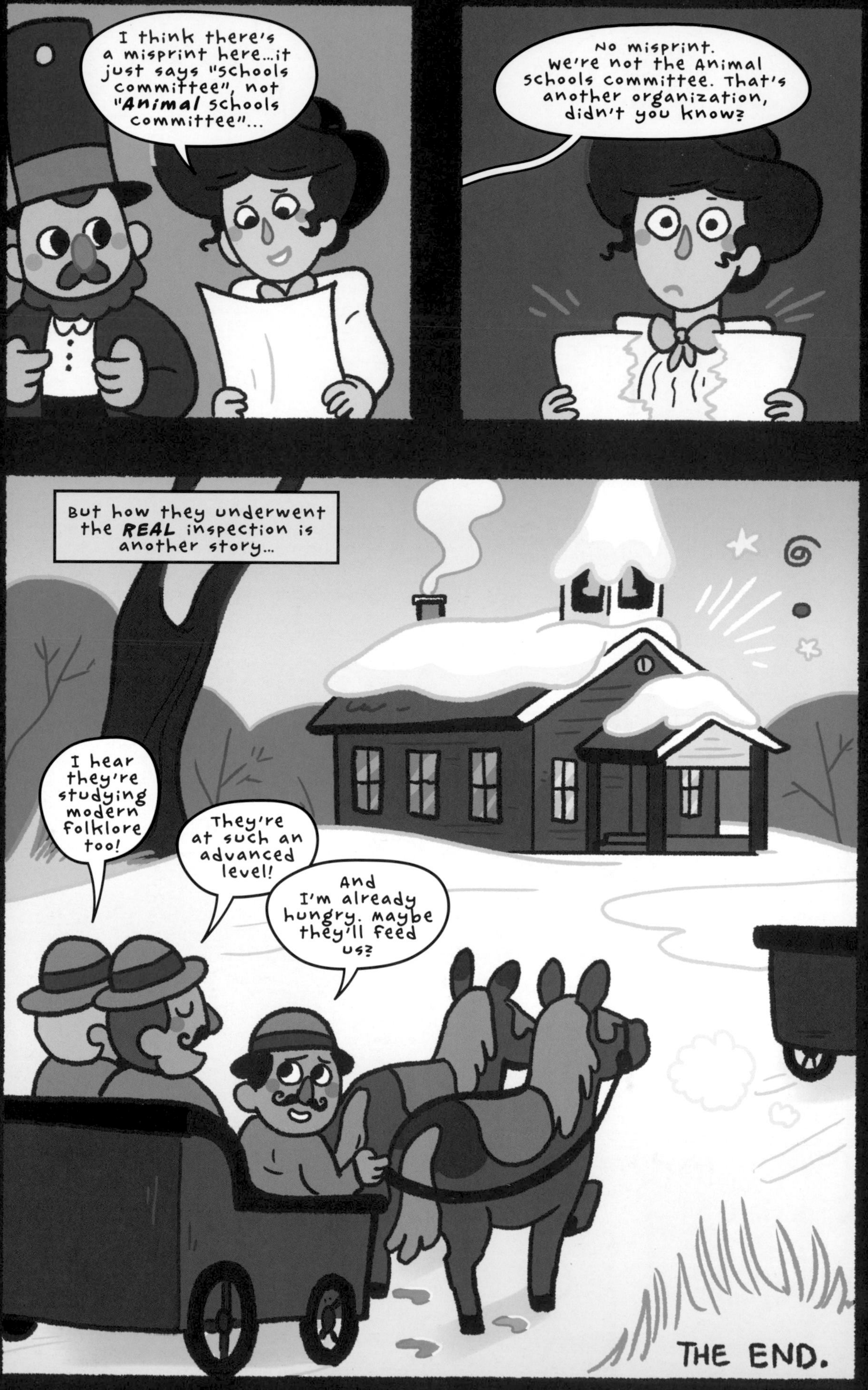
I think there's a misprint here...it just says "schools committee", not "*Animal* schools committee"...
No misprint. We're not the Animal schools committee. That's another organization, didn't you know?
But how they underwent the ***REAL*** inspection is another story...
I hear they're studying modern folklore too!
They're at such an advanced level!
And I'm already hungry. Maybe they'll feed us?
THE END.

Cover Gallery

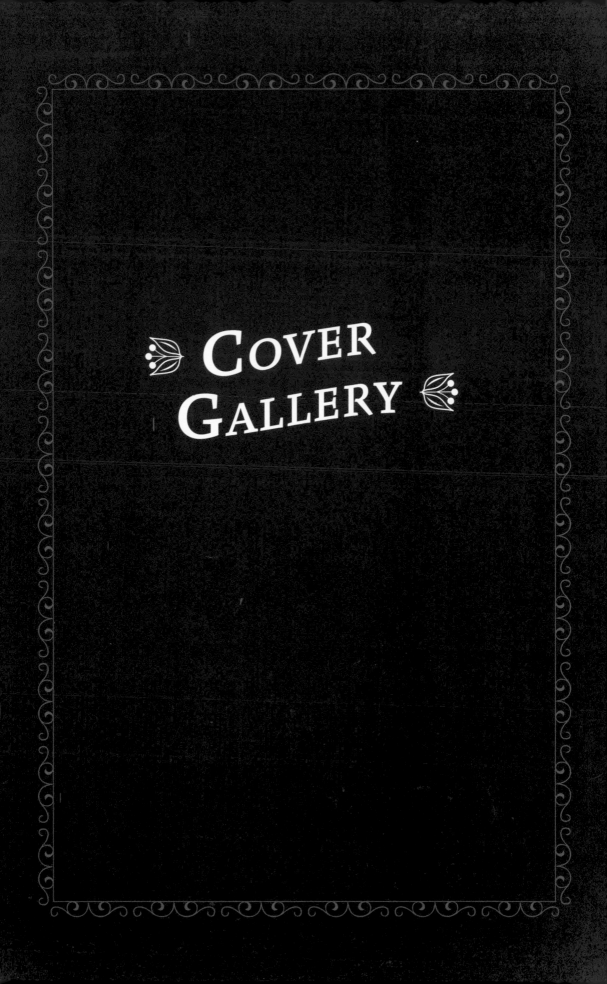

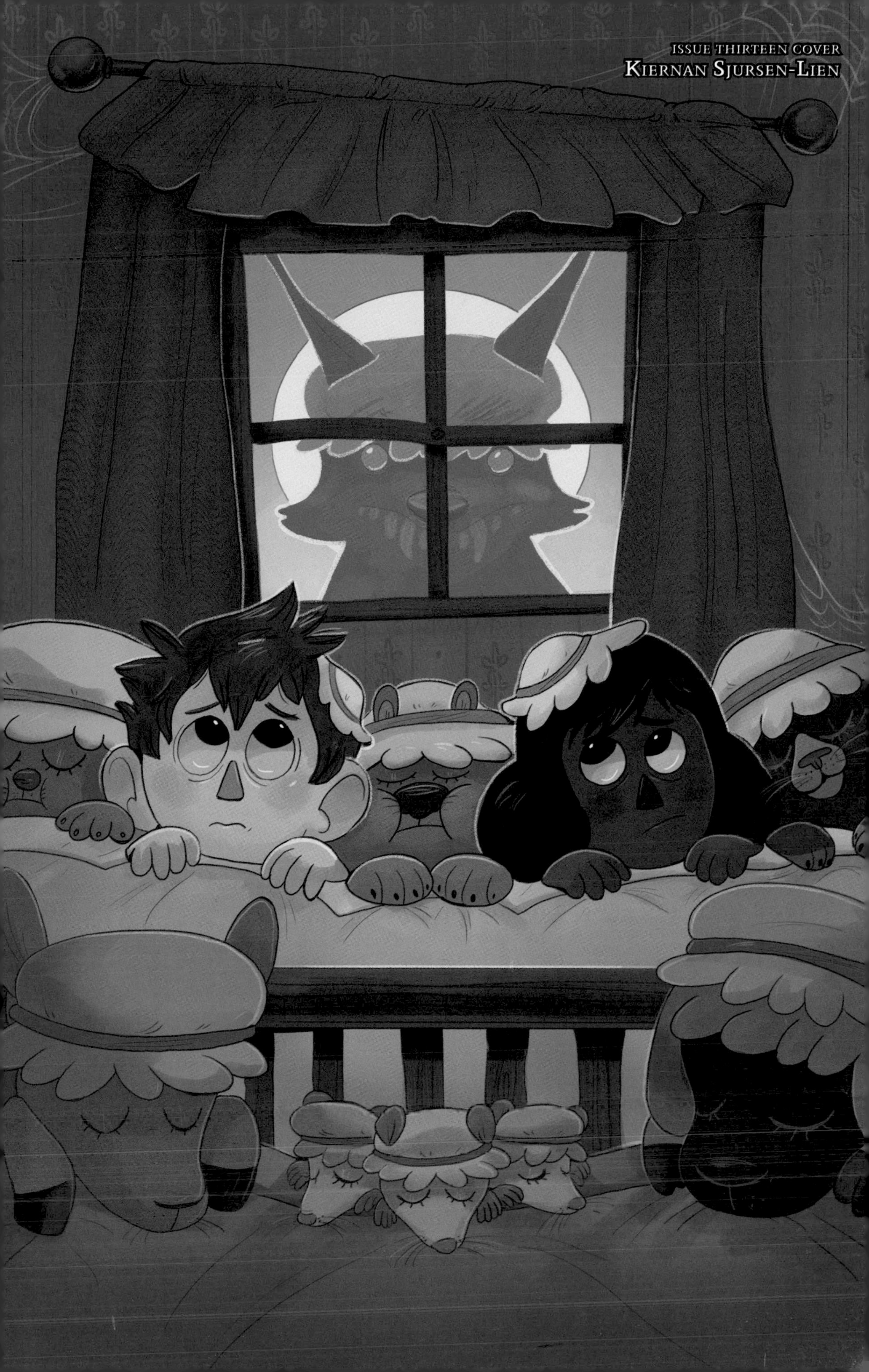

ISSUE THIRTEEN COVER
KIERNAN SJURSEN-LIEN

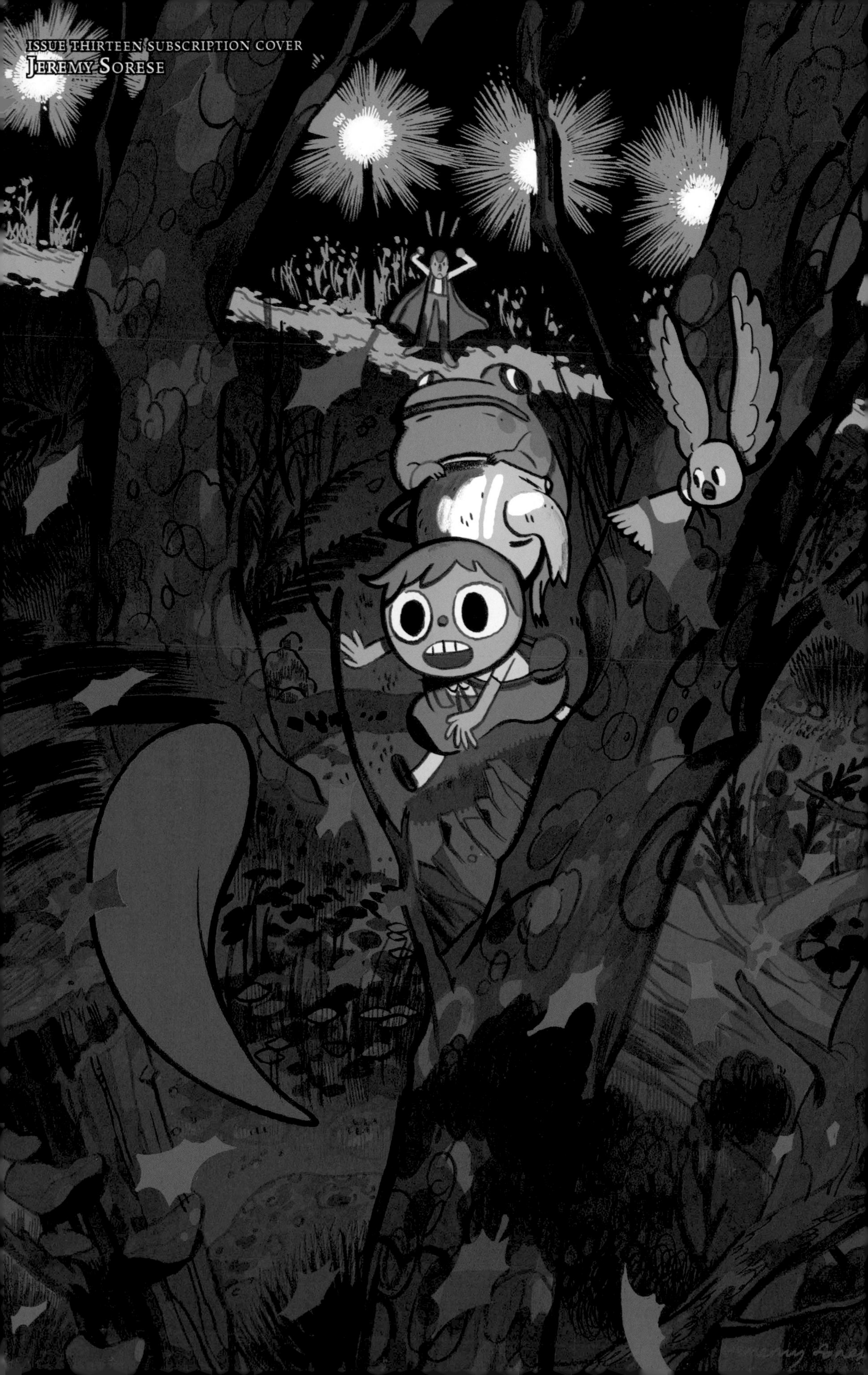

ISSUE THIRTEEN SUBSCRIPTION COVER
JEREMY SORESE

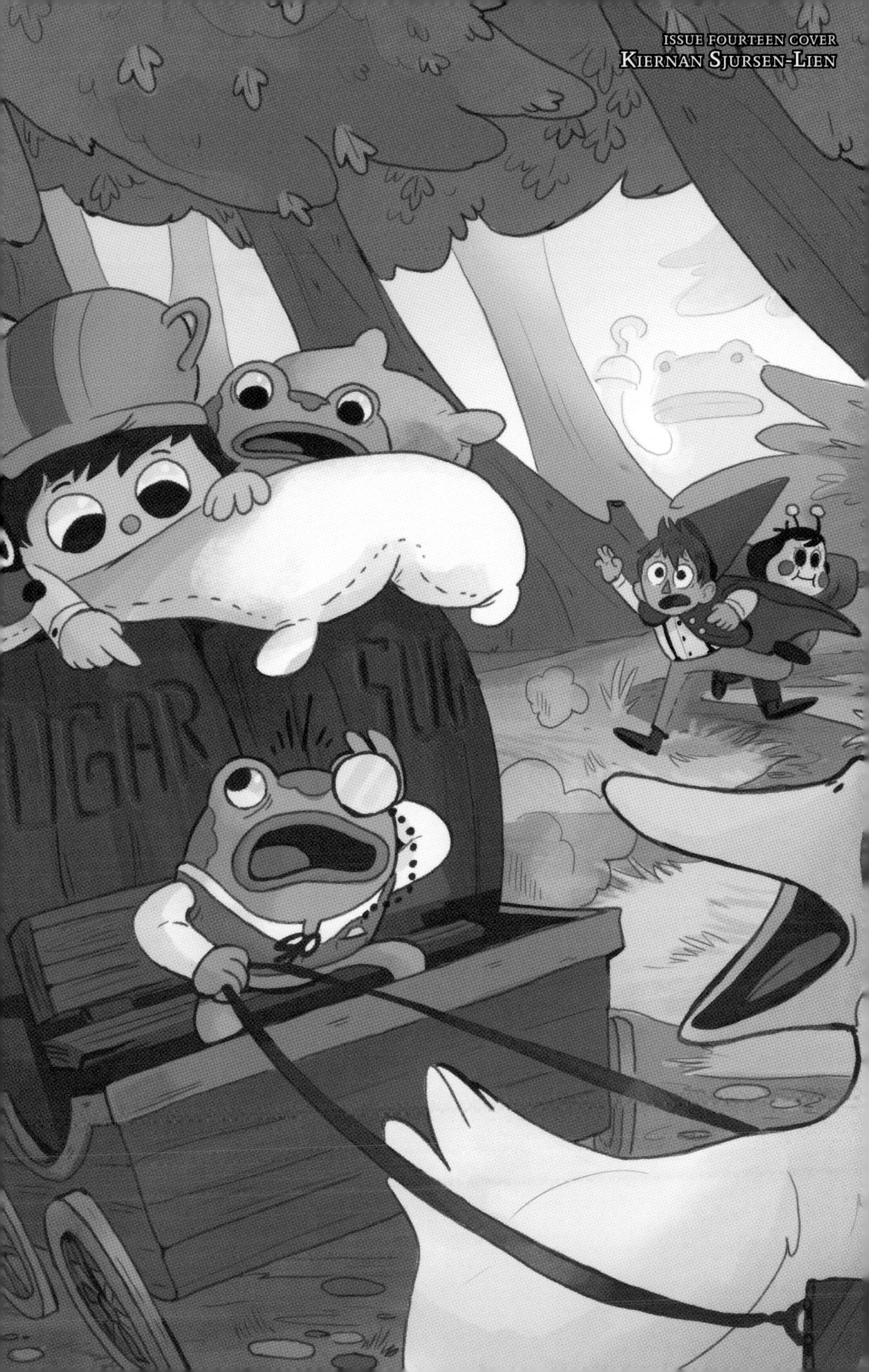

ISSUE FOURTEEN COVER
KIERNAN SJURSEN-LIEN

ISSUE FOURTEEN SUBSCRIPTION COVER
KATIE CHINASKI

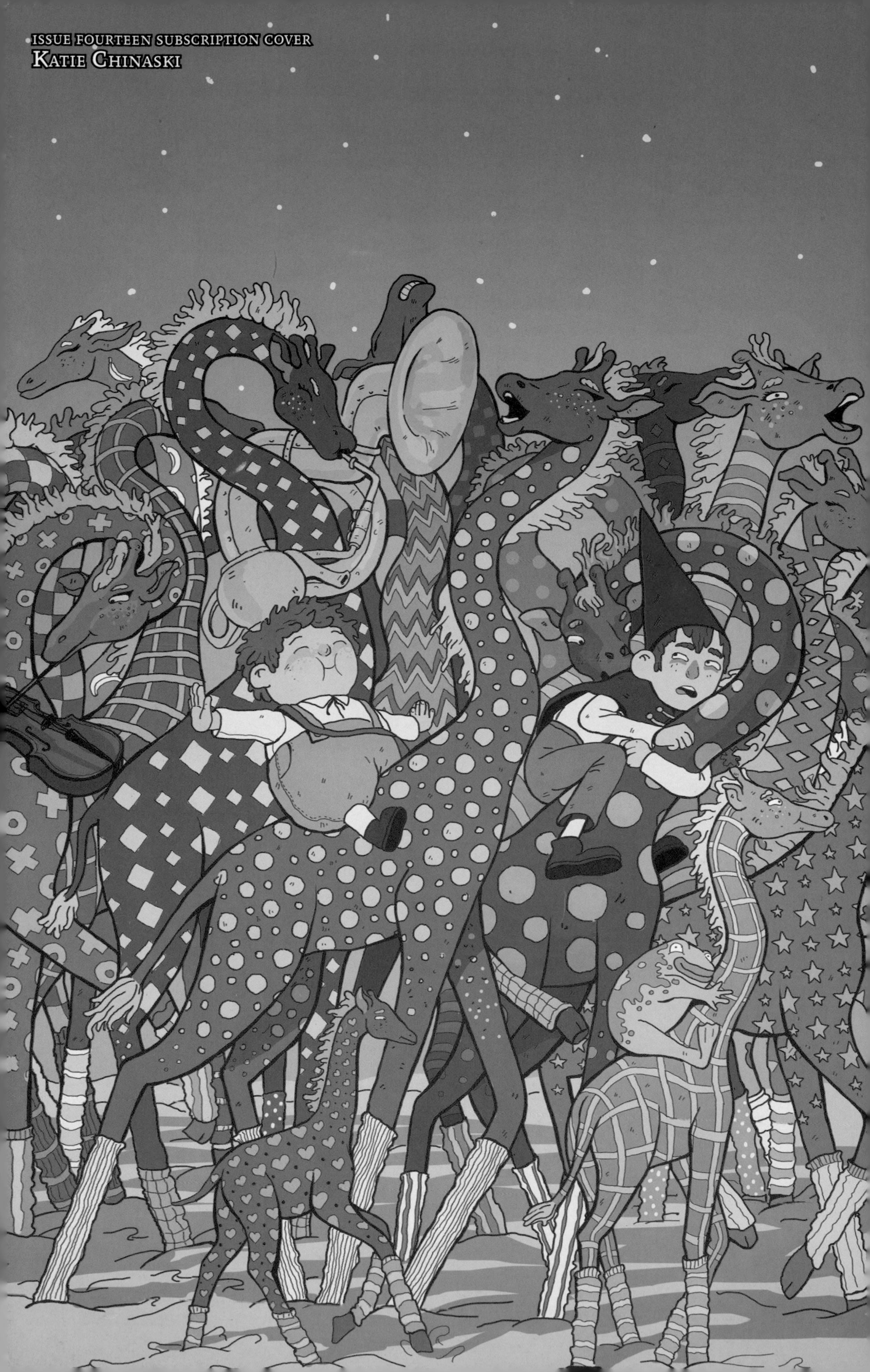

ISSUE FIFTEEN COVER
KIERNAN SJURSEN-LIEN

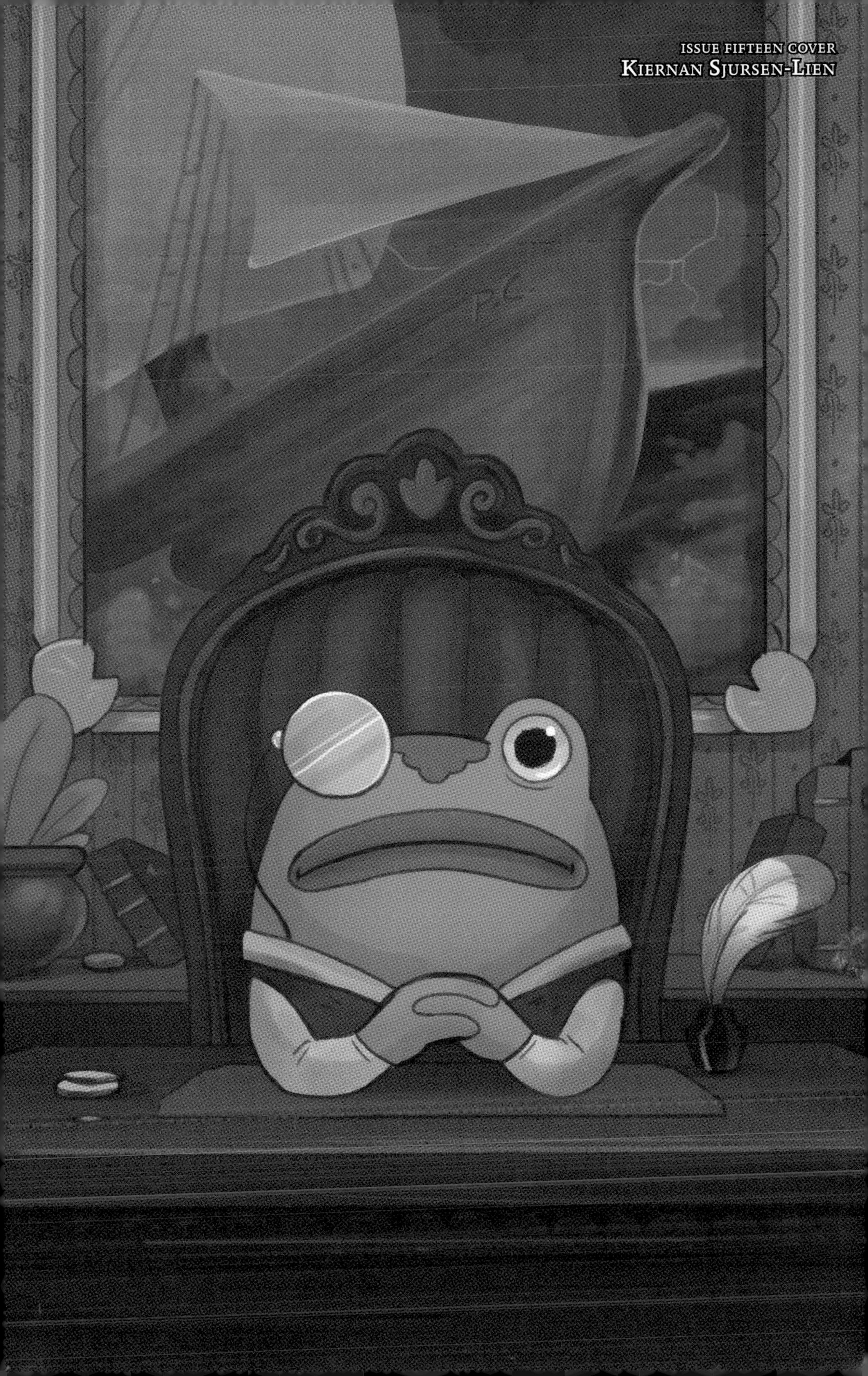

ISSUE FIFTEEN SUBSCRIPTION COVER
VICTORIA MADERNA

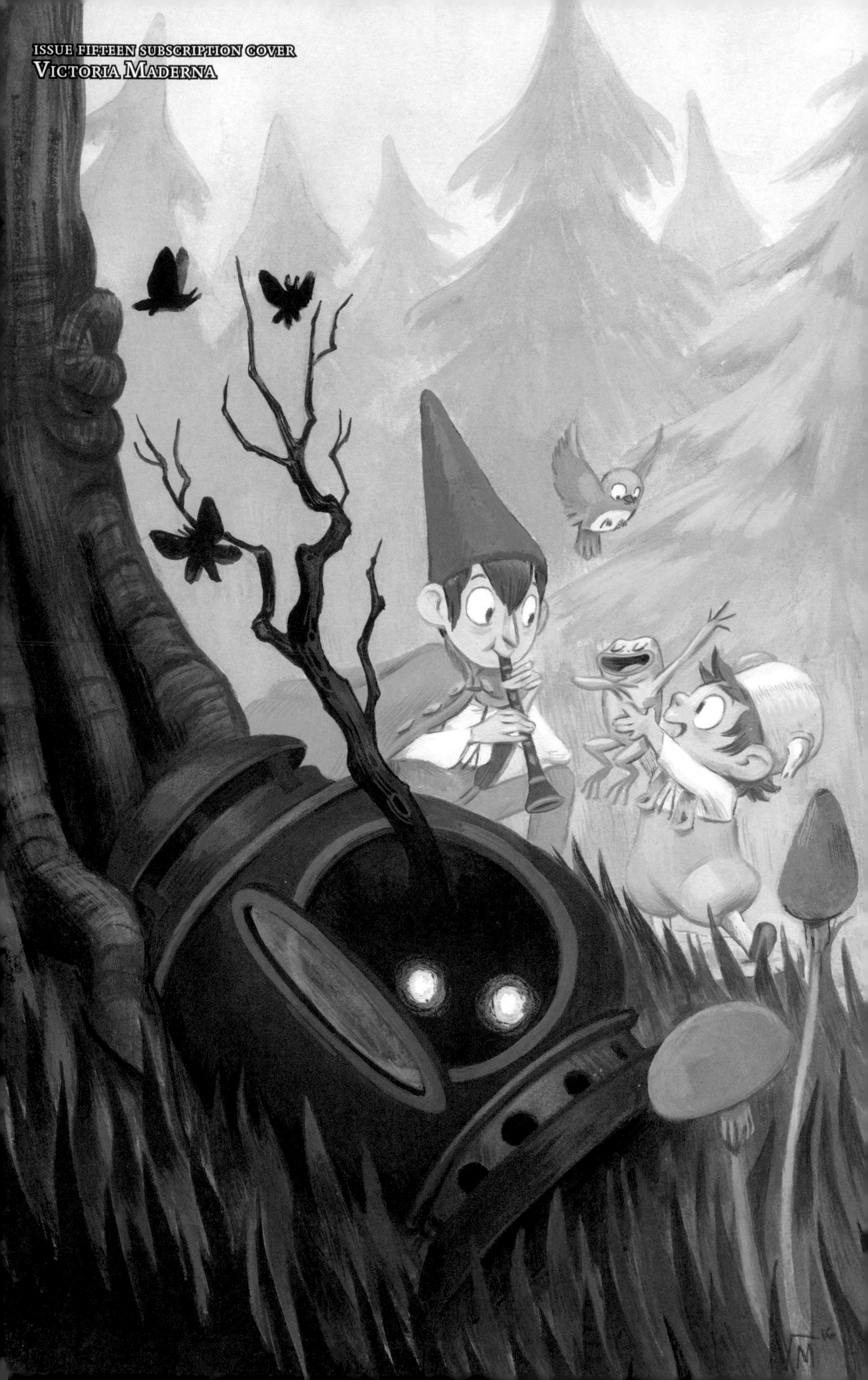

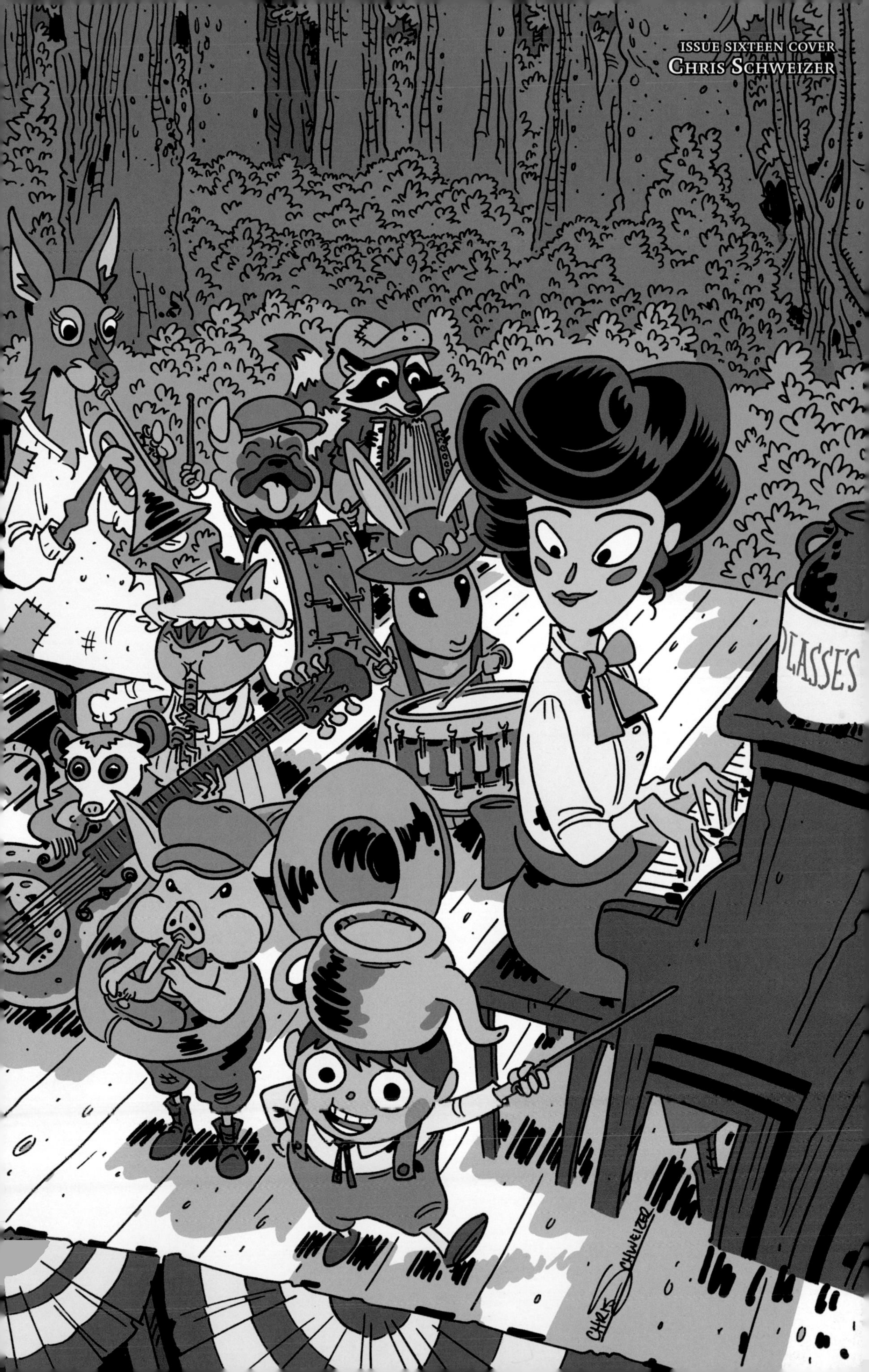
PLASSE'S
CHRIS SCHWEIZER

ISSUE SIXTEEN COVER
CHRIS SCHWEIZER

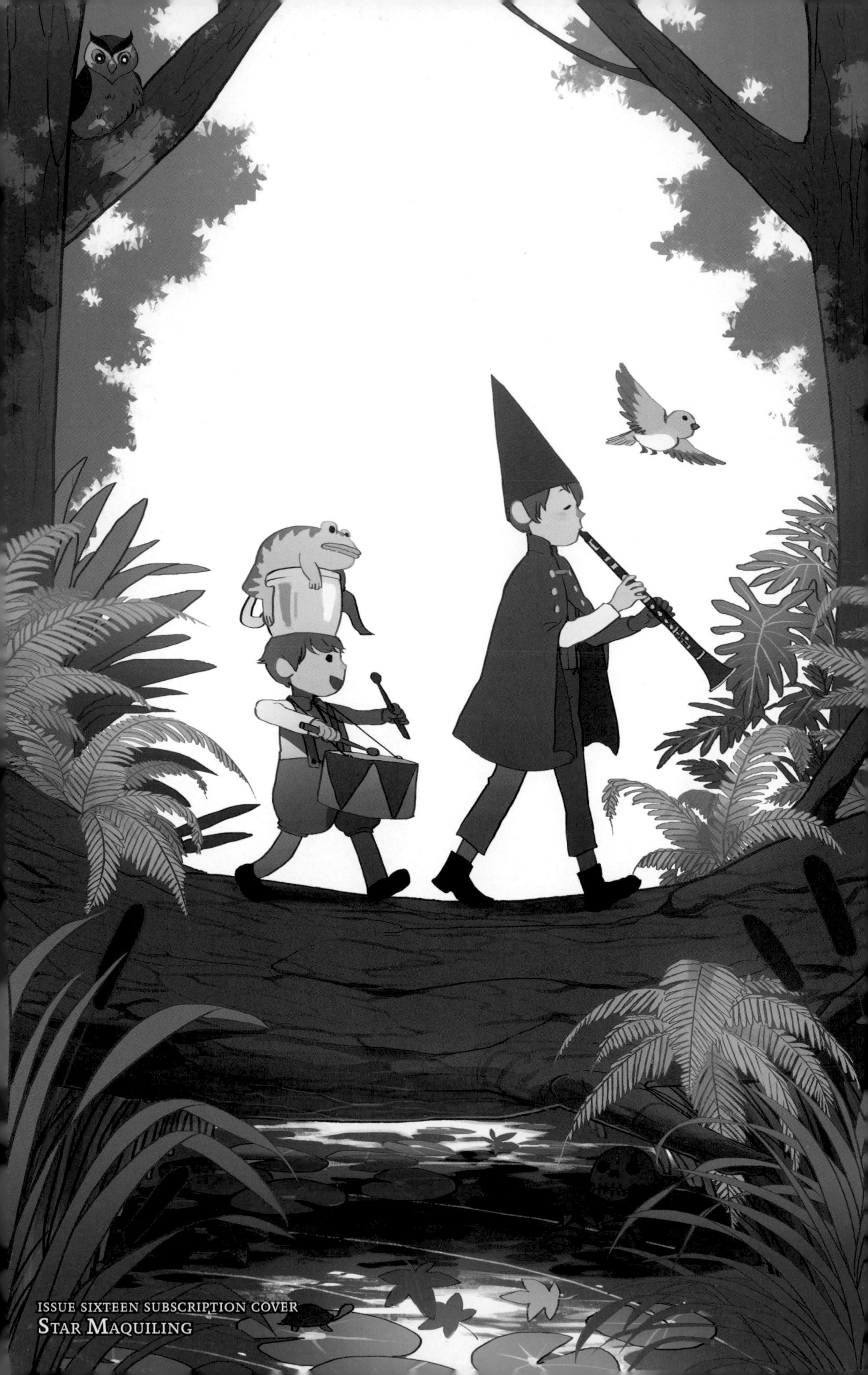

ISSUE SIXTEEN SUBSCRIPTION COVER
STAR MAQUILING

DISCOVER
EXPLOSIVE NEW WORLDS

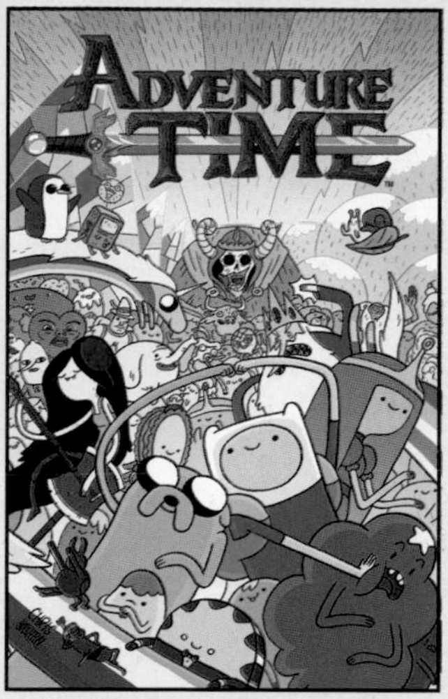
ADVENTURE TIME

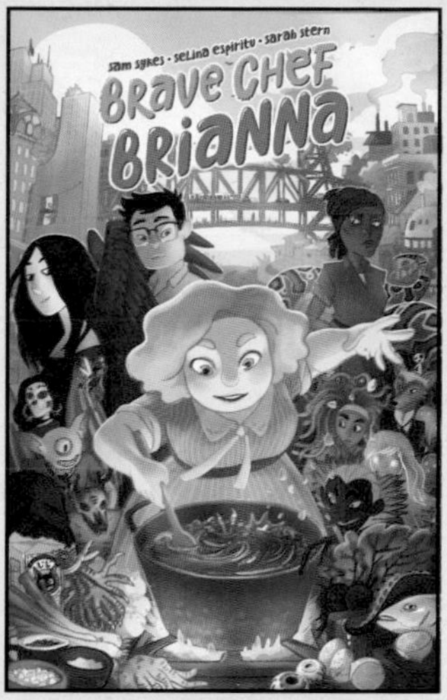
Sam Sykes · Selina Espiritu · Sarah Stern
BRAVE CHEF BRIANNA

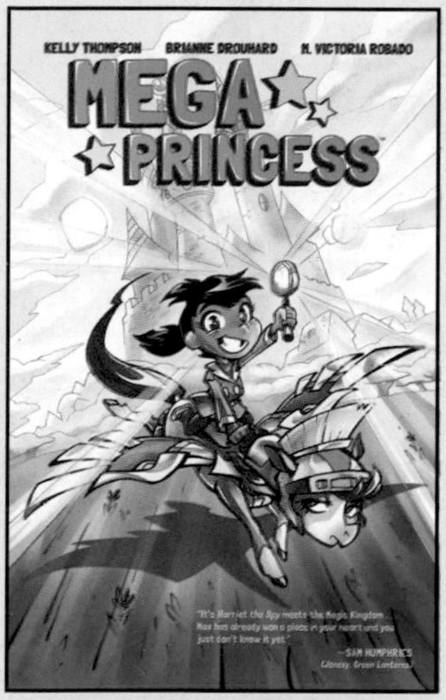
KELLY THOMPSON BRIANNE DROUHARD M. VICTORIA ROBADO
MEGA PRINCESS

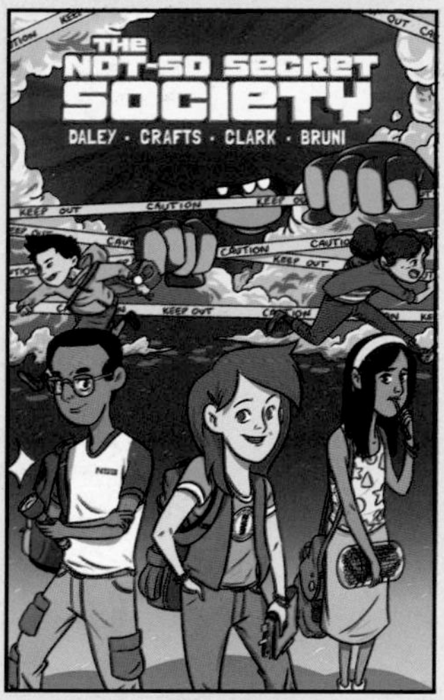
THE NOT-SO SECRET SOCIETY
DALEY · CRAFTS · CLARK · BRUNI

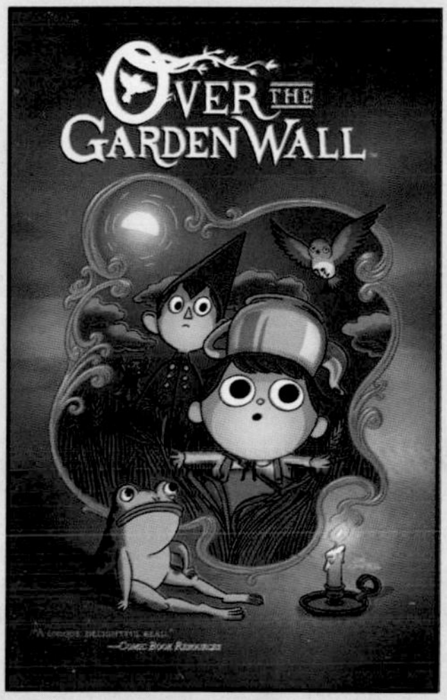
OVER THE GARDEN WALL

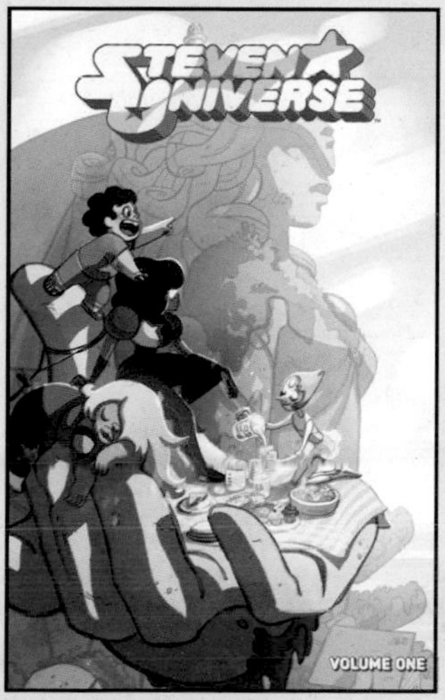
STEVEN UNIVERSE
VOLUME ONE

kaboom!™

AVAILABLE AT YOUR LOCAL COMICS SHOP AND BOOKSTORE

To find a comics shop in your area, call 1-888-266-4226

WWW.**BOOM-STUDIOS**.COM

Adventure Time
Pendleton Ward and Others
Volume 1
ISBN: 978-1-60886-280-1 | $14.99 US
Volume 2
ISBN: 978-1-60886-323-5 | $14.99 US
Adventure Time: Islands
ISBN: 978-1-60886-972-5 | $9.99 US

The Amazing World of Gumball
Ben Bocquelet and Others
Volume 1
ISBN: 978-1-60886-488-1 | $14.99 US
Volume 2
ISBN: 978-1-60886-793-6 | $14.99 US

Brave Chef Brianna
Sam Sykes, Selina Espiritu
ISBN: 978-1-68415-050-2 | $14.99 US

Mega Princess
Kelly Thompson, Brianne Drouhard
ISBN: 978-1-68415-007-6 | $14.99 US

The Not-So Secret Society
Matthew Daley, Arlene Daley, Wook Jin Clark
ISBN: 978-1-60886-997-8 | $9.99 US

Over the Garden Wall
Patrick McHale, Jim Campbell and Others
Volume 1
ISBN: 978-1-60886-940-4 | $14.99 US
Volume 2
ISBN: 978-1-68415-006-9 | $14.99 US

Steven Universe
Rebecca Sugar and Others
Volume 1
ISBN: 978-1-60886-706-6 | $14.99 US
Volume 2
ISBN: 978-1-60886-796-7 | $14.99 US

Steven Universe & The Crystal Gems
ISBN: 978-1-60886-921-3 | $14.99 US

Steven Universe: Too Cool for School
ISBN: 978-1-60886-771-4 | $14.99 US